AMERICAN FAIRY TALES
AND THE SEA FAIRIES

L. FRANK BAUM

FV EDITIONS

CONTENTS

AMERICAN FAIRY TALES

THE SEA FAIRIES

AMERICAN FAIRY TALES

CHAPTER I
THE BOX OF ROBBERS

No one intended to leave Martha alone that afternoon, but it happened that everyone was called away, for one reason or another. Mrs. McFarland was attending the weekly card party held by the Women's Anti-Gambling League. Sister Nell's young man had called quite unexpectedly to take her for a long drive. Papa was at the office, as usual. It was Mary Ann's day out. As for Emeline, she certainly should have stayed in the house and looked after the little girl; but Emeline had a restless nature.

"Would you mind, miss, if I just crossed the alley to speak a word to Mrs. Carleton's girl?" she asked Martha.

"'Course not," replied the child. "You'd better lock the back door, though, and take the key, for I shall be upstairs."

"Oh, I'll do that, of course, miss," said the delighted maid, and ran away to spend the afternoon with her friend, leaving Martha quite alone in the big house, and locked in, into the bargain.

The little girl read a few pages in her new book, sewed a few stitches in her embroidery and started to "play visiting" with her four favorite dolls. Then she remembered that in the attic was a doll's playhouse that hadn't been used for months, so she decided she would dust it and put it in order.

Filled with this idea, the girl climbed the winding stairs to the big room under the roof. It was well lighted by three dormer windows and was warm and pleasant. Around the walls were rows of boxes and trunks, piles of old carpeting, pieces of damaged furniture, bundles of discarded clothing and other odds and ends of more or less value. Every well-regulated house has an attic of this sort, so I need not describe it.

The doll's house had been moved, but after a search Martha found it away over in a corner near the big chimney.

She drew it out and noticed that behind it was a black wooden chest which Uncle Walter had sent over from Italy years and years ago—before Martha was born, in fact. Mamma had told her about it one day; how there was no key to it, because Uncle Walter wished it to remain unopened until he returned home; and how this wandering uncle, who was a mighty hunter, had gone into Africa to hunt elephants and had never been heard from afterwards.

The little girl looked at the chest curiously, now that it had by accident attracted her attention.

It was quite big—bigger even than mamma's traveling trunk—and was studded all over with tarnished brassheaded nails. It was heavy, too, for when Martha tried to lift one end of it she found she could not stir it a bit. But there was a place in the side of the cover for a key. She stooped to examine the lock, and saw that it would take a rather big key to open it.

Then, as you may suspect, the little girl longed to open Uncle Walter's big box and see what was in it. For we are all curious, and little girls are just as curious as the rest of us.

"I don't b'lieve Uncle Walter'll ever come back," she thought. "Papa said once that some elephant must have killed him. If I only had a key—" She stopped and clapped her little hands together gayly as she remembered a big basket of keys on the shelf in the linen closet. They were of all sorts and sizes; perhaps one of them would unlock the mysterious chest!

She flew down the stairs, found the basket and returned with it to the attic. Then she sat down before the brass-studded box and began trying one key after another in the curious old lock. Some were too large, but most were too small. One would go into the lock but would not turn; another stuck so fast that she feared for a time that she would never get it out again. But at last, when the basket was almost empty, an oddly-shaped, ancient brass key slipped easily into the lock. With a cry of joy Martha turned the key with both hands; then she heard a sharp "click," and the next moment the heavy lid flew up of its own accord!

The little girl leaned over the edge of the chest an instant, and the sight that met her eyes caused her to start back in amazement.

Slowly and carefully a man unpacked himself from the chest, stepped out upon the floor, stretched his limbs and then took off his hat and bowed politely to the astonished child.

He was tall and thin and his face seemed badly tanned or sunburnt.

Then another man emerged from the chest, yawning and rubbing his eyes like a sleepy schoolboy. He was of middle size and his skin seemed as badly tanned as that of the first.

While Martha stared open-mouthed at the remarkable sight a third man crawled from the chest. He had the same complexion as his fellows, but was short and fat.

All three were dressed in a curious manner. They wore short jackets of red velvet braided with gold, and knee breeches of sky-blue satin with silver buttons. Over their stockings were laced wide ribbons of red and yellow and blue, while their hats had broad brims with high, peaked crowns, from which fluttered yards of bright-colored ribbons.

They had big gold rings in their ears and rows of knives and pistols in their belts. Their eyes were black and glittering and they wore long, fierce mustaches, curling at the ends like a pig's tail.

"My! but you were heavy," exclaimed the fat one,

when he had pulled down his velvet jacket and brushed the dust from his sky-blue breeches. "And you squeezed me all out of shape."

"It was unavoidable, Luigi," responded the thin man, lightly; "the lid of the chest pressed me down upon you. Yet I tender you my regrets."

"As for me," said the middle-sized man, carelessly rolling a cigarette and lighting it, "you must acknowledge I have been your nearest friend for years; so do not be disagreeable."

"You mustn't smoke in the attic," said Martha, recovering herself at sight of the cigarette. "You might set the house on fire."

The middle-sized man, who had not noticed her before, at this speech turned to the girl and bowed.

"Since a lady requests it," said he, "I shall abandon my cigarette," and he threw it on the floor and extinguished it with his foot.

"Who are you?" asked Martha, who until now had been too astonished to be frightened.

"Permit us to introduce ourselves," said the thin man, flourishing his hat gracefully. "This is Lugui," the fat man nodded; "and this is Beni," the middle-sized man bowed; "and I am Victor. We are three bandits—Italian bandits."

"Bandits!" cried Martha, with a look of horror.

"Exactly. Perhaps in all the world there are not three other bandits so terrible and fierce as ourselves," said Victor, proudly.

"'Tis so," said the fat man, nodding gravely.

"But it's wicked!" exclaimed Martha.

"Yes, indeed," replied Victor. "We are extremely

and tremendously wicked. Perhaps in all the world you could not find three men more wicked than those who now stand before you."

"'Tis so," said the fat man, approvingly.

"But you shouldn't be so wicked," said the girl; "it's—it's—naughty!"

Victor cast down his eyes and blushed.

"Naughty!" gasped Beni, with a horrified look.

"'Tis a hard word," said Luigi, sadly, and buried his face in his hands.

"I little thought," murmured Victor, in a voice broken by emotion, "ever to be so reviled—and by a lady! Yet, perhaps you spoke thoughtlessly. You must consider, miss, that our wickedness has an excuse. For how are we to be bandits, let me ask, unless we are wicked?"

Martha was puzzled and shook her head, thoughtfully. Then she remembered something.

"You can't remain bandits any longer," said she, "because you are now in America."

"America!" cried the three, together.

"Certainly. You are on Prairie avenue, in Chicago. Uncle Walter sent you here from Italy in this chest."

The bandits seemed greatly bewildered by this announcement. Lugui sat down on an old chair with a broken rocker and wiped his forehead with a yellow silk handkerchief. Beni and Victor fell back upon the chest and looked at her with pale faces and staring eyes.

When he had somewhat recovered himself Victor spoke.

"Your Uncle Walter has greatly wronged us," he

said, reproachfully. "He has taken us from our beloved Italy, where bandits are highly respected, and brought us to a strange country where we shall not know whom to rob or how much to ask for a ransom."

"'Tis so!" said the fat man, slapping his leg sharply.

"And we had won such fine reputations in Italy!" said Beni, regretfully.

"Perhaps Uncle Walter wanted to reform you," suggested Martha.

"Are there, then, no bandits in Chicago?" asked Victor.

"Well," replied the girl, blushing in her turn, "we do not call them bandits."

"Then what shall we do for a living?" inquired Beni, despairingly.

"A great deal can be done in a big American city," said the child. "My father is a lawyer" (the bandits shuddered), "and my mother's cousin is a police inspector."

"Ah," said Victor, "that is a good employment. The police need to be inspected, especially in Italy."

"Everywhere!" added Beni.

"Then you could do other things," continued Martha, encouragingly. "You could be motor men on trolley cars, or clerks in a department store. Some people even become aldermen to earn a living."

The bandits shook their heads sadly.

"We are not fitted for such work," said Victor. "Our business is to rob."

Martha tried to think.

"It is rather hard to get positions in the gas office," she said, "but you might become politicians."

"No!" cried Beni, with sudden fierceness; "we must not abandon our high calling. Bandits we have always been, and bandits we must remain!"

"'Tis so!" agreed the fat man.

"Even in Chicago there must be people to rob," remarked Victor, with cheerfulness.

Martha was distressed.

"I think they have all been robbed," she objected.

"Then we can rob the robbers, for we have experience and talent beyond the ordinary," said Beni.

"Oh, dear; oh, dear!" moaned the girl; "why did Uncle Walter ever send you here in this chest?"

The bandits became interested.

"That is what we should like to know," declared Victor, eagerly.

"But no one will ever know, for Uncle Walter was lost while hunting elephants in Africa," she continued, with conviction.

"Then we must accept our fate and rob to the best of our ability," said Victor. "So long as we are faithful to our beloved profession we need not be ashamed."

"'Tis so!" cried the fat man.

"Brothers! we will begin now. Let us rob the house we are in."

"Good!" shouted the others and sprang to their feet.

Beni turned threateningly upon the child.

"Remain here!" he commanded. "If you stir one step your blood will be on your own head!" Then he added, in a gentler voice: "Don't be afraid; that's the way all bandits talk to their captives. But of course we wouldn't hurt a young lady under any circumstances."

"Of course not," said Victor.

The fat man drew a big knife from his belt and flourished it about his head.

"S'blood!" he ejaculated, fiercely.

"S'bananas!" cried Beni, in a terrible voice.

"Confusion to our foes!" hissed Victor.

And then the three bent themselves nearly double and crept stealthily down the stairway with cocked pistols in their hands and glittering knives between their teeth, leaving Martha trembling with fear and too horrified to even cry for help.

How long she remained alone in the attic she never knew, but finally she heard the catlike tread of the returning bandits and saw them coming up the stairs in single file.

All bore heavy loads of plunder in their arms, and Lugui was balancing a mince pie on the top of a pile of her mother's best evening dresses. Victor came next with an armful of bric-a-brac, a brass candelabra and the parlor clock. Beni had the family Bible, the basket of silverware from the sideboard, a copper kettle and papa's fur overcoat.

"Oh, joy!" said Victor, putting down his load; "it is pleasant to rob once more."

"Oh, ecstacy!" said Beni; but he let the kettle drop on his toe and immediately began dancing around in anguish, while he muttered queer words in the Italian language.

"We have much wealth," continued Victor, holding the mince pie while Lugui added his spoils to the heap; "and all from one house! This America must be a rich place."

With a dagger he then cut himself a piece of the pie and handed the remainder to his comrades. Whereupon all three sat upon the floor and consumed the pie while Martha looked on sadly.

"We should have a cave," remarked Beni; "for we must store our plunder in a safe place. Can you tell us of a secret cave?" he asked Martha.

"There's a Mammoth cave," she answered, "but it's in Kentucky. You would be obliged to ride on the cars a long time to get there."

The three bandits looked thoughtful and munched their pie silently, but the next moment they were startled by the ringing of the electric doorbell, which was heard plainly even in the remote attic.

"What's that?" demanded Victor, in a hoarse voice, as the three scrambled to their feet with drawn daggers.

Martha ran to the window and saw it was only the postman, who had dropped a letter in the box and gone away again. But the incident gave her an idea of how to get rid of her troublesome bandits, so she began wringing her hands as if in great distress and cried out:

"It's the police!"

The robbers looked at one another with genuine alarm, and Lugui asked, tremblingly:

"Are there many of them?"

"A hundred and twelve!" exclaimed Martha, after pretending to count them.

"Then we are lost!" declared Beni; "for we could never fight so many and live."

"Are they armed?" inquired Victor, who was shivering as if cold.

"Oh, yes," said she. "They have guns and swords and pistols and axes and—and—"

"And what?" demanded Lugui.

"And cannons!"

The three wicked ones groaned aloud and Beni said, in a hollow voice:

"I hope they will kill us quickly and not put us to the torture. I have been told these Americans are painted Indians, who are bloodthirsty and terrible."

"'Tis so!" gasped the fat man, with a shudder.

Suddenly Martha turned from the window.

"You are my friends, are you not?" she asked.

"We are devoted!" answered Victor.

"We adore you!" cried Beni.

"We would die for you!" added Lugui, thinking he was about to die anyway.

"Then I will save you," said the girl.

"How?" asked the three, with one voice.

"Get back into the chest," she said. "I will then close the lid, so they will be unable to find you."

They looked around the room in a dazed and ir-resolute way, but she exclaimed:

"You must be quick! They will soon be here to arrest you."

Then Lugui sprang into the chest and lay flat upon the bottom. Beni tumbled in next and packed himself in the back side. Victor followed after pausing to kiss her hand to the girl in a graceful manner.

Then Martha ran up to press down the lid, but could not make it catch.

"You must squeeze down," she said to them.

Lugui groaned.

"I am doing my best, miss," said Victor, who was nearest the top; "but although we fitted in very nicely before, the chest now seems rather small for us."

"'Tis so!" came the muffled voice of the fat man from the bottom.

"I know what takes up the room," said Beni.

"What?" inquired Victor, anxiously.

"The pie," returned Beni.

"'Tis so!" came from the bottom, in faint accents.

Then Martha sat upon the lid and pressed it down with all her weight. To her great delight the lock caught, and, springing down, she exerted all her strength and turned the key.

THIS STORY SHOULD TEACH us not to interfere in matters that do not concern us. For had Martha refrained from opening Uncle Walter's mysterious chest she would not have been obliged to carry downstairs all the plunder the robbers had brought into the attic.

CHAPTER 2

THE GLASS DOG

An accomplished wizard once lived on the top floor of a tenement house and passed his time in thoughtful study and studious thought. What he didn't know about wizardry was hardly worth knowing, for he possessed all the books and recipes of all the wizards who had lived before him; and, moreover, he had invented several wizardments himself.

This admirable person would have been completely happy but for the numerous interruptions to his studies caused by folk who came to consult him about their troubles (in which he was not interested), and by the loud knocks of the iceman, the milkman, the baker's boy, the laundryman and the peanut woman. He never dealt with any of these people; but they rapped at his door every day to see him about this or that or to try to sell him their wares. Just when he was most deeply interested in his books or engaged in watching the bubbling of a cauldron there would come a knock at his door. And after sending the intruder away he always found he had lost his train of thought or ruined his compound.

At length these interruptions aroused his anger, and he decided he must have a dog to keep people away from his door. He didn't know where to find a dog, but in the next room lived a poor glass-blower with whom he had a slight acquaintance; so he went into the man's apartment and asked:

"Where can I find a dog?"

"What sort of a dog?" inquired the glass-blower.

"A good dog. One that will bark at people and drive them away. One that will be no trouble to keep and won't expect to be fed. One that has no fleas and is neat in his habits. One that will obey me when I speak to him. In short, a good dog," said the wizard.

"Such a dog is hard to find," returned the glass-blower, who was busy making a blue glass flower pot with a pink glass rosebush in it, having green glass leaves and yellow glass roses.

The wizard watched him thoughtfully.

"Why cannot you blow me a dog out of glass?" he asked, presently.

"I can," declared the glass-blower; "but it would not bark at people, you know."

"Oh, I'll fix that easily enough," replied the other. "If I could not make a glass dog bark I would be a mighty poor wizard."

"Very well; if you can use a glass dog I'll be

pleased to blow one for you. Only, you must pay for my work."

"Certainly," agreed the wizard. "But I have none of that horrid stuff you call money. You must take some of my wares in exchange."

The glass-blower considered the matter for a moment.

"Could you give me something to cure my rheumatism?" he asked.

"Oh, yes; easily."

"Then it's a bargain. I'll start the dog at once. What color of glass shall I use?"

"Pink is a pretty color," said the wizard, "and it's unusual for a dog, isn't it?"

"Very," answered the glass-blower; "but it shall be pink."

So the wizard went back to his studies and the glass-blower began to make the dog.

Next morning he entered the wizard's room with the glass dog under his arm and set it carefully upon the table. It was a beautiful pink in color, with a fine coat of spun glass, and about its neck was twisted a blue glass ribbon. Its eyes were specks of black glass and sparkled intelligently, as do many of the glass eyes worn by men.

The wizard expressed himself pleased with the glass-blower's skill and at once handed him a small vial.

"This will cure your rheumatism," he said.

"But the vial is empty!" protested the glass-blower.

"Oh, no; there is one drop of liquid in it," was the wizard's reply.

"Will one drop cure my rheumatism?" inquired the glass-blower, in wonder.

"Most certainly. That is a marvelous remedy. The one drop contained in the vial will cure instantly any kind of disease ever known to humanity. Therefore it is especially good for rheumatism. But guard it well, for it is the only drop of its kind in the world, and I've forgotten the recipe."

"Thank you," said the glass-blower, and went back to his room.

Then the wizard cast a wizzy spell and mumbled several very learned words in the wizardese language over the glass dog. Whereupon the little animal first wagged its tail from side to side, then winked his left eye knowingly, and at last began barking in a most frightful manner—that is, when you stop to consider the noise came from a pink glass dog. There is something almost astonishing in the magic arts of wizards; unless, of course, you know how to do the things yourself, when you are not expected to be surprised at them.

The wizard was as delighted as a school teacher at the success of his spell, although he was not astonished. Immediately he placed the dog outside his door, where it would bark at anyone who dared knock and so disturb the studies of its master.

The glass-blower, on returning to his room, decided not to use the one drop of wizard cure-all just then.

"My rheumatism is better to-day," he reflected,

"and I will be wise to save the medicine for a time when I am very ill, when it will be of more service to me."

So he placed the vial in his cupboard and went to work blowing more roses out of glass. Presently he happened to think the medicine might not keep, so he started to ask the wizard about it. But when he reached the door the glass dog barked so fiercely that he dared not knock, and returned in great haste to his own room. Indeed, the poor man was quite upset at so unfriendly a reception from the dog he had himself so carefully and skillfully made.

The next morning, as he read his newspaper, he noticed an article stating that the beautiful Miss Mydas, the richest young lady in town, was very ill, and the doctors had given up hope of her recovery.

The glass-blower, although miserably poor, hard-working and homely of feature, was a man of ideas. He suddenly recollected his precious medicine, and determined to use it to better advantage than relieving his own ills. He dressed himself in his best clothes, brushed his hair and combed his whiskers, washed his hands and tied his necktie, blackened his shoes and sponged his vest, and then put the vial of magic cure-all in his pocket. Next he locked his door, went downstairs and walked through the streets to the grand mansion where the wealthy Miss Mydas resided.

The butler opened the door and said:

"No soap, no chromos, no vegetables, no hair oil, no books, no baking powder. My young lady is dying and we're well supplied for the funeral."

The glass-blower was grieved at being taken for a peddler.

"My friend," he began, proudly; but the butler interrupted him, saying:

"No tombstones, either; there's a family grave-yard and the monument's built."

"The graveyard won't be needed if you will permit me to speak," said the glass-blower.

"No doctors, sir; they've given up my young lady, and she's given up the doctors," continued the butler, calmly.

"I'm no doctor," returned the glass-blower.

"Nor are the others. But what is your errand?"

"I called to cure your young lady by means of a magical compound."

"Step in, please, and take a seat in the hall. I'll speak to the housekeeper," said the butler, more politely.

So he spoke to the housekeeper and the housekeeper mentioned the matter to the steward and the steward consulted the chef and the chef kissed the lady's maid and sent her to see the stranger. Thus are the very wealthy hedged around with ceremony, even when dying.

When the lady's maid heard from the glass-blower that he had a medicine which would cure her mistress, she said:

"I'm glad you came."

"But," said he, "if I restore your mistress to health she must marry me."

"I'll make inquiries and see if she's willing," answered the maid, and went at once to consult Miss Mydas.

The young lady did not hesitate an instant.

"I'd marry any old thing rather than die!" she cried. "Bring him here at once!"

So the glass-blower came, poured the magic drop into a little water, gave it to the patient, and the next minute Miss Mydas was as well as she had ever been in her life.

"Dear me!" she exclaimed; "I've an engagement at the Fritters' reception to-night. Bring my pearl-colored silk, Marie, and I will begin my toilet at once. And don't forget to cancel the order for the funeral flowers and your mourning gown."

"But, Miss Mydas," remonstrated the glass-blower, who stood by, "you promised to marry me if I cured you."

"I know," said the young lady, "but we must have time to make proper announcement in the society papers and have the wedding cards engraved. Call to-morrow and we'll talk it over."

The glass-blower had not impressed her favorably as a husband, and she was glad to find an excuse for getting rid of him for a time. And she did not want to miss the Fritters' reception.

Yet the man went home filled with joy; for he thought his stratagem had succeeded and he was about to marry a rich wife who would keep him in luxury forever afterward.

The first thing he did on reaching his room was to smash his glass-blowing tools and throw them out of the window.

He then sat down to figure out ways of spending his wife's money.

The following day he called upon Miss Mydas, who was reading a novel and eating chocolate creams as happily as if she had never been ill in her life.

"Where did you get the magic compound that cured me?" she asked.

"From a learned wizard," said he; and then, thinking it would interest her, he told how he had made the glass dog for the wizard, and how it barked and kept everybody from bothering him.

"How delightful!" she said. "I've always wanted a glass dog that could bark."

"But there is only one in the world," he answered, "and it belongs to the wizard."

"You must buy it for me," said the lady.

"The wizard cares nothing for money," replied the glass-blower.

"Then you must steal it for me," she retorted. "I can never live happily another day unless I have a glass dog that can bark."

The glass-blower was much distressed at this, but said he would see what he could do. For a man should always try to please his wife, and Miss Mydas has promised to marry him within a week.

On his way home he purchased a heavy sack, and when he passed the wizard's door and the pink glass dog ran out to bark at him he threw the sack over the dog, tied the opening with a piece of twine, and carried him away to his own room.

The next day he sent the sack by a messenger

boy to Miss Mydas, with his compliments, and later in the afternoon he called upon her in person, feeling quite sure he would be received with gratitude for stealing the dog she so greatly desired.

But when he came to the door and the butler opened it, what was his amazement to see the glass dog rush out and begin barking at him furiously.

"Call off your dog," he shouted, in terror.

"I can't, sir," answered the butler. "My young lady has ordered the glass dog to bark whenever you call here. You'd better look out, sir," he added, "for if it bites you, you may have glassophobia!"

This so frightened the poor glass-blower that he went away hurriedly. But he stopped at a drug store and put his last dime in the telephone box so he could talk to Miss Mydas without being bitten by the dog.

"Give me Pelf 6742!" he called.

"Hello! What is it?" said a voice.

"I want to speak with Miss Mydas," said the glass-blower.

Presently a sweet voice said: "This is Miss Mydas. What is it?"

"Why have you treated me so cruelly and set the glass dog on me?" asked the poor fellow.

"Well, to tell the truth," said the lady, "I don't like your looks. Your cheeks are pale and baggy, your hair is coarse and long, your eyes are small and red, your hands are big and rough, and you are bow-legged."

"But I can't help my looks!" pleaded the glass-blower; "and you really promised to marry me."

"If you were better looking I'd keep my promise," she returned. "But under the circumstances you are no fit mate for me, and unless you keep away from my mansion I shall set my glass dog on you!" Then she dropped the 'phone and would have nothing more to say.

The miserable glass-blower went home with a heart bursting with disappointment and began tying a rope to the bedpost by which to hang himself.

Some one knocked at the door, and, upon opening it, he saw the wizard.

"I've lost my dog," he announced.

"Have you, indeed?" replied the glass-blower tying a knot in the rope.

"Yes; some one has stolen him."

"That's too bad," declared the glass-blower, indifferently.

"You must make me another," said the wizard.

"But I cannot; I've thrown away my tools."

"Then what shall I do?" asked the wizard.

"I do not know, unless you offer a reward for the dog."

"But I have no money," said the wizard.

"Offer some of your compounds, then," suggested the glass-blower, who was making a noose in the rope for his head to go through.

"The only thing I can spare," replied the wizard, thoughtfully, "is a Beauty Powder."

"What!" cried the glass-blower, throwing down the rope, "have you really such a thing?"

"Yes, indeed. Whoever takes the powder will become the most beautiful person in the world."

"If you will offer that as a reward," said the glass-blower, eagerly, "I'll try to find the dog for you, for above everything else I long to be beautiful."

"But I warn you the beauty will only be skin deep," said the wizard.

"That's all right," replied the happy glass-blower; "when I lose my skin I shan't care to remain beautiful."

"Then tell me where to find my dog and you shall have the powder," promised the wizard.

So the glass-blower went out and pretended to search, and by-and-by he returned and said:

"I've discovered the dog. You will find him in the mansion of Miss Mydas."

The wizard went at once to see if this were true, and, sure enough, the glass dog ran out and began barking at him. Then the wizard spread out his hands and chanted a magic spell which sent the dog fast asleep, when he picked him up and carried him to his own room on the top floor of the tenement house.

Afterward he carried the Beauty Powder to the glass-blower as a reward, and the fellow immediately swallowed it and became the most beautiful man in the world.

The next time he called upon Miss Mydas there was no dog to bark at him, and when the young lady saw him she fell in love with his beauty at once.

"If only you were a count or a prince," she sighed, "I'd willingly marry you."

"But I am a prince," he answered; "the Prince of Dogblowers."

"Ah!" said she; "then if you are willing to accept an allowance of four dollars a week I'll order the wedding cards engraved."

The man hesitated, but when he thought of the rope hanging from his bedpost he consented to the terms.

So they were married, and the bride was very jealous of her husband's beauty and led him a dog's life. So he managed to get into debt and made her miserable in turn.

As for the glass dog, the wizard set him barking again by means of his wizardness and put him outside his door. I suppose he is there yet, and am rather sorry, for I should like to consult the wizard about the moral to this story.

CHAPTER 3
THE QUEEN OF QUOK

A king once died, as kings are apt to do, being as liable to shortness of breath as other mortals.

It was high time this king abandoned his earth life, for he had lived in a sadly extravagant manner, and his subjects could spare him without the slightest inconvenience.

His father had left him a full treasury, both money and jewels being in abundance. But the foolish king just deceased had squandered every penny in riotous living. He had then taxed his subjects until most of them became paupers, and this money vanished in more riotous living. Next he sold all the grand old furniture in the palace; all the silver and gold plate and bric-a-brac; all the rich carpets and furnishings and even his own kingly wardrobe, reserving only a soiled and moth-eaten ermine robe to fold over his threadbare raiment. And he spent the money in further riotous living.

Don't ask me to explain what riotous living is. I only know, from hearsay, that it is an excellent way to get rid of money. And so this spendthrift king found it.

He now picked all the magnificent jewels from this kingly crown and from the round ball on the top of his scepter, and sold them and spent the money. Riotous living, of course. But at last he was at the end of his resources. He couldn't sell the crown itself, because no one but the king had the right to wear it. Neither could he sell the royal palace, because only the king had the right to live there.

So, finally, he found himself reduced to a bare palace, containing only a big mahogany bedstead that he slept in, a small stool on which he sat to pull off his shoes and the moth-eaten ermine robe.

In this straight he was reduced to the necessity of borrowing an occasional dime from his chief counselor, with which to buy a ham sandwich. And the chief counselor hadn't many dimes. One who counseled his king so foolishly was likely to ruin his own prospects as well.

So the king, having nothing more to live for, died suddenly and left a ten-year-old son to inherit the dismantled kingdom, the moth-eaten robe and the jewel-stripped crown.

No one envied the child, who had scarcely been thought of until he became king himself. Then he was recognized as a personage of some importance, and the politicians and hangers-on, headed by the chief counselor of the kingdom, held a meeting to determine what could be done for him.

These folk had helped the old king to live riotously while his money lasted, and now they were poor and too proud to work. So they tried to think of a plan that would bring more money into the little king's treasury, where it would be handy for them to help themselves.

After the meeting was over the chief counselor came to the young king, who was playing peg-top in the courtyard, and said:

"Your majesty, we have thought of a way to restore your kingdom to its former power and magnificence."

"All right," replied his majesty, carelessly. "How will you do it?"

"By marrying you to a lady of great wealth," replied the counselor.

"Marrying me!" cried the king. "Why, I am only ten years old!"

"I know; it is to be regretted. But your majesty will grow older, and the affairs of the kingdom demand that you marry a wife."

"Can't I marry a mother, instead?" asked the poor little king, who had lost his mother when a baby.

"Certainly not," declared the counselor. "To marry a mother would be illegal; to marry a wife is right and proper."

"Can't you marry her yourself?" inquired his majesty, aiming his peg-top at the chief counselor's toe, and laughing to see how he jumped to escape it.

"Let me explain," said the other. "You haven't a penny in the world, but you have a kingdom. There are many rich women who would be glad to give their wealth in exchange for a queen's coronet—even if the king is but a child. So we have decided to advertise that the one who bids the highest shall become the queen of Quok."

"If I must marry at all," said the king, after a moment's thought, "I prefer to marry Nyana, the armorer's daughter."

"She is too poor," replied the counselor.

"Her teeth are pearls, her eyes are amethysts, and her hair is gold," declared the little king.

"True, your majesty. But consider that your wife's wealth must be used. How would Nyana look after you have pulled her teeth of pearls, plucked out her amethyst eyes and shaved her golden head?"

The boy shuddered.

"Have your own way," he said, despairingly. "Only let the lady be as dainty as possible and a good playfellow."

"We shall do our best," returned the chief counselor, and went away to advertise throughout the neighboring kingdoms for a wife for the boy king of Quok.

There were so many applicants for the privilege of marrying the little king that it was decided to put him up at auction, in order that the largest possible sum of money should be brought into the kingdom. So, on the day appointed, the ladies gathered at the palace from all the surrounding kingdoms—from

Bilkon, Mulgravia, Junkum and even as far away as the republic of Macvelt.

The chief counselor came to the palace early in the morning and had the king's face washed and his hair combed; and then he padded the inside of the crown with old newspapers to make it small enough to fit his majesty's head. It was a sorry looking crown, having many big and little holes in it where the jewels had once been; and it had been neglected and knocked around until it was quite battered and tarnished. Yet, as the counselor said, it was the king's crown, and it was quite proper he should wear it on the solemn occasion of his auction.

Like all boys, be they kings or paupers, his majesty had torn and soiled his one suit of clothes, so that they were hardly presentable; and there was no money to buy new ones. Therefore the counselor wound the old ermine robe around the king and sat him upon the stool in the middle of the otherwise empty audience chamber.

And around him stood all the courtiers and politicians and hangers-on of the kingdom, consisting of such people as were too proud or lazy to work for a living. There was a great number of them, you may be sure, and they made an imposing appearance.

Then the doors of the audience chamber were thrown open, and the wealthy ladies who aspired to being queen of Quok came trooping in. The king looked them over with much anxiety, and decided they were each and all old enough to be his grandmother, and ugly enough to scare away the crows from the royal cornfields. After which he lost interest in them.

But the rich ladies never looked at the poor little king squatting upon his stool. They gathered at once about the chief counselor, who acted as auctioneer.

"How much am I offered for the coronet of the queen of Quok?" asked the counselor, in a loud voice.

"Where is the coronet?" inquired a fussy old lady who had just buried her ninth husband and was worth several millions.

"There isn't any coronet at present," explained the chief counselor, "but whoever bids highest will have the right to wear one, and she can then buy it."

"Oh," said the fussy old lady, "I see." Then she added: "I'll bid fourteen dollars."

"Fourteen thousand dollars!" cried a sour-looking woman who was thin and tall and had wrinkles all over her skin—"like a frosted apple," the king thought.

The bidding now became fast and furious, and the poverty-stricken courtiers brightened up as the sum began to mount into the millions.

"He'll bring us a very pretty fortune, after all," whispered one to his comrade, "and then we shall have the pleasure of helping him spend it."

The king began to be anxious. All the women who looked at all kind-hearted or pleasant had stopped bidding for lack of money, and the slender old dame with the wrinkles seemed determined to get the coronet at any price, and with it the boy husband. This ancient creature finally became so excited that her wig got crosswise of her head and her false teeth kept slipping out, which horrified the little king greatly; but she would not give up.

At last the chief counselor ended the auction by crying out:

"Sold to Mary Ann Brodjinsky de la Porkus for three million, nine hundred thousand, six hundred and twenty-four dollars and sixteen cents!" And the sour-looking old woman paid the money in cash and on the spot, which proves this is a fairy story.

The king was so disturbed at the thought that he must marry this hideous creature that he began to wail and weep; whereupon the woman boxed his ears soundly. But the counselor reproved her for punishing her future husband in public, saying:

"You are not married yet. Wait until to-morrow, after the wedding takes place. Then you can abuse him as much as you wish. But at present we prefer to have people think this is a love match."

The poor king slept but little that night, so filled was he with terror of his future wife. Nor could he get the idea out of his head that he preferred to marry the armorer's daughter, who was about his own age. He tossed and tumbled around upon his hard bed until the moonlight came in at the window and lay like a great white sheet upon the bare floor. Finally, in turning over for the hundredth time, his hand struck against a secret spring in the headboard of the big mahogany bedstead, and at once, with a sharp click, a panel flew open.

The noise caused the king to look up, and, seeing the open panel, he stood upon tiptoe, and, reaching within, drew out a folded paper. It had several leaves fastened together like a book, and upon the first page was written:

"When the king is in trouble
This leaf he must double
And set it on fire
To obtain his desire."

This was not very good poetry, but when the king had spelled it out in the moonlight he was filled with joy.

"There's no doubt about my being in trouble," he exclaimed; "so I'll burn it at once, and see what happens."

He tore off the leaf and put the rest of the book in its secret hiding place. Then, folding the paper double, he placed it on the top of his stool, lighted a match and set fire to it.

It made a horrid smudge for so small a paper, and the king sat on the edge of the bed and watched it eagerly.

When the smoke cleared away he was surprised to see, sitting upon the stool, a round little man, who, with folded arms and crossed legs, sat calmly facing the king and smoking a black briarwood pipe.

"Well, here I am," said he.

"So I see," replied the little king. "But how did you get here?"

"Didn't you burn the paper?" demanded the round man, by way of answer.

"Yes, I did," acknowledged the king.

"Then you are in trouble, and I've come to help you out of it. I'm the Slave of the Royal Bedstead."

"Oh!" said the king. "I didn't know there was one."

"Neither did your father, or he would not have been so foolish as to sell everything he had for money. By the way, it's lucky for you he did not sell this bedstead. Now, then, what do you want?"

"I'm not sure what I want," replied the king; "but I know what I don't want, and that is the old woman who is going to marry me."

"That's easy enough," said the Slave of the Royal Bedstead. "All you need do is to return her the money she paid the chief counselor and declare the match off. Don't be afraid. You are the king, and your word is law."

"To be sure," said the majesty. "But I am in great need of money. How am I going to live if the chief counselor returns to Mary Ann Brodjinski her millions?"

"Phoo! that's easy enough," again answered the man, and, putting his hand in his pocket, he drew out and tossed to the king an old-fashioned leather purse. "Keep that with you," said he, "and you will always be rich, for you can take out of the purse as many twenty-five-cent silver pieces as you wish, one at a time. No matter how often you take one out, another will instantly appear in its place within the purse."

"Thank you," said the king, gratefully. "You have rendered me a rare favor; for now I shall have money for all my needs and will not be obliged to marry anyone. Thank you a thousand times!"

"Don't mention it," answered the other, puffing his pipe slowly and watching the smoke curl into the moonlight. "Such things are easy to me. Is that all you want?"

"All I can think of just now," returned the king.

"Then, please close that secret panel in the bedstead," said the man; "the other leaves of the book may be of use to you some time."

The boy stood upon the bed as before and, reaching up, closed the opening so that no one else could discover it. Then he turned to face his visitor, but the Slave of the Royal Bedstead had disappeared.

"I expected that," said his majesty; "yet I am sorry he did not wait to say good-by."

With a lightened heart and a sense of great relief the boy king placed the leathern purse underneath his pillow, and climbing into bed again slept soundly until morning.

When the sun rose his majesty rose also, refreshed and comforted, and the first thing he did was to send for the chief counselor.

That mighty personage arrived looking glum and unhappy, but the boy was too full of his own good fortune to notice it. Said he:

"I have decided not to marry anyone, for I have just come into a fortune of my own. Therefore I command you return to that old woman the money she has paid you for the right to wear the coronet of the queen of Quok. And make public declaration that the wedding will not take place."

Hearing this the counselor began to tremble, for he saw the young king had decided to reign in earnest; and he looked so guilty that his majesty inquired:

"Well! what is the matter now?"

"Sire," replied the wretch, in a shaking voice, "I cannot return the woman her money, for I have lost it!"

"Lost it!" cried the king, in mingled astonishment and anger.

"Even so, your majesty. On my way home from the auction last night I stopped at the drug store to get some potash lozenges for my throat, which was dry and hoarse with so much loud talking; and your majesty will admit it was through my efforts the woman was induced to pay so great a price. Well, going into the drug store I carelessly left the package of money lying on the seat of my carriage, and when I came out again it was gone. Nor was the thief anywhere to be seen."

"Did you call the police?" asked the king.

"Yes, I called; but they were all on the next block, and although they have promised to search for the robber I have little hope they will ever find him."

The king sighed.

"What shall we do now?" he asked.

"I fear you must marry Mary Ann Brodjinski," answered the chief counselor; "unless, indeed, you order the executioner to cut her head off."

"That would be wrong," declared the king. "The woman must not be harmed. And it is just that we return her money, for I will not marry her under any circumstances."

"Is that private fortune you mentioned large enough to repay her?" asked the counselor.

"Why, yes," said the king, thoughtfully, "but it will take some time to do it, and that shall be your task. Call the woman here."

The counselor went in search of Mary Ann, who, when she heard she was not to become a queen, but would receive her money back, flew into a violent passion and boxed the chief counselor's ears so viciously that they stung for nearly an hour. But she followed him into the king's audience chamber, where she demanded her money in a loud voice, claiming as well the interest due upon it over night.

"The counselor has lost your money," said the boy king, "but he shall pay you every penny out of my own private purse. I fear, however, you will be obliged to take it in small change."

"That will not matter," she said, scowling upon the counselor as if she longed to reach his ears again; "I don't care how small the change is so long as I get every penny that belongs to me, and the interest. Where is it?"

"Here," answered the king, handing the counselor the leathern purse. "It is all in silver quarters, and they must be taken from the purse one at a time; but there will be plenty to pay your demands, and to spare."

So, there being no chairs, the counselor sat down upon the floor in one corner and began counting out silver twenty-five-cent pieces from the purse, one by one. And the old woman sat upon the floor opposite him and took each piece of money from his hand.

It was a large sum: three million, nine hundred thousand, six hundred and twenty-four dollars and sixteen cents. And it takes four times as many twenty-five-cent pieces as it would dollars to make up the amount.

The king left them sitting there and went to school, and often thereafter he came to the counselor and interrupted him long enough to get from the purse what money he needed to reign in a proper and dignified manner. This somewhat delayed the counting, but as it was a long job, anyway, that did not matter much.

The king grew to manhood and married the pretty daughter of the armorer, and they now have two lovely children of their own. Once in awhile they go into the big audience chamber of the palace and let the little ones watch the aged, hoary-headed counselor count out silver twenty-five-cent pieces to a withered old woman, who watched his every movement to see that he does not cheat her.

It is a big sum, three million, nine hundred thousand, six hundred and twenty-four dollars and sixteen cents in twenty-five-cent pieces.

But this is how the counselor was punished for being so careless with the woman's money. And this is how Mary Ann Brodjinski de la Porkus was also punished for wishing to marry a ten-year-old king in order that she might wear the coronet of the queen of Quok.

CHAPTER 4
THE GIRL WHO OWNED A BEAR

Mamma had gone down-town to shop. She had asked Nora to look after Jane Gladys, and Nora promised she would. But it was her afternoon for polishing the silver, so she stayed in the pantry and left Jane Gladys to amuse herself alone in the big sitting-room upstairs.

The little girl did not mind being alone, for she was working on her first piece of embroidery—a sofa pillow for papa's birthday present. So she crept into the big bay window and curled herself up on the broad sill while she bent her brown head over her work.

Soon the door opened and closed again, quietly. Jane Gladys thought it was Nora, so she didn't look up until she had taken a couple more stitches on a forget-me-not. Then she raised her eyes and was astonished to find a strange man in the middle of the room, who regarded her earnestly.

He was short and fat, and seemed to be breathing heavily from his climb up the stairs. He held a work silk hat in one hand and underneath his other elbow was tucked a good-sized book. He was dressed in a black suit that looked old and rather shabby, and his head was bald upon the top.

"Excuse me," he said, while the child gazed at him in solemn surprise. "Are you Jane Gladys Brown?"

"Yes, sir," she answered.

"Very good; very good, indeed!" he remarked, with a queer sort of smile. "I've had quite a hunt to find you, but I've succeeded at last."

"How did you get in?" inquired Jane Gladys, with a growing distrust of her visitor.

"That is a secret," he said, mysteriously.

This was enough to put the girl on her guard. She looked at the man and the man looked at her, and both looks were grave and somewhat anxious.

"What do you want?" she asked, straightening herself up with a dignified air.

"Ah!—now we are coming to business," said the man, briskly. "I'm going to be quite frank with you. To begin with, your father has abused me in a most ungentlemanly manner."

Jane Gladys got off the window sill and pointed her small finger at the door.

"Leave this room 'meejitly!" she cried, her voice trembling with indignation. "My papa is the best man in the world. He never 'bused anybody!"

"Allow me to explain, please," said the visitor, without paying any attention to her request to go

41

away. "Your father may be very kind to you, for you are his little girl, you know. But when he's downtown in his office he's inclined to be rather severe, especially on book agents. Now, I called on him the other day and asked him to buy the 'Complete Works of Peter Smith,' and what do you suppose he did?"

She said nothing.

"Why," continued the man, with growing excitement, "he ordered me from his office, and had me put out of the building by the janitor! What do you think of such treatment as that from the 'best papa in the world,' eh?"

"I think he was quite right," said Jane Gladys.

"Oh, you do? Well," said the man, "I resolved to be revenged for the insult. So, as your father is big and strong and a dangerous man, I have decided to be revenged upon his little girl."

Jane Gladys shivered.

"What are you going to do?" she asked.

"I'm going to present you with this book," he answered, taking it from under his arm. Then he sat down on the edge of a chair, placed his hat on the rug and drew a fountain pen from his vest pocket.

"I'll write your name in it," said he. "How do you spell Gladys?"

"G-l-a-d-y-s," she replied.

"Thank you. Now this," he continued, rising and handing her the book with a bow, "is my revenge for your father's treatment of me. Perhaps he'll be sorry he didn't buy the 'Complete Works of Peter Smith.' Good-by, my dear."

He walked to the door, gave her another bow, and left the room, and Jane Gladys could see that he was laughing to himself as if very much amused.

When the door had closed behind the queer little man the child sat down in the window again and glanced at the book. It had a red and yellow cover and the word "Thingamajigs" was across the front in big letters.

Then she opened it, curiously, and saw her name written in black letters upon the first white leaf.

"He was a funny little man," she said to herself, thoughtfully.

She turned the next leaf, and saw a big picture of a clown, dressed in green and red and yellow, and having a very white face with three-cornered spots of red on each cheek and over the eyes. While she looked at this the book trembled in her hands, the leaf crackled and creaked and suddenly the clown jumped out of it and stood upon the floor beside her, becoming instantly as big as any ordinary clown.

After stretching his arms and legs and yawning in a rather impolite manner, he gave a silly chuckle and said:

"This is better! You don't know how cramped one gets, standing so long upon a page of flat paper."

Perhaps you can imagine how startled Jane Gladys was, and how she stared at the clown who had just leaped out of the book.

"You didn't expect anything of this sort, did you?" he asked, leering at her in clown fashion. Then he turned around to take a look at the room and Jane Gladys laughed in spite of her astonishment.

"What amuses you?" demanded the clown.

"Why, the back of you is all white!" cried the girl. "You're only a clown in front of you."

"Quite likely," he returned, in an annoyed tone. "The artist made a front view of me. He wasn't expected to make the back of me, for that was against the page of the book."

"But it makes you look so funny!" said Jane Gladys, laughing until her eyes were moist with tears.

The clown looked sulky and sat down upon a chair so she couldn't see his back.

"I'm not the only thing in the book," he remarked, crossly.

This reminded her to turn another page, and she had scarcely noted that it contained the picture of a monkey when the animal sprang from the book with a great crumpling of paper and landed upon the window seat beside her.

"He-he-he-he-he!" chattered the creature, springing to the girl's shoulder and then to the center table. "This is great fun! Now I can be a real monkey instead of a picture of one."

"Real monkeys can't talk," said Jane Gladys, reprovingly.

"How do you know? Have you ever been one yourself?" inquired the animal; and then he laughed loudly, and the clown laughed, too, as if he enjoyed the remark.

The girl was quite bewildered by this time. She thoughtlessly turned another leaf, and before she had time to look twice a gray donkey leaped from the book and stumbled from the window seat to the floor with a great clatter.

"You're clumsy enough, I'm sure!" said the child, indignantly, for the beast had nearly upset her.

"Clumsy! And why not?" demanded the donkey, with angry voice. "If the fool artist had drawn you out of perspective, as he did me, I guess you'd be clumsy yourself."

"What's wrong with you?" asked Jane Gladys.

"My front and rear legs on the left side are nearly six inches too short, that's what's the matter! If that artist didn't know how to draw properly why did he try to make a donkey at all?"

"I don't know," replied the child, seeing an answer was expected.

"I can hardly stand up," grumbled the donkey; "and the least little thing will topple me over."

"Don't mind that," said the monkey, making a spring at the chandelier and swinging from it by his tail until Jane Gladys feared he would knock all the globes off; "the same artist has made my ears as big as that clown's and everyone knows a monkey hasn't any ears to speak of—much less to draw."

"He should be prosecuted," remarked the clown, gloomily. "I haven't any back."

Jane Gladys looked from one to the other with a puzzled expression upon her sweet face, and turned another page of the book.

Swift as a flash there sprang over her shoulder a tawney, spotted leopard, which landed upon the back of a big leather armchair and turned upon the others with a fierce movement.

The monkey climbed to the top of the chandelier and chattered with fright. The donkey tried to run and straightway tipped over on his left side. The clown grew paler than ever, but he sat still in his chair and gave a low whistle of surprise.

The leopard crouched upon the back of the chair, lashed his tail from side to side and glared at all of them, by turns, including Jane Gladys.

"Which of us are you going to attack first?" asked the donkey, trying hard to get upon his feet again.

"I can't attack any of you," snarled the leopard. "The artist made my mouth shut, so I haven't any teeth; and he forgot to make my claws. But I'm a frightful looking creature, nevertheless; am I not?"

"Oh, yes;" said the clown, indifferently. "I suppose you're frightful looking enough. But if you have no teeth nor claws we don't mind your looks at all."

This so annoyed the leopard that he growled horribly, and the monkey laughed at him.

Just then the book slipped from the girl's lap, and as she made a movement to catch it one of the pages near the back opened wide. She caught a glimpse of a fierce grizzly bear looking at her from the page, and quickly threw the book from her. It fell with a crash in the middle of the room, but beside it stood the great grizzly, who had wrenched himself from the page before the book closed.

"Now," cried the leopard from his perch, "you'd better look out for yourselves! You can't laugh at him as you did at me. The bear has both claws and teeth."

"Indeed I have," said the bear, in a low, deep, growling voice. "And I know how to use them, too. If you read in that book you'll find I'm described as a horrible, cruel and remorseless grizzly, whose only business in life is to eat up little girls—shoes, dresses, ribbons and all! And then, the author says, I smack my lips and glory in my wickedness."

"That's awful!" said the donkey, sitting upon his haunches and shaking his head sadly. "What do you suppose possessed the author to make you so hungry for girls? Do you eat animals, also?"

"The author does not mention my eating anything but little girls," replied the bear.

"Very good," remarked the clown, drawing a long breath of relief. "you may begin eating Jane Gladys as soon as you wish. She laughed because I had no back."

"And she laughed because my legs are out of perspective," brayed the donkey.

"But you also deserve to be eaten," screamed the leopard from the back of the leather chair; "for you laughed and poked fun at me because I had no claws nor teeth! Don't you suppose Mr. Grizzly, you could manage to eat a clown, a donkey and a monkey after you finish the girl?"

"Perhaps so, and a leopard into the bargain," growled the bear. "It will depend on how hungry I am. But I must begin on the little girl first, because the author says I prefer girls to anything."

Jane Gladys was much frightened on hearing this conversation, and she began to realize what the man meant when he said he gave her the book to be revenged. Surely papa would be sorry he hadn't bought the "Complete Works of Peter Smith" when he came home and found his little girl eaten up by a grizzly bear—shoes, dress, ribbons and all!

The bear stood up and balanced himself on his rear legs.

"This is the way I look in the book," he said. "Now watch me eat the little girl."

He advanced slowly toward Jane Gladys, and the monkey, the leopard, the donkey and the clown all stood around in a circle and watched the bear with much interest.

But before the grizzly reached her the child had a sudden thought, and cried out:

"Stop! You mustn't eat me. It would be wrong."

"Why?" asked the bear, in surprise.

"Because I own you. You're my private property," she answered.

"I don't see how you make that out," said the bear, in a disappointed tone.

"Why, the book was given to me; my name's on the front leaf. And you belong, by rights, in the book. So you mustn't dare to eat your owner!"

The Grizzly hesitated.

"Can any of you read?" he asked.

"I can," said the clown.

"Then see if she speaks the truth. Is her name really in the book?"

The clown picked it up and looked at the name.

"It is," said he. "'Jane Gladys Brown;' and written quite plainly in big letters."

The bear sighed.

"Then, of course, I can't eat her," he decided. "That author is as disappointing as most authors are."

"But he's not as bad as the artist," exclaimed the donkey, who was still trying to stand up straight.

"The fault lies with yourselves," said Jane Gladys, severely. "Why didn't you stay in the book, where you were put?"

The animals looked at each other in a foolish way, and the clown blushed under his white paint.

"Really—" began the bear, and then he stopped short.

The door bell rang loudly.

"It's mamma!" cried Jane Gladys, springing to her feet. "She's come home at last. Now, you stupid creatures—"

But she was interrupted by them all making a rush for the book. There was a swish and a whirr and a rustling of leaves, and an instant later the book lay upon the floor looking just like any other book, while Jane Gladys' strange companions had all disappeared.

THIS STORY SHOULD TEACH us to think quickly and clearly upon all occasions; for had Jane Gladys not remembered that she owned the bear he probably would have eaten her before the bell rang.

CHAPTER 5
THE ENCHANTED TYPES

One time a knook became tired of his beautiful life and longed for something new to do. The knooks have more wonderful powers than any other immortal folk—except, perhaps, the fairies and ryls. So one would suppose that a knook who might gain anything he desired by a simple wish could not be otherwise than happy and contented. But such was not the case with Popopo, the knook we are speaking of. He had lived thousands of years, and had enjoyed all the wonders he could think of. Yet life had become as tedious to him now as it might be to one who was unable to gratify a single wish.

Finally, by chance, Popopo thought of the earth people who dwell in cities, and so he resolved to visit them and see how they lived. This would surely be fine amusement, and serve to pass away many wearisome hours.

Therefore one morning, after a breakfast so dainty that you could scarcely imagine it, Popopo set out for the earth and at once was in the midst of a big city.

His own dwelling was so quiet and peaceful that the roaring noise of the town startled him. His nerves were so shocked that before he had looked around three minutes he decided to give up the adventure, and instantly returned home.

This satisfied for a time his desire to visit the earth cities, but soon the monotony of his existence again made him restless and gave him another thought. At night the people slept and the cities would be quiet. He would visit them at night.

So at the proper time Popopo transported himself in a jiffy to a great city, where he began wandering about the streets. Everyone was in bed. No wagons rattled along the pavements; no throngs of busy men shouted and halloaed. Even the policemen slumbered slyly and there happened to be no prowling thieves abroad.

His nerves being soothed by the stillness, Popopo began to enjoy himself. He entered many of the houses and examined their rooms with much curiosity. Locks and bolts made no difference to a knook, and he saw as well in darkness as in daylight.

After a time he strolled into the business portion of the city. Stores are unknown among the immortals, who have no need of money or of barter and exchange; so Popopo was greatly interested by the novel sight of so many collections of goods and merchandise.

During his wanderings he entered a millinery shop, and was surprised to see within a large glass case a great number of women's hats, each bearing in one position or another a stuffed bird. Indeed, some of the most elaborate hats had two or three birds upon them.

Now knooks are the especial guardians of birds, and love them dearly. To see so many of his little friends shut up in a glass case annoyed and grieved Popopo, who had no idea they had purposely been placed upon the hats by the milliner. So he slid back one of the doors of the case, gave the little chirruping whistle of the knooks that all birds know well, and called:

"Come, friends; the door is open—fly out!"

Popopo did not know the birds were stuffed; but, stuffed or not, every bird is bound to obey a knook's whistle and a knook's call. So they left the hats, flew out of the case and began fluttering about the room.

"Poor dears!" said the kind-hearted knook, "you long to be in the fields and forests again."

Then he opened the outer door for them and cried: "Off with you! Fly away, my beauties, and be happy again."

The astonished birds at once obeyed, and when they had soared away into the night air the knook closed the door and continued his wandering through the streets.

By dawn he saw many interesting sights, but day broke before he had finished the city, and he resolved to come the next evening a few hours earlier.

As soon as it was dark the following day he came

again to the city and on passing the millinery shop noticed a light within. Entering he found two women, one of whom leaned her head upon the table and sobbed bitterly, while the other strove to comfort her.

Of course Popopo was invisible to mortal eyes, so he stood by and listened to their conversation.

"Cheer up, sister," said one. "Even though your pretty birds have all been stolen the hats themselves remain."

"Alas!" cried the other, who was the milliner, "no one will buy my hats partly trimmed, for the fashion is to wear birds upon them. And if I cannot sell my goods I shall be utterly ruined."

Then she renewed her sobbing and the knook stole away, feeling a little ashamed to realized that in his love for the birds he had unconsciously wronged one of the earth people and made her unhappy.

This thought brought him back to the millinery shop later in the night, when the two women had gone home. He wanted, in some way, to replace the birds upon the hats, that the poor woman might be happy again. So he searched until he came upon a nearby cellar full of little gray mice, who lived quite undisturbed and gained a livelihood by gnawing through the walls into neighboring houses and stealing food from the pantries.

"Here are just the creatures," thought Popopo, "to place upon the woman's hats. Their fur is almost as soft as the plumage of the birds, and it strikes me the mice are remarkably pretty and graceful animals.

Moreover, they now pass their lives in stealing, and were they obliged to remain always upon women's hats their morals would be much improved."

So he exercised a charm that drew all the mice from the cellar and placed them upon the hats in the glass case, where they occupied the places the birds had vacated and looked very becoming—at least, in the eyes of the unworldly knook. To prevent their running about and leaving the hats Popopo rendered them motionless, and then he was so pleased with his work that he decided to remain in the shop and witness the delight of the milliner when she saw how daintily her hats were now trimmed.

She came in the early morning, accompanied by her sister, and her face wore a sad and resigned expression. After sweeping and dusting the shop and drawing the blinds she opened the glass case and took out a hat.

But when she saw a tiny gray mouse nestling among the ribbons and laces she gave a loud shriek, and, dropping the hat, sprang with one bound to the top of the table. The sister, knowing the shriek to be one of fear, leaped upon a chair and exclaimed:

"What is it? Oh! what is it?"

"A mouse!" gasped the milliner, trembling with terror.

Popopo, seeing this commotion, now realized that mice are especially disagreeable to human beings, and that he had made a grave mistake in placing them upon the hats; so he gave a low whistle of command that was heard only by the mice.

Instantly they all jumped from the hats, dashed

out the open door of the glass case and scampered away to their cellar. But this action so frightened the milliner and her sister that after giving several loud screams they fell upon their backs on the floor and fainted away.

Popopo was a kind-hearted knook, but on witnessing all this misery, caused by his own ignorance of the ways of humans, he straightway wished himself at home, and so left the poor women to recover as best they could.

Yet he could not escape a sad feeling of responsibility, and after thinking upon the matter he decided that since he had caused the milliner's unhappiness by freeing the birds, he could set the matter right by restoring them to the glass case. He loved the birds, and disliked to condemn them to slavery again; but that seemed the only way to end the trouble.

So he set off to find the birds. They had flown a long distance, but it was nothing to Popopo to reach them in a second, and he discovered them sitting upon the branches of a big chestnut tree and singing gayly.

When they saw the knook the birds cried:

"Thank you, Popopo. Thank you for setting us free."

"Do not thank me," returned the knook, "for I have come to send you back to the millinery shop."

"Why?" demanded a blue jay, angrily, while the others stopped their songs.

"Because I find the woman considers you her property, and your loss has caused her much unhappiness," answered Popopo.

"But remember how unhappy we were in her glass case," said a robin redbreast, gravely. "And as for being her property, you are a knook, and the natural guardian of all birds; so you know that Nature created us free. To be sure, wicked men shot and stuffed us, and sold us to the milliner; but the idea of our being her property is nonsense!"

Popopo was puzzled.

"If I leave you free," he said, "wicked men will shoot you again, and you will be no better off than before."

"Pooh!" exclaimed the blue jay, "we cannot be shot now, for we are stuffed. Indeed, two men fired several shots at us this morning, but the bullets only ruffled our feathers and buried themselves in our stuffing. We do not fear men now."

"Listen!" said Popopo, sternly, for he felt the birds were getting the best of the argument; "the poor milliner's business will be ruined if I do not return you to her shop. It seems you are necessary to trim the hats properly. It is the fashion for women to wear birds upon their headgear. So the poor milliner's wares, although beautified by lace and ribbons, are worthless unless you are perched upon them."

"Fashions," said a black bird, solemnly, "are made by men. What law is there, among birds or knooks, that requires us to be the slaves of fashion?"

"What have we to do with fashions, anyway?" screamed a linnet. "If it were the fashion to wear knooks perched upon women's hats would you be contented to stay there? Answer me, Popopo!"

But Popopo was in despair. He could not wrong the birds by sending them back to the milliner, nor did he wish the milliner to suffer by their loss. So he went home to think what could be done.

After much meditation he decided to consult the king of the knooks, and going at once to his majesty he told him the whole story.

The king frowned.

"This should teach you the folly of interfering with earth people," he said. "But since you have caused all this trouble, it is your duty to remedy it. Our birds cannot be enslaved, that is certain; therefore you must have the fashions changed, so it will no longer be stylish for women to wear birds upon their hats."

"How shall I do that?" asked Popopo.

"Easily enough. Fashions often change among the earth people, who tire quickly of any one thing. When they read in their newspapers and magazines that the style is so-and-so, they never question the matter, but at once obey the mandate of fashion. So you must visit the newspapers and magazines and enchant the types."

"Enchant the types!" echoed Popopo, in wonder.

"Just so. Make them read that it is no longer the fashion to wear birds upon hats. That will afford relief to your poor milliner and at the same time set free thousands of our darling birds who have been so cruelly used."

Popopo thanked the wise king and followed his advice.

The office of every newspaper and magazine in

the city was visited by the knook, and then he went to other cities, until there was not a publication in the land that had not a "new fashion note" in its pages. Sometimes Popopo enchanted the types, so that whoever read the print would see only what the knook wished them to. Sometimes he called upon the busy editors and befuddled their brains until they wrote exactly what he wanted them to. Mortals seldom know how greatly they are influenced by fairies, knooks and ryls, who often put thoughts into their heads that only the wise little immortals could have conceived.

The following morning when the poor milliner looked over her newspaper she was overjoyed to read that "no woman could now wear a bird upon her hat and be in style, for the newest fashion required only ribbons and laces."

Popopo after this found much enjoyment in visiting every millinery shop he could find and giving new life to the stuffed birds which were carelessly tossed aside as useless. And they flew to the fields and forests with songs of thanks to the good knook who had rescued them.

Sometimes a hunter fires his gun at a bird and then wonders why he did not hit it. But, having read this story, you will understand that the bird must have been a stuffed one from some millinery shop, which cannot, of course, be killed by a gun.

CHAPTER 6
THE LAUGHING HIPPOPOTAMUS

On one of the upper branches of the Congo river lived an ancient and aristocratic family of hippopotamuses, which boasted a pedigree dating back beyond the days of Noah—beyond the existence of mankind—far into the dim ages when the world was new.

They had always lived upon the banks of this same river, so that every curve and sweep of its waters, every pit and shallow of its bed, every rock and stump and wallow upon its bank was as familiar to them as their own mothers. And they are living there yet, I suppose.

Not long ago the queen of this tribe of hippopotamuses had a child which she named Keo, because it was so fat and round. Still, that you may not be misled, I will say that in the hippopotamus language "Keo," properly translated, means "fat and lazy" instead of fat and round. However, no one called the queen's attention to this error, because her tusks were monstrous long and sharp, and she thought Keo the sweetest baby in the world.

He was, indeed, all right for a hippopotamus. He rolled and played in the soft mud of the river bank, and waddled inland to nibble the leaves of the wild cabbage that grew there, and was happy and contented from morning till night. And he was the jolliest hippopotamus that ancient family had ever known. His little red eyes were forever twinkling with fun, and he laughed his merry laugh on all occasions, whether there was anything to laugh at or not.

Therefore the black people who dwelt in that region called him "Ippi"—the jolly one, although they dared not come anigh him on account of his fierce mother, and his equally fierce uncles and aunts and cousins, who lived in a vast colony upon the river bank.

And while these black people, who lived in little villages scattered among the trees, dared not openly attack the royal family of hippopotamuses, they were amazingly fond of eating hippopotamus meat whenever they could get it. This was no secret to the hippopotamuses. And, again, when the blacks managed to catch these animals alive, they had a trick of riding them through the jungles as if they were horses, thus reducing them to a condition of slavery.

Therefore, having these things in mind, whenever the tribe of hippopotamuses smelled the oily odor of black people they were accustomed to charge upon them furiously, and if by chance they overtook one of the enemy they would rip him with their sharp tusks or stamp him into the earth with their huge feet.

It was continual warfare between the hippopotamuses and the black people.

Gouie lived in one of the little villages of the blacks. He was the son of the chief's brother and grandson of the village sorcerer, the latter being an aged man known as the "the boneless wonder," because he could twist himself into as many coils as a serpent and had no bones to hinder his bending his flesh into any position. This made him walk in a wabbly fashion, but the black people had great respect for him.

Gouie's hut was made of branches of trees stuck together with mud, and his clothing consisted of a grass mat tied around his middle. But his relationship to the chief and the sorcerer gave him a certain dignity, and he was much addicted to solitary thought. Perhaps it was natural that these thoughts frequently turned upon his enemies, the hippopotamuses, and that he should consider many ways of capturing them.

Finally he completed his plans, and set about digging a great pit in the ground, midway between two sharp curves of the river. When the pit was finished he covered it over with small branches of trees, and strewed earth upon them, smoothing the surface so artfully that no one would suspect there was a big hole underneath. Then Gouie laughed softly to himself and went home to supper.

That evening the queen said to Keo, who was growing to be a fine child for his age:

"I wish you'd run across the bend and ask your Uncle Nikki to come here. I have found a strange plant, and want him to tell me if it is good to eat."

The jolly one laughed heartily as he started upon his errand, for he felt as important as a boy does when he is sent for the first time to the corner grocery to buy a yeast cake.

"Guk-uk-uk-uk! guk-uk-uk-uk!" was the way he laughed; and if you think a hippopotamus does not laugh this way you have but to listen to one and you will find I am right.

He crawled out of the mud where he was wallowing and tramped away through the bushes, and the last his mother heard as she lay half in and half out of the water was his musical "guk-uk-uk-uk!" dying away in the distance.

Keo was in such a happy mood that he scarcely noticed where he stepped, so he was much surprised when, in the middle of a laugh, the ground gave way beneath him, and he fell to the bottom of Gouie's deep pit. He was not badly hurt, but had bumped his nose severely as he went down; so he stopped laughing and began to think how he should get out again. Then he found the walls were higher than his head, and that he was a prisoner.

So he laughed a little at his own misfortune, and the laughter soothed him to sleep, so that he snored all through the night until daylight came.

When Gouie peered over the edge of the pit next morning he exclaimed:

"Why, 'tis Ippi—the Jolly One!"

Keo recognized the scent of a black man and tried to raise his head high enough to bite him. Seeing which Gouie spoke in the hippopotamus language, which he had learned from his grandfather, the sorcerer.

"Have peace, little one; you are my captive."

"Yes; I will have a piece of your leg, if I can reach it," retorted Keo; and then he laughed at his own joke: "Guk-uk-uk-uk!"

But Gouie, being a thoughtful black man, went away without further talk, and did not return until the following morning. When he again leaned over the pit Keo was so weak from hunger that he could hardly laugh at all.

"Do you give up?" asked Gouie, "or do you still wish to fight?"

"What will happen if I give up?" inquired Keo.

The black man scratched his woolly head in perplexity.

"It is hard to say, Ippi. You are too young to work, and if I kill you for food I shall lose your tusks, which are not yet grown. Why, O Jolly One, did you fall into my hole? I wanted to catch your mother or one of your uncles."

"Guk-uk-uk-uk!" laughed Keo. "You must let me go, after all, black man; for I am of no use to you!"

"That I will not do," declared Gouie; "unless," he added, as an afterthought, "you will make a bargain with me."

"Let me hear about the bargain, black one, for I am hungry," said Keo.

"I will let your go if you swear by the tusks of your grandfather that you will return to me in a year and a day and become my prisoner again."

The youthful hippopotamus paused to think, for he knew it was a solemn thing to swear by the tusks of his grandfather; but he was exceedingly hungry, and a year and a day seemed a long time off; so he said, with another careless laugh:

"Very well; if you will now let me go I swear by the tusks of my grandfather to return to you in a year and a day and become your prisoner."

Gouie was much pleased, for he knew that in a year and a day Keo would be almost full grown. So he began digging away one end of the pit and filling it up with the earth until he had made an incline which would allow the hippopotamus to climb out.

Keo was so pleased when he found himself upon the surface of the earth again that he indulged in a merry fit of laughter, after which he said:

"Good-by, Gouie; in a year and a day you will see me again."

Then he waddled away toward the river to see his mother and get his breakfast, and Gouie returned to his village.

During the months that followed, as the black man lay in his hut or hunted in the forest, he heard at times the faraway "Guk-uk-uk-uk!" of the laughing hippopotamus. But he only smiled to himself and thought: "A year and a day will soon pass away!"

Now when Keo returned to his mother safe and well every member of his tribe was filled with joy, for the Jolly One was a general favorite. But when he told them that in a year and a day he must again become the slave of the black man, they began to wail and weep, and so many were their tears that the river rose several inches.

Of course Keo only laughed at their sorrow; but a great meeting of the tribe was called and the matter discussed seriously.

"Having sworn by the tusks of his grandfather," said Uncle Nikki, "he must keep his promise. But it is our duty to try in some way to rescue him from death or a life of slavery."

To this all agreed, but no one could think of any method of saving Keo from his fate. So months passed away, during which all the royal hippopotamuses were sad and gloomy except the Jolly One himself.

Finally but a week of freedom remained to Keo, and his mother, the queen, became so nervous and worried that another meeting of the tribe was called. By this time the laughing hippopotamus had grown to enormous size, and measured nearly fifteen feet long and six feet high, while his sharp tusks were whiter and harder than those of an elephant.

"Unless something is done to save my child," said the mother, "I shall die of grief."

Then some of her relations began to make foolish suggestions; but presently Uncle Nep, a wise and very big hippopotamus, said:

"We must go to Glinkomok and implore his aid."

Then all were silent, for it was a bold thing to

face the mighty Glinkomok. But the mother's love was equal to any heroism.

"I will myself go to him, if Uncle Nep will accompany me," she said, quickly.

Uncle Nep thoughtfully patted the soft mud with his fore foot and wagged his short tail leisurely from side to side.

"We have always been obedient to Glinkomok, and shown him great respect," said he. "Therefore I fear no danger in facing him. I will go with you."

All the others snorted approval, being very glad they were not called upon to go themselves.

So the queen and Uncle Nep, with Keo swimming between them, set out upon their journey. They swam up the river all that day and all the next, until they came at sundown to a high, rocky wall, beneath which was the cave where the mighty Glinkomok dwelt.

This fearful creature was part beast, part man, part fowl and part fish. It had lived since the world began. Through years of wisdom it had become part sorcerer, part wizard, part magician and part fairy. Mankind knew it not, but the ancient beasts knew and feared it.

The three hippopotamuses paused before the cave, with their front feet upon the bank and their bodies in the water, and called in chorus a greeting to Glinkomok. Instantly thereafter the mouth of the cave darkened and the creature glided silently toward them.

The hippopotamuses were afraid to look upon it, and bowed their heads between their legs.

"We come, O Glinkomok, to implore your mercy
and friendly assistance!" began Uncle Nep; and then
he told the story of Keo's capture, and how he had
promised to return to the black man.

"He must keep his promise," said the creature, in
a voice that sounded like a sigh.

The mother hippopotamus groaned aloud.

"But I will prepare him to overcome the black
man, and to regain his liberty," continued
Glinkomok.

Keo laughed.

"Lift your right paw," commanded Glinkomok.
Keo obeyed, and the creature touched it with its
long, hairy tongue. Then it held four skinny hands
over Keo's bowed head and mumbled some words in
a language unknown to man or beast or fowl or fish.
After this it spoke again in hippopotamese:

"Your skin has now become so tough that no
man can hurt you. Your strength is greater than that
of ten elephants. Your foot is so swift that you can
distance the wind. Your wit is sharper than the
bulthorn. Let the man fear, but drive fear from your
own breast forever; for of all your race you are the
mightiest!"

Then the terrible Glinkomok leaned over, and
Keo felt its fiery breath scorch him as it whispered
some further instructions in his ear. The next moment it glided back into its cave, followed by the
loud thanks of the three hippopotamuses, who slid
into the water and immediately began their journey
home.

The mother's heart was full of joy; Uncle Nep

shivered once or twice as he remembered a glimpse he had caught of Glinkomok; but Keo was as jolly as possible, and, not content to swim with his dignified elders, he dived under their bodies, raced all around them and laughed merrily every inch of the way home.

Then all the tribe held high jinks and praised the mighty Glinkomok for befriending their queen's son. And when the day came for the Jolly One to give himself up to the black man they all kissed him good-by without a single fear for his safety.

Keo went away in good spirits, and they could hear his laughing "guk-uk-uk-uk!" long after he was lost in sight in the jungle.

Gouie had counted the days and knew when to expect Keo; but he was astonished at the monstrous size to which his captive had grown, and congratulated himself on the wise bargain he had made. And Keo was so fat that Gouie determined to eat him— that is, all of him he possibly could, and the remainder of the carcass he would trade off to his fellow villagers.

So he took a knife and tried to stick it into the hippopotamus, but the skin was so tough the knife was blunted against it. Then he tried other means; but Keo remained unhurt.

And now indeed the Jolly One laughed his most gleeful laugh, till all the forest echoed the "guk-uk-uk-uk-uk!" And Gouie decided not to kill him, since that was impossible, but to use him for a beast of burden. He mounted upon Keo's back and commanded him to march. So Keo trotted briskly through the village, his little eyes twinkling with merriment.

The other blacks were delighted with Gouie's captive, and begged permission to ride upon the Jolly One's back. So Gouie bargained with them for bracelets and shell necklaces and little gold ornaments, until he had acquired quite a heap of trinkets. Then a dozen black men climbed upon Keo's back to enjoy a ride, and the one nearest his nose cried out:

"Run, Mud-dog—run!"

And Keo ran. Swift as the wind he strode, away from the village, through the forest and straight up the river bank. The black men howled with fear; the Jolly One roared with laughter; and on, on, on they rushed!

Then before them, on the opposite side of the river, appeared the black mouth of Glinkomok's cave. Keo dashed into the water, dived to the bottom and left the black people struggling to swim out. But Glinkomok had heard the laughter of Keo and knew what to do. When the Jolly One rose to the surface and blew the water from his throat there was no black man to be seen.

Keo returned alone to the village, and Gouie asked, with surprise:

"Where are my brothers:"

"I do not know," answered Keo. "I took them far away, and they remained where I left them."

Gouie would have asked more questions then, but another crowd of black men impatiently waited to ride on the back of the laughing hippopotamus.

So they paid the price and climbed to their seats, after which the foremost said:

"Run, mud-wallower—run!"

And Keo ran as before and carried them to the mouth of Glinkomok's cave, and returned alone.

But now Gouie became anxious to know the fate of his fellows, for he was the only black man left in his village. So he mounted the hippopotamus and cried:

"Run, river-hog—run!"

Keo laughed his jolly "guk-uk-uk-uk!" and ran with the speed of the wind. But this time he made straight for the river bank where his own tribe lived, and when he reached it he waded into the river, dived to the bottom and left Gouie floating in the middle of the stream.

The black man began swimming toward the right bank, but there he saw Uncle Nep and half the royal tribe waiting to stamp him into the soft mud. So he turned toward the left bank, and there stood the queen mother and Uncle Nikki, red-eyed and angry, waiting to tear him with their tusks.

Then Gouie uttered loud screams of terror, and, spying the Jolly One, who swam near him, he cried:

"Save me, Keo! Save me, and I will release you from slavery!"

"That is not enough," laughed Keo.

"I will serve you all my life!" screamed Gouie; "I will do everything you bid me!"

"Will you return to me in a year and a day and become my captive, if I allow you to escape?" asked Keo.

"I will! I will! I will!" cried Gouie.

"Swear it by the bones of your grandfather!" commanded Keo, remembering that black men have no tusks to swear by.

And Gouie swore it by the bones of his grandfather.

Then Keo swam to the black one, who clambered upon his back again. In this fashion they came to the bank, where Keo told his mother and all the tribe of the bargain he had made with Gouie, who was to return in a year and a day and become his slave.

Therefore the black man was permitted to depart in peace, and once more the Jolly One lived with his own people and was happy.

When a year and a day had passed Keo began watching for the return of Gouie; but he did not come, then or ever afterwards.

For the black man had made a bundle of his bracelets and shell necklaces and little gold ornaments and had traveled many miles into another country, where the ancient and royal tribe of hippopotamuses was unknown. And he set up for a great chief, because of his riches, and people bowed down before him.

By day he was proud and swaggering. But at night he tumbled and tossed upon his bed and could not sleep. His conscience troubled him.

For he had sworn by the bones of his grandfather; and his grandfather had no bones.

THE MAGIC BON BONS

There lived in Boston a wise and ancient chemist by the name of Dr. Daws, who dabbled somewhat in magic. There also lived in Boston a young lady by the name of Claribel Sudds, who was possessed of much money, little wit and an intense desire to go upon the stage.

So Claribel went to Dr. Daws and said:

"I can neither sing nor dance; I cannot recite verse nor play upon the piano; I am no acrobat nor leaper nor high kicker; yet I wish to go upon the stage. What shall I do?"

"Are you willing to pay for such accomplishments?" asked the wise chemist.

"Certainly," answered Claribel, jingling her purse.

"Then come to me to-morrow at two o'clock," said he.

All that night he practiced what is known as

chemical sorcery; so that when Claribel Sudds came next day at two o'clock he showed her a small box filled with compounds that closely resembled French bonbons.

"This is a progressive age," said the old man, "and I flatter myself your Uncle Daws keeps right along with the procession. Now, one of your old-fashioned sorcerers would have made you some nasty, bitter pills to swallow; but I have consulted your taste and convenience. Here are some magic bonbons. If you eat this one with the lavender color you can dance thereafter as lightly and gracefully as if you had been trained a lifetime. After you consume the pink confection you will sing like a nightingale. Eating the white one will enable you to become the finest elocutionist in the land. The chocolate piece will charm you into playing the piano better than Rubenstein, while after eating the lemon-yellow bonbon you can easily kick six feet above your head."

"How delightful!" exclaimed Claribel, who was truly enraptured. "You are certainly a most clever sorcerer as well as a considerate compounder," and she held out her hand for the box.

"Ahem!" said the wise one; "a check, please."

"Oh, yes; to be sure! How stupid of me to forget it," she returned.

He considerately retained the box in his own hand while she signed a check for a large amount of money, after which he allowed her to hold the box herself.

"Are you sure you have made them strong

enough?" she inquired, anxiously; "it usually takes a great deal to affect me."

"My only fear," replied Dr. Daws, "is that I have made them too strong. For this is the first time I have ever been called upon to prepare these wonderful confections."

"Don't worry," said Claribel; "the stronger they act the better I shall act myself."

She went away, after saying this, but stopping in at a dry goods store to shop, she forgot the precious box in her new interest and left it lying on the ribbon counter.

Then little Bessie Bostwick came to the counter to buy a hair ribbon and laid her parcels beside the box. When she went away she gathered up the box with her other bundles and trotted off home with it.

Bessie never knew, until after she had hung her coat in the hall closet and counted up her parcels, that she had one too many. Then she opened it and exclaimed:

"Why, it's a box of candy! Someone must have mislaid it. But it is too small a matter to worry about; there are only a few pieces." So she dumped the contents of the box into a bonbon dish that stood upon the hall table and picking out the chocolate piece—she was fond of chocolates—ate it daintily while she examined her purchases.

These were not many, for Bessie was only twelve years old and was not yet trusted by her parents to expend much money at the stores. But while she tried on the hair ribbon she suddenly felt a great desire to play upon the piano, and the desire at last became so overpowering that she went into the parlor and opened the instrument.

The little girl had, with infinite pains, contrived to learn two "pieces" which she usually executed with a jerky movement of her right hand and a left hand that forgot to keep up and so made dreadful discords. But under the influence of the chocolate bonbon she sat down and ran her fingers lightly over the keys producing such exquisite harmony that she was filled with amazement at her own performance.

That was the prelude, however. The next moment she dashed into Beethoven's seventh sonata and played it magnificently.

Her mother, hearing the unusual burst of melody, came downstairs to see what musical guest had arrived; but when she discovered it was her own little daughter who was playing so divinely she had an attack of palpitation of the heart (to which she was subject) and sat down upon a sofa until it should pass away.

Meanwhile Bessie played one piece after another with untiring energy. She loved music, and now found that all she need do was to sit at the piano and listen and watch her hands twinkle over the keyboard.

Twilight deepened in the room and Bessie's father came home and hung up his hat and overcoat and placed his umbrella in the rack. Then he peeped into the parlor to see who was playing.

"Great Caesar!" he exclaimed. But the mother came to him softly with her finger on her lips and whispered: "Don't interrupt her, John. Our child seems to be in a trance. Did you ever hear such superb music?"

"Why, she's an infant prodigy!" gasped the astounded father. "Beats Blind Tom all hollow! It's—it's wonderful!"

As they stood listening the senator arrived, having been invited to dine with them that evening. And before he had taken off his coat the Yale professor—a man of deep learning and scholarly attainments—joined the party.

Bessie played on; and the four elders stood in a huddled but silent and amazed group, listening to the music and waiting for the sound of the dinner gong.

Mr. Bostwick, who was hungry, picked up the bonbon dish that lay on the table beside him and ate the pink confection. The professor was watching him, so Mr. Bostwick courteously held the dish toward him. The professor ate the lemon-yellow piece and the senator reached out his hand and took the lavender piece. He did not eat it, however, for, chancing to remember that it might spoil his dinner, he put it in his vest pocket. Mrs. Bostwick, still intently listening to her precocious daughter, without thinking what she did, took the remaining piece, which was the white one, and slowly devoured it.

The dish was now empty, and Claribel Sudds' precious bonbons had passed from her possession forever!

Suddenly Mr. Bostwick, who was a big man, began to sing in a shrill, tremolo soprano voice. It was not the same song Bessie was playing, and the discord was shocking that the professor smiled, the senator put his hands to his ears and Mrs. Bostwick cried in a horrified voice:

"William!"

Her husband continued to sing as if endeavoring to emulate the famous Christine Nillson, and paid no attention whatever to his wife or his guests.

Fortunately the dinner gong now sounded, and Mrs. Bostwick dragged Bessie from the piano and ushered her guests into the dining-room. Mr. Bostwick followed, singing "The Last Rose of Summer" as if it had been an encore demanded by a thousand delighted hearers.

The poor woman was in despair at witnessing her husband's undignified actions and wondered what she might do to control him. The professor seemed more grave than usual; the senator's face wore an offended expression, and Bessie kept moving her fingers as if she still wanted to play the piano.

Mrs. Bostwick managed to get them all seated, although her husband had broken into another aria; and then the maid brought in the soup.

When she carried a plate to the professor, he cried, in an excited voice:

"Hold it higher! Higher—I say!" And springing up he gave it a sudden kick that sent it nearly to the ceiling, from whence the dish descended to scatter soup over Bessie and the maid and to smash in pieces upon the crown of the professor's bald head.

At this atrocious act the senator rose from his

seat with an exclamation of horror and glanced at his hostess.

For some time Mrs. Bostwick had been staring straight ahead, with a dazed expression; but now, catching the senator's eye, she bowed gracefully and began reciting "The Charge of the Light Brigade" in forceful tones.

The senator shuddered. Such disgraceful rioting he had never seen nor heard before in a decent private family. He felt that his reputation was at stake, and, being the only sane person, apparently, in the room, there was no one to whom he might appeal.

The maid had run away to cry hysterically in the kitchen; Mr. Bostwick was singing "O Promise Me;" the professor was trying to kick the globes off the chandelier; Mrs. Bostwick had switched her recitation to "The Boy Stood on the Burning Deck," and Bessie had stolen into the parlor and was pounding out the overture from the "Flying Dutchman."

The senator was not at all sure he would not go crazy himself, presently; so he slipped away from the turmoil, and, catching up his had and coat in the hall, hurried from the house.

That night he sat up late writing a political speech he was to deliver the next afternoon at Faneuil hall, but his experiences at the Bostwicks' had so unnerved him that he could scarcely collect his thoughts, and often he would pause and shake his head pityingly as he remembered the strange things he had seen in that usually respectable home.

The next day he met Mr. Bostwick in the street, but passed him by with a stony glare of oblivion. He felt he really could not afford to know this gentleman in the future. Mr. Bostwick was naturally indignant at the direct snub; yet in his mind lingered a faint memory of some quite unusual occurrences at his dinner party the evening before, and he hardly knew whether he dared resent the senator's treatment or not.

The political meeting was the feature of the day, for the senator's eloquence was well known in Boston. So the big hall was crowded with people, and in one of the front rows sat the Bostwick family, with the learned Yale professor beside them. They all looked tired and pale, as if they had passed a rather dissipated evening, and the senator was rendered so nervous by seeing them that he refused to look in their direction a second time.

While the mayor was introducing him the great man sat fidgeting in his chair; and, happening to put his thumb and finger into his vest pocket, he found the lavender-colored bonbon he had placed there the evening before.

"This may clear my throat," thought the senator, and slipped the bonbon into his mouth.

A few minutes afterwards he arose before the vast audience, which greeted him with enthusiastic plaudits.

"My friends," began the senator, in a grave voice, "this is a most impressive and important occasion."

Then he paused, balanced himself upon his left foot, and kicked his right leg into the air in the way favored by ballet-dancers!

There was a hum of amazement and horror from

the spectators, but the senator appeared not to notice it. He whirled around upon the tips of his toes, kicked right and left in a graceful manner, and startled a bald-headed man in the front row by casting a languishing glance in his direction.

Suddenly Claribel Sudds, who happened to be present, uttered a scream and sprang to her feet. Pointing an accusing finger at the dancing senator, she cried in a loud voice:

"That's the man who stole my bonbons! Seize him! Arrest him! Don't let him escape!"

But the ushers rushed her out of the hall, thinking she had gone suddenly insane; and the senator's friends seized him firmly and carried him out the stage entrance to the street, where they put him into an open carriage and instructed the driver to take him home.

The effect of the magic bonbon was still powerful enough to control the poor senator, who stood upon the rear seat of the carriage and danced energetically all the way home, to the delight of the crowd of small boys who followed the carriage and the grief of the sober-minded citizens, who shook their heads sadly and whispered that "another good man had gone wrong."

It took the senator several months to recover from the shame and humiliation of this escapade; and, curiously enough, he never had the slightest idea what had induced him to act in so extraordinary a manner. Perhaps it was fortunate the last bonbon had now been eaten, for they might easily have caused considerably more trouble than they did.

Of course Claribel went again to the wise chemist and signed a check for another box of magic bonbons; but she must have taken better care of these, for she is now a famous vaudeville actress.

THIS STORY SHOULD TEACH us the folly of condemning others for actions that we do not understand, for we never know what may happen to ourselves. It may also serve as a hint to be careful about leaving parcels in public places, and, incidentally, to let other people's packages severely alone.

CHAPTER 8
THE CAPTURE OF FATHER TIME

Jim was the son of a cowboy, and lived on the broad plains of Arizona. His father had trained him to lasso a bronco or a young bull with perfect accuracy, and had Jim possessed the strength to back up his skill he would have been as good a cowboy as any in all Arizona.

When he was twelve years old he made his first visit to the east, where Uncle Charles, his father's brother, lived. Of course Jim took his lasso with him, for he was proud of his skill in casting it, and wanted to show his cousins what a cowboy could do.

At first the city boys and girls were much interested in watching Jim lasso posts and fence pickets, but they soon tired of it, and even Jim decided it was not the right sort of sport for cities.

But one day the butcher asked Jim to ride one of his horses into the country, to a pasture that had been engaged, and Jim eagerly consented. He had been longing for a horseback ride, and to make it seem like old times he took his lasso with him.

He rode through the streets demurely enough, but on reaching the open country roads his spirits broke forth into wild jubilation, and, urging the butcher's horse to full gallop, he dashed away in true cowboy fashion.

Then he wanted still more liberty, and letting down the bars that led into a big field he began riding over the meadow and throwing his lasso at imaginary cattle, while he yelled and whooped to his heart's content.

Suddenly, on making a long cast with his lasso, the loop caught upon something and rested about three feet from the ground, while the rope drew taut and nearly pulled Jim from his horse.

This was unexpected. More than that, it was wonderful; for the field seemed bare of even a stump. Jim's eyes grew big with amazement, but he knew he had caught something when a voice cried out:

"Here, let go! Let go, I say! Can't you see what you've done?"

No, Jim couldn't see, nor did he intend to let go until he found out what was holding the loop of the lasso. So he resorted to an old trick his father had taught him and, putting the butcher's horse to a run, began riding in a circle around the spot where his lasso had caught.

As he thus drew nearer and nearer his quarry he saw the rope coil up, yet it looked to be coiling over nothing but air. One end of the lasso was made fast to a ring in the saddle, and when the rope was almost wound up and the horse began to pull away and snort with fear, Jim dismounted. Holding the reins of the bridle in one hand, he followed the rope, and an instant later saw an old man caught fast in the coils of the lasso.

His head was bald and uncovered, but long white whiskers grew down to his waist. About his body was thrown a loose robe of fine white linen. In one hand he bore a great scythe, and beneath the other arm he carried an hourglass.

While Jim gazed wonderingly upon him, this venerable old man spoke in an angry voice:

"Now, then—get that rope off as fast as you can! You've brought everything on earth to a standstill by your foolishness! Well—what are you staring at? Don't you know who I am?"

"No," said Jim, stupidly.

"Well, I'm Time—Father Time! Now, make haste and set me free—if you want the world to run properly."

"How did I happen to catch you?" asked Jim, without making a move to release his captive.

"I don't know. I've never been caught before," growled Father Time. "But I suppose it was because you were foolishly throwing your lasso at nothing."

"I didn't see you," said Jim.

"Of course you didn't. I'm invisible to the eyes of human beings unless they get within three feet of me, and I take care to keep more than that distance away from them. That's why I was crossing this field, where I supposed no one would be. And I

84

should have been perfectly safe had it not been for your beastly lasso. Now, then," he added, crossly, "are you going to get that rope off?"

"Why should I?" asked Jim.

"Because everything in the world stopped moving the moment you caught me. I don't suppose you want to make an end of all business and pleasure, and war and love, and misery and ambition and everything else, do you? Not a watch has ticked since you tied me up here like a mummy!"

Jim laughed. It really was funny to see the old man wound round and round with coils of rope from his knees up to his chin.

"It'll do you good to rest," said the boy. "From all I've heard you lead a rather busy life."

"Indeed I do," replied Father Time, with a sigh. "I'm due in Kamchatka this very minute. And to think one small boy is upsetting all my regular habits!"

"Too bad!" said Jim, with a grin. "But since the world has stopped anyhow, it won't matter if it takes a little longer recess. As soon as I let you go Time will fly again. Where are your wings?"

"I haven't any," answered the old man. "That is a story cooked up by some one who never saw me. As a matter of fact, I move rather slowly."

"I see, you take your time," remarked the boy. "What do you use that scythe for?"

"To mow down the people," said the ancient one. "Every time I swing my scythe some one dies."

"Then I ought to win a life-saving medal by

keeping you tied up," said Jim. "Some folks will live this much longer."

"But they won't know it," said Father Time, with a sad smile; "so it will do them no good. You may as well untie me at once."

"No," said Jim, with a determined air. "I may never capture you again; so I'll hold you for awhile and see how the world wags without you."

Then he swung the old man, bound as he was, upon the back of the butcher's horse, and, getting into the saddle himself, started back toward town, one hand holding his prisoner and the other guiding the reins.

When he reached the road his eye fell on a strange tableau. A horse and buggy stood in the middle of the road, the horse in the act of trotting, with his head held high and two legs in the air, but perfectly motionless. In the buggy a man and a woman were seated; but had they been turned into stone they could not have been more still and stiff.

"There's no Time for them!" sighed the old man. "Won't you let me go now?"

"Not yet," replied the boy.

He rode on until he reached the city, where all the people stood in exactly the same positions they were in when Jim lassoed Father Time. Stopping in front of a big dry goods store, the boy hitched his horse and went in. The clerks were measuring out goods and showing patterns to the rows of customers in front of them, but everyone seemed suddenly to have become a statue.

There was something very unpleasant in this

scene, and a cold shiver began to run up and down Jim's back; so he hurried out again.

On the edge of the sidewalk sat a poor, crippled beggar, holding out his hat, and beside him stood a prosperous-looking gentleman who was about to drop a penny into the beggar's hat. Jim knew this gentleman to be very rich but rather stingy, so he ventured to run his hand into the man's pocket and take out his purse, in which was a $20 gold piece. This glittering coin he put in the gentleman's fingers instead of the penny and then restored the purse to the rich man's pocket.

"That donation will surprise him when he comes to life," thought the boy.

He mounted the horse again and rode up the street. As he passed the shop of his friend, the butcher, he noticed several pieces of meat hanging outside.

"I'm afraid that meat'll spoil," he remarked.

"It takes Time to spoil meat," answered the old man.

This struck Jim as being queer, but true.

"It seems Time meddles with everything," said he.

"Yes; you've made a prisoner of the most important personage in the world," groaned the old man; "and you haven't enough sense to let him go again."

Jim did not reply, and soon they came to his uncle's house, where he again dismounted. The street was filled with teams and people, but all were motionless. His two little cousins were just coming out the gate on their way to school, with their books and slates underneath their arms; so Jim had to jump over the fence to avoid knocking them down.

In the front room sat his aunt, reading her Bible. She was just turning a page when Time stopped. In the dining-room was his uncle, finishing his luncheon. His mouth was open and his fork poised just before it, while his eyes were fixed upon the newspaper folded beside him. Jim helped himself to his uncle's pie, and while he ate it he walked out to his prisoner.

"There's one thing I don't understand," said he.

"What's that?" asked Father Time.

"Why is it that I'm able to move around while everyone else is—is—froze up?"

"That is because I'm your prisoner," answered the other. "You can do anything you wish with Time now. But unless you are careful you'll do something you will be sorry for."

Jim threw the crust of his pie at a bird that was suspended in the air, where it had been flying when Time stopped.

"Anyway," he laughed, "I'm living longer than anyone else. No one will ever be able to catch up with me again."

"Each life has its allotted span," said the old man. "When you have lived your proper time my scythe will mow you down."

"I forgot your scythe," said Jim, thoughtfully.

Then a spirit of mischief came into the boy's head, for he happened to think that the present opportunity to have fun would never occur again. He tied Father Time to his uncle's hitching post, that he might not escape, and then crossed the road to the corner grocery.

The grocer had scolded Jim that very morning for stepping into a basket of turnips by accident. So the boy went to the back end of the grocery and turned on the faucet of the molasses barrel.

"That'll make a nice mess when Time starts the molasses running all over the floor," said Jim, with a laugh.

A little further down the street was a barber shop, and sitting in the barber's chair Jim saw the man that all the boys declared was the "meanest man in town." He certainly did not like the boys and the boys knew it. The barber was in the act of shampooing this person when Time was captured. Jim ran to the drug store, and, getting a bottle of mucilage, he returned and poured it over the ruffled hair of the unpopular citizen.

"That'll probably surprise him when he wakes up," thought Jim.

Near by was the schoolhouse. Jim entered it and found that only a few of the pupils were assembled. But the teacher sat at his desk, stern and frowning as usual.

Taking a piece of chalk, Jim marked upon the blackboard in big letters the following words:

"Every scholar is requested to yell the minute he enters the room. He will also please throw his books at the teacher's head. Signed, Prof. Sharpe."

"That ought to raise a nice rumpus," murmured the mischiefmaker, as he walked away.

On the corner stood Policeman Mulligan, talking

with old Miss Scrapple, the worst gossip in town, who always delighted in saying something disagreeable about her neighbors. Jim thought this opportunity was too good to lose. So he took off the policeman's cap and brass-buttoned coat and put them on Miss Scrapple, while the lady's feathered and ribboned hat he placed jauntily upon the policeman's head.

The effect was so comical that the boy laughed aloud, and as a good many people were standing near the corner Jim decided that Miss Scrapple and Officer Mulligan would create a sensation when Time started upon his travels.

Then the young cowboy remembered his prisoner, and, walking back to the hitching post, he came within three feet of it and saw Father Time still standing patiently within the toils of the lasso. He looked angry and annoyed, however, and growled out:

"Well, when do you intend to release me?"

"I've been thinking about that ugly scythe of yours," said Jim.

"What about it?" asked Father Time.

"Perhaps if I let you go you'll swing it at me the first thing, to be revenged," replied the boy.

Father Time gave him a severe look, but said:

"I've known boys for thousands of years, and of course I know they're mischievous and reckless. But I like boys, because they grow up to be men and people my world. Now, if a man had caught me by accident, as you did, I could have scared him into letting me go instantly; but boys are harder to scare. I don't know as I blame you. I was a boy myself, long ago, when the world was new. But surely you've had enough fun with me by this time, and now I hope you'll show the respect that is due to old age. Let me go, and in return I will promise to forget all about my capture. The incident won't do much harm, anyway, for no one will ever know that Time has halted the last three hours or so."

"All right," said Jim, cheerfully, "since you've promised not to mow me down, I'll let you go." But he had a notion some people in the town would suspect Time had stopped when they returned to life.

He carefully unwound the rope from the old man, who, when he was free, at once shouldered his scythe, rearranged his white robe and nodded farewell.

The next moment he had disappeared, and with a rustle and rumble and roar of activity the world came to life again and jogged along as it always had before.

Jim wound up his lasso, mounted the butcher's horse and rode slowly down the street.

Loud screams came from the corner, where a great crowd of people quickly assembled. From his seat on the horse Jim saw Miss Scrapple, attired in the policeman's uniform, angrily shaking her fists in Mulligan's face, while the officer was furiously stamping upon the lady's hat, which he had torn from his own head amidst the jeers of the crowd.

As he rode past the schoolhouse he heard a tremendous chorus of yells, and knew Prof. Sharpe was having a hard time to quell the riot caused by the sign on the blackboard.

Through the window of the barber shop he saw the "mean man" frantically belaboring the barber with a hair brush, while his hair stood up stiff as bayonets in all directions. And the grocer ran out of his door and yelled "Fire!" while his shoes left a track of molasses wherever he stepped.

Jim's heart was filled with joy. He was fairly reveling in the excitement he had caused when some one caught his leg and pulled him from the horse.

"What're ye doin' hear, ye rascal?" cried the butcher, angrily; "didn't ye promise to put that beast inter Plympton's pasture? An' now I find ye ridin' the poor nag around like a gentleman o' leisure!"

"That's a fact," said Jim, with surprise; "I clean forgot about the horse!"

THIS STORY SHOULD TEACH us the supreme importance of Time and the folly of trying to stop it. For should you succeed, as Jim did, in bringing Time to a standstill, the world would soon become a dreary place and life decidedly unpleasant.

CHAPTER 9
THE WONDERFUL PUMP

Not many years ago there lived on a stony, barren New England farm a man and his wife. They were sober, honest people, working hard from early morning until dark to enable them to secure a scanty living from their poor land.

Their house, a small, one-storied building, stood upon the side of a steep hill, and the stones lay so thickly about it that scarce anything green could grow from the ground. At the foot of the hill, a quarter of a mile from the house by the winding path, was a small brook, and the woman was obliged to go there for water and to carry it up the hill to the house. This was a tedious task, and with the other hard work that fell to her share had made her gaunt and bent and lean.

Yet she never complained, but meekly and faithfully performed her duties, doing the housework, carrying the water and helping her husband hoe the scanty crop that grew upon the best part of their land.

One day, as she walked down the path to the brook, her big shoes scattering the pebbles right and left, she noticed a large beetle lying upon its back and struggling hard with its little legs to turn over, that its feet might again touch the ground. But this it could not accomplish; so the woman, who had a kind heart, reached down and gently turned the beetle with her finger. At once it scampered from the path and she went on to the brook.

The next day, as she came for water, she was surprised to see the beetle again lying upon its back and struggling helplessly to turn. Once more the woman stopped and set him upon his feet; and then, as she stooped over the tiny creature, she heard a small voice say:

"Oh, thank you! Thank you so much for saving me!"

Half frightened at hearing a beetle speak in her own language, the woman started back and exclaimed:

"La sakes! Surely you can't talk like humans!" Then, recovering from her alarm, she again bent over the beetle, who answered her:

"Why shouldn't I talk, if I have anything to say?

"'Cause you're a bug," replied the woman.

"That is true; and you saved my life—saved me from my enemies, the sparrows. And this is the second time you have come to my assistance, so I owe you a debt of gratitude. Bugs value their lives as much as human beings, and I am a more important creature than you, in your ignorance, may suppose. But, tell me, why do you come each day to the brook?"

"For water," she answered, staring stupidly down at the talking beetle.

"Isn't it hard work?" the creature inquired.

"Yes; but there's no water on the hill," said she.

"Then dig a well and put a pump in it," replied the beetle.

She shook her head.

"My man tried it once; but there was no water," she said, sadly.

"Try it again," commanded the beetle; "and in return for your kindness to me I will make this promise: if you do not get water from the well you will get that which is more precious to you. I must go now. Do not forget. Dig a well."

And then, without pausing to say good-by, it ran swiftly away and was lost among the stones.

The woman returned to the house much perplexed by what the beetle had said, and when her husband came in from his work she told him the whole story.

The poor man thought deeply for a time, and then declared:

"Wife, there may be truth in what the bug told you. There must be magic in the world yet, if a beetle can speak; and if there is such a thing as magic we may get water from the well. The pump I bought to use in the well which proved to be dry is now lying in the barn, and the only expense in following the talking bug's advice will be the labor of digging the hole. Labor I am used to; so I will dig the well."

Next day he set about it, and dug so far down in the ground that he could hardly reach the top to climb out again; but not a drop of water was found.

"Perhaps you did not dig deep enough," his wife said, when he told her of his failure.

So the following day he made a long ladder, which he put into the hole; and then he dug, and dug, and dug, until the top of the ladder barely reached the top of the hole. But still there was no water.

When the woman next went to the brook with her pail she saw the beetle sitting upon a stone beside her path. So she stopped and said:

"My husband has dug the well; but there is no water."

"Did he put the pump in the well?" asked the beetle.

"No," she answered.

"Then do as I commanded; put in the pump, and if you do not get water I promise you something still more precious."

Saying which, the beetle swiftly slid from the stone and disappeared. The woman went back to the house and told her husband what the bug had said.

"Well," replied the simple fellow, "there can be no harm in trying."

So he got the pump from the barn and placed it in the well, and then he took hold of the handle and began to pump, while his wife stood by to watch what would happen.

No water came, but after a few moments a gold piece dropped from the spout of the pump, and then another, and another, until several handfuls of gold lay in a little heap upon the ground.

The man stopped pumping then and ran to help his wife gather the gold pieces into her apron; but their hands trembled so greatly through excitement and joy that they could scarcely pick up the sparkling coins.

At last she gathered them close to her bosom and together they ran to the house, where they emptied the precious gold upon the table and counted the pieces.

All were stamped with the design of the United States mint and were worth five dollars each. Some were worn and somewhat discolored from use, while others seemed bright and new, as if they had not been much handled. When the value of the pieces was added together they were found to be worth three hundred dollars.

Suddenly the woman spoke.

"Husband, the beetle said truly when he declared we should get something more precious than water from the well. But run at once and take away the handle from the pump, lest anyone should pass this way and discover our secret."

So the man ran to the pump and removed the handle, which he carried to the house and hid underneath the bed.

They hardly slept a wink that night, lying awake

to think of their good fortune and what they should do with their store of yellow gold. In all their former lives they had never possessed more than a few dollars at a time, and now the cracked teapot was nearly full of gold coins.

The following day was Sunday, and they arose early and ran to see if their treasure was safe. There it lay, heaped snugly within the teapot, and they were so willing to feast their eyes upon it that it was long before the man could leave it to build the fire or the woman to cook the breakfast.

While they ate their simple meal the woman said:

"We will go to church to-day and return thanks for the riches that have come to us so suddenly. And I will give the pastor one of the gold pieces."

"It is well enough to go to church," replied her husband, "and also to return thanks. But in the night I decided how we will spend all our money; so there will be none left for the pastor."

"We can pump more," said the woman.

"Perhaps; and perhaps not," he answered, cautiously. "What we have we can depend upon, but whether or not there be more in the well I cannot say."

"Then go and find out," she returned, "for I am anxious to give something to the pastor, who is a poor man and deserving."

So the man got the pump handle from beneath the bed, and, going to the pump, fitted it in place. Then he set a large wooden bucket under the spout and began to pump. To their joy the gold pieces soon began flowing into the pail, and, seeing it about to run over the brim, the woman brought another pail. But now the stream suddenly stopped, and the man said, cheerfully:

"That is enough for to-day, good wife! We have added greatly to our treasure, and the parson shall have his gold piece. Indeed, I think I shall also put a coin into the contribution box."

Then, because the teapot would hold no more gold, the farmer emptied the pail into the wood-box, covering the money with dried leaves and twigs, that no one might suspect what lay underneath.

Afterward they dressed themselves in their best clothing and started for the church, each taking a bright gold piece from the teapot as a gift to the pastor.

Over the hill and down into the valley beyond they walked, feeling so gay and light-hearted that they did not mind the distance at all. At last they came to the little country church and entered just as the services began.

Being proud of their wealth and of the gifts they had brought for the pastor, they could scarcely wait for the moment when the deacon passed the contribution box. But at last the time came, and the farmer held his hand high over the box and dropped the gold piece so that all the congregation could see what he had given. The woman did likewise, feeling important and happy at being able to give the good parson so much.

The parson, watching from the pulpit, saw the gold drop into the box, and could hardly believe that his eyes did not deceive him. However, when the box was laid upon his desk there were the two gold pieces, and he was so surprised that he nearly forgot his sermon.

When the people were leaving the church at the close of the services the good man stopped the farmer and his wife and asked:

"Where did you get so much gold?"

The woman gladly told him how she had rescued the beetle, and how, in return, they had been rewarded with the wonderful pump. The pastor listened to it all gravely, and when the story was finished he said:

"According to tradition strange things happened in this world ages ago, and now I find that strange things may also happen to-day. For by your tale you have found a beetle that can speak and also has power to bestow upon you great wealth." Then he looked carefully at the gold pieces and continued: "Either this money is fairy gold or it is genuine metal, stamped at the mint of the United States government. If it is fairy gold it will disappear within 24 hours, and will therefore do no one any good. If it is real money, then your beetle must have robbed some one of the gold and placed it in your well. For all money belongs to some one, and if you have not earned it honestly, but have come by it in the mysterious way you mention, it was surely taken from the persons who owned it, without their consent. Where else could real money come from?"

The farmer and his wife were confused by this

statement and looked guiltily at each other, for they were honest people and wished to wrong no one.

"Then you think the beetle stole the money?" asked the woman.

"By his magic powers he probably took it from its rightful owners. Even bugs which can speak have no consciences and cannot tell the difference between right and wrong. With a desire to reward you for your kindness the beetle took from its lawful possessors the money you pumped from the well."

"Perhaps it really is fairy gold," suggested the man. "If so, we must go to the town and spend the money before it disappears."

"That would be wrong," answered the pastor; "for then the merchants would have neither money nor goods. To give them fairy gold would be to rob them."

"What, then, shall we do?" asked the poor woman, wringing her hands with grief and disappointment.

"Go home and wait until to-morrow. If the gold is then in your possession it is real money and not fairy gold. But if it is real money you must try to restore it to its rightful owners. Take, also, these pieces which you have given me, for I cannot accept gold that is not honestly come by."

Sadly the poor people returned to their home, being greatly disturbed by what they had heard. Another sleepless night was passed, and on Monday morning they arose at daylight and ran to see if the gold was still visible.

"It is real money, after all!" cried the man; "for not a single piece has disappeared."

When the woman went to the brook that day she looked for the beetle, and, sure enough, there he sat upon the flat stone.

"Are you happy now?" asked the beetle, as the woman paused before him.

"We are very unhappy," she answered; "for, although you have given us much gold, our good parson says it surely belongs to some one else, and was stolen by you to reward us."

"Your parson may be a good man," returned the beetle, with some indignation, "but he certainly is not overwise. Nevertheless, if you do not want the gold I can take it from you as easily as I gave it."

"But we do want it!" cried the woman, fearfully. "That is," she added, "if it is honestly come by."

"It is not stolen," replied the beetle, sulkily, "and now belongs to no one but yourselves. When you saved my life I thought how I might reward you; and, knowing you to be poor, I decided gold would make you happier than anything else.

"You must know," he continued, "that although I appear so small and insignificant, I am really king of all the insects, and my people obey my slightest wish. Living, as they do, close to the ground, the insects often come across gold and other pieces of money which have been lost by men and have fallen into cracks or crevasses or become covered with earth or hidden by grass or weeds. Whenever my people find money in this way they report the fact to me; but I have always let it lie, because it could be of no possible use to an insect.

"However, when I decided to give you gold I knew just where to obtain it without robbing any of your fellow creatures. Thousands of insects were at once sent by me in every direction to bring the pieces of lost gold to this hill. It cost my people several days of hard labor, as you may suppose; but by the time your husband had finished the well the gold began to arrive from all parts of the country, and during the night my subjects dumped it all into the well. So you may use it with a clear conscience, knowing that you wrong no one."

This explanation delighted the woman, and when she returned to the house and reported to her husband what the beetle had said he also was overjoyed.

So they at once took a number of the gold pieces and went to the town to purchase provisions and clothing and many things of which they had long stood in need; but so proud were they of their newly acquired wealth that they took no pains to conceal it. They wanted everyone to know they had money, and so it was no wonder that when some of the wicked men in the village saw the gold they longed to possess it themselves.

"If they spend this money so freely," whispered one to another, "there must be a great store of gold at their home."

"That is true," was the answer. "Let us hasten there before they return and ransack the house."

So they left the village and hurried away to the

farm on the hill, where they broke down the door and turned everything topsy turvy until they had discovered the gold in the wood-box and the teapot. It did not take them long to make this into bundles, which they slung upon their backs and carried off, and it was probably because they were in a great hurry that they did not stop to put the house in order again.

Presently the good woman and her husband came up the hill from the village with their arms full of bundles and followed by a crowd of small boys who had been hired to help carry the purchases. Then followed others, youngsters and country louts, attracted by the wealth and prodigality of the pair, who, from simple curiosity, trailed along behind like the tail of a comet and helped swell the concourse into a triumphal procession. Last of all came Guggins, the shopkeeper, carrying with much tenderness a new silk dress which was to be paid for when they reached the house, all the money they had taken to the village having been lavishly expended.

The farmer, who had formerly been a modest man, was now so swelled with pride that he tipped the rim of his hat over his left ear and smoked a big cigar that was fast making him ill. His wife strutted along beside him like a peacock, enjoying to the full the homage and respect her wealth had won from those who formerly deigned not to notice her, and glancing from time to time at the admiring procession in the rear.

But, alas for their new-born pride! when they reached the farmhouse they found the door broken in, the furniture strewn in all directions and their treasure stolen to the very last gold piece.

The crowd grinned and made slighting remarks of a personal nature, and Guggins, the shopkeeper, demanded in a loud voice the money for the silk dress he had brought.

Then the woman whispered to her husband to run and pump some more gold while she kept the crowd quiet, and he obeyed quickly. But after a few moments he returned with a white face to tell her the pump was dry, and not a gold piece could now be coaxed from the spout.

The procession marched back to the village laughing and jeering at the farmer and his wife, who had pretended to be so rich; and some of the boys were naughty enough to throw stones at the house from the top of the hill. Mr. Guggins carried away his dress after severely scolding the woman for deceiving him, and when the couple at last found themselves alone their pride had turned to humiliation and their joy to bitter grief.

Just before sundown the woman dried her eyes and, having resumed her ordinary attire, went to the brook for water. When she came to the flat stone she saw the King Beetle sitting upon it.

"The well is dry!" she cried out, angrily.

"Yes," answered the beetle, calmly, "you have pumped from it all the gold my people could find."

"But we are now ruined," said the woman, sitting down in the path beginning to weep; "for robbers have stolen from us every penny we possessed."

"I'm sorry," returned the beetle; "but it is your

own fault. Had you not made so great a show of your wealth no one would have suspected you possessed a treasure, or thought to rob you. As it is, you have merely lost the gold which others have lost before you. It will probably be lost many times more before the world comes to an end."

"But what are we to do now?" she asked.

"What did you do before I gave you the money?"

"We worked from morning 'til night," said she.

"Then work still remains for you," remarked the beetle, composedly; "no one will ever try to rob you of that, you may be sure!" And he slid from the stone and disappeared for the last time.

THIS STORY SHOULD TEACH us to accept good fortune with humble hearts and to use it with moderation. For, had the farmer and his wife resisted the temptation to display their wealth ostentatiously, they might have retained it to this very day.

CHAPTER 10
THE DUMMY THAT LIVED

In all Fairyland there is no more mischievous a person than Tanko-Mankie the Yellow Ryl. He flew through the city one afternoon—quite invisible to mortal eyes, but seeing everything himself—and noticed a figure of a wax lady standing behind the big plate glass window of Mr. Floman's department store.

The wax lady was beautifully dressed, and extended in her stiff left hand was a card bearing the words:

> *"RARE BARGIN!*
> *This Stylish Costume*
> *(Imported from Paris)*
> *Former Price, $20,*
> *REDUCED TO ONLY $19.98."*

This impressive announcement had drawn before the window a crowd of women shoppers, who stood looking at the wax lady with critical eyes.

Tanko-Mankie laughed to himself the low, gurgling little laugh that always means mischief. Then he flew close to the wax figure and breathed twice upon its forehead.

From that instant the dummy began to live, but so dazed and astonished was she at the unexpected sensation that she continued to stand stupidly staring at the women outside and holding out the placard as before.

The ryl laughed again and flew away. Anyone but Tanko-Mankie would have remained to help the wax lady out of the troubles that were sure to overtake her; but this naughty elf thought it rare fun to turn the inexperienced lady loose in a cold and heartless world and leave her to shift for herself.

Fortunately it was almost six o'clock when the dummy first realized that she was alive, and before she had collected her new thoughts and decided what to do a man came around and drew down all the window shades, shutting off the view from the curious shoppers.

Then the clerks and cashiers and floorwalkers and cash girls went home and the store was closed for the night, although the sweepers and scrubbers remained to clean the floors for the following day.

The window inhabited by the wax lady was boxed in, like a little room, one small door being left at the side for the window-trimmer to creep in and out of. So the scrubbers never noticed that the dummy, when left to herself, dropped the placard to the floor and sat down upon a pile of silks to wonder who she was, where she was, and how she happened to be alive.

For you must consider, dear reader, that in spite of her size and her rich costume, in spite of her pink cheeks and fluffy yellow hair, this lady was very young—no older, in reality, than a baby born but half an hour. All she knew of the world was contained in the glimpse she had secured of the busy street facing her window; all she knew of people lay in the actions of the group of women which had stood before her on the other side of the window pane and criticised the fit of her dress or remarked upon its stylish appearance.

So she had little enough to think about, and her thoughts moved somewhat slowly; yet one thing she really decided upon, and that was not to remain in the window and be insolently stared at by a lot of women who were not nearly so handsome or well dressed as herself.

By the time she reached this important conclusion, it was after midnight; but dim lights were burning in the big, deserted store, so she crept through the door of her window and walked down the long aisles, pausing now and then to look with much curiosity at the wealth of finery confronting her on every side.

When she came to the glass cases filled with trimmed hats she remembered having seen upon the heads of the women in the street similar creations. So she selected one that suited her fancy and placed it carefully upon her yellow locks. I won't attempt to explain what instinct it was that made her glance into a near-by mirror to see if the hat was straight, but this she certainly did. It didn't correspond with her dress very well, but the poor thing was too young to have much taste in matching colors.

When she reached the glove counter she remembered that gloves were also worn by the women she had seen. She took a pair from the case and tried to fit them upon her stiff, wax-coated fingers; but the gloves were too small and ripped in the seams. Then she tried another pair, and several others, as well; but hours passed before she finally succeeded in getting her hands covered with a pair of pea-green kids.

Next she selected a parasol from a large and varied assortment in the rear of the store. Not that she had any idea what it was used for; but other ladies carried such things, so she also would have one.

When she again examined herself critically in the mirror she decided her outfit was now complete, and to her inexperienced eyes there was no perceptible difference between her and the women who had stood outside the window. Whereupon she tried to leave the store, but found every door fast locked.

The wax lady was in no hurry. She inherited patience from her previous existence. Just to be alive and to wear beautiful clothes was sufficient enjoyment for her at present. So she sat down upon a stool and waited quietly until daylight.

When the janitor unlocked the door in the morning the wax lady swept past him and walked with stiff but stately strides down the street. The poor fellow was so completely whuckered at seeing the well-known wax lady leave her window and march away from the store that he fell over in a heap and only saved himself from fainting by striking his funny bone against the doorstep. When he recovered his wits she had turned the corner and disappeared.

The wax lady's immature mind had reasoned that, since she had come to life, her evident duty was to mix with the world and do whatever other folks did. She could not realize how different she was from people of flesh and blood; nor did she know she was the first dummy that had ever lived, or that she owed her unique experience to Tanko-Mankie's love of mischief. So ignorance gave her a confidence in herself that she was not justly entitled to.

It was yet early in the day, and the few people she met were hurrying along the streets. Many of them turned into restaurants and eating houses, and following their example the wax lady also entered one and sat upon a stool before a lunch counter.

"Coffee 'n' rolls!" said a shop girl on the next stool.

"Coffee 'n' rolls!" repeated the dummy, and soon the waiter placed them before her. Of course she had no appetite, as her constitution, being mostly wood, did not require food; but she watched the shop girl, and saw her put the coffee to her mouth and drink it. Therefore the wax lady did the same, and the next instant was surprised to feel the hot liquid trickling out between her wooden ribs. The coffee also blistered her wax lips, and so disagreeable was the experience that she arose and left the restaurant, paying no attention to the demands of the waiter for "20 cents, mum." Not that she intended to defraud him, but the poor creature had no idea what he meant by "20 cents, mum."

As she came out she met the window trimmer at Floman's store. The man was rather near-sighted, but seeing something familiar in the lady's features he politely raised his hat. The wax lady also raised her hat, thinking it the proper thing to do, and the man hurried away with a horrified face.

Then a woman touched her arm and said:

"Beg pardon, ma'am; but there's a price-mark hanging on your dress behind."

"Yes, I know," replied the wax lady, stiffly; "it was originally $20, but it's been reduced to $19.98."

The woman looked surprised at such indifference and walked on. Some carriages were standing at the edge of the sidewalk, and seeing the dummy hesitate a driver approached her and touched his cap.

"Cab, ma'am?" he asked.

"No," said she, misunderstanding him; "I'm wax."

"Oh!" he exclaimed, and looked after her wonderingly.

"Here's yer mornin' paper!" yelled a newsboy.

"Mine, did you say?" she asked.

"Sure! Chronicle, 'Quirer, R'public 'n' 'Spatch! Wot'll ye 'ave?"

"What are they for?" inquired the wax lady, simply.

"W'y, ter read, o' course. All the news, you know."

She shook her head and glanced at a paper.

"It looks all speckled and mixed up," she said. "I'm afraid I can't read."

"Ever ben to school?" asked the boy, becoming interested.

"No; what's school?" she inquired.

The boy gave her an indignant look.

"Say!" he cried, "ye'r just a dummy, that's wot ye are!" and ran away to seek a more promising customer.

"I wonder that he means," thought the poor lady. "Am I really different in some way from all the others? I look like them, certainly; and I try to act like them; yet that boy called me a dummy and seemed to think I acted queerly."

This idea worried her a little, but she walked on to the corner, where she noticed a street car stop to let some people on. The wax lady, still determined to do as others did, also boarded the car and sat down quietly in a corner.

After riding a few blocks the conductor approached her and said:

"Fare, please!"

"What's that?" she inquired, innocently.

"Your fare!" said the man, impatiently.

She stared at him stupidly, trying to think what he meant.

"Come, come!" growled the conductor, "either pay up or get off!"

Still she did not understand, and he grabbed her rudely by the arm and lifted her to her feet. But when his hand came in contact with the hard wood of which her arm was made the fellow was filled with surprise. He stooped down and peered into her face, and, seeing it was wax instead of flesh, he gave a yell of fear and jumped from the car, running as if he had seen a ghost.

At this the other passengers also yelled and sprang from the car, fearing a collision; and the motorman, knowing something was wrong, followed suit. The wax lady, seeing the others run, jumped from the car last of all, and stepped in front of another car coming at full speed from the opposite direction.

She heard cries of fear and of warning on all sides, but before she understood her danger she was knocked down and dragged for half a block.

When the car was brought to a stop a policeman reached down and pulled her from under the wheels. Her dress was badly torn and soiled. Her left ear was entirely gone, and the left side of her head was caved in; but she quickly scrambled to her feet and asked for her hat. This a gentleman had already picked up, and when the policeman handed it to her and noticed the great hole in her head and the hollow place it disclosed, the poor fellow trembled so frightfully that his knees actually knocked together.

"Why—why, ma'am, you're killed!" he gasped.

"What does it mean to be killed?" asked the wax lady.

The policeman shuddered and wiped the perspiration from his forehead.

"You're it!" he answered, with a groan.

The crowd that had collected were looking upon the lady wonderingly, and a middle-aged gentleman now exclaimed:

"Why, she's wax!"

"Wax!" echoed the policeman.

"Certainly. She's one of those dummies they put in the windows," declared the middle-aged man.

The people who had collected shouted: "You're right!" "That's what she is!" "She's a dummy!"

"Are you?" inquired the policeman, sternly.

The wax lady did not reply. She began to fear she was getting into trouble, and the staring crowd seemed to embarrass her.

Suddenly a bootblack attempted to solve the problem by saying: "You guys is all wrong! Can a dummy talk? Can a dummy walk? Can a dummy live?"

"Hush!" murmured the policeman. "Look here!" and he pointed to the hole in the lady's head. The newsboy looked, turned pale and whistled to keep himself from shivering.

A second policeman now arrived, and after a brief conference it was decided to take the strange creature to headquarters. So they called a hurry-up wagon, and the damaged wax lady was helped inside and driven to the police station. There the policeman locked her in a cell and hastened to tell Inspector Mugg their wonderful story.

Inspector Mugg had just eaten a poor breakfast, and was not in a pleasant mood; so he roared and stormed at the unlucky policemen, saying they were themselves dummies to bring such a fairy tale to a man of sense. He also hinted that they had been guilty of intemperance.

The policemen tried to explain, but Inspector Mugg would not listen; and while they were still disputing in rushed Mr. Floman, the owner of the department store.

"I want a dozen detectives, at once, inspector!" he cried.

"What for?" demanded Mugg.

"One of the wax ladies has escaped from my store and eloped with a $19.98 costume, a $4.23 hat, a $2.19 parasol and a 76-cent pair of gloves, and I want her arrested!"

While he paused for breath the inspector glared at him in amazement.

"Is everybody going crazy at the same time?" he inquired, sarcastically. "How could a wax dummy run away?"

"I don't know; but she did. When my janitor opened the door this morning he saw her run out."

"Why didn't he stop her?" asked Mugg.

"He was too frightened. But she's stolen my property, your honor, and I want her arrested!" declared the storekeeper.

The inspector thought for a moment.

"You wouldn't be able to prosecute her," he said, "for there's no law against dummies stealing."

Mr. Floman sighed bitterly.

"Am I to lose that $19.98 costume and the $4.25 hat and—"

"By no means," interrupted Inspector Mugg. "The police of this city are ever prompt to act in defense of our worthy citizens. We have already arrested the wax lady, and she is locked up in cell No. 16. You may go there and recover your property, if you wish, but before you prosecute her for stealing you'd better hunt up a law that applies to dummies."

"All I want," said Mr. Floman, "is that $19.98 costume and—"

"Come along!" interrupted the policeman. "I'll take you to the cell."

But when they entered No. 16 they found only a lifeless dummy lying prone upon the floor. Its wax was cracked and blistered, its head was badly damaged, and the bargain costume was dusty, soiled and much bedraggled. For the mischief-loving Tanko-Mankie had flown by and breathed once more upon the poor wax lady, and in that instant her brief life ended.

"It's just as I thought," said Inspector Mugg, leaning back in his chair contentedly. "I knew all the time the thing was a fake. It seems sometimes as though the whole world would go crazy if there wasn't some level-headed man around to bring 'em to their senses. Dummies are wood an' wax, an' that's all there is of 'em."

"That may be the rule," whispered the policeman to himself, "but this one were a dummy as lived!"

CHAPTER II
THE KING OF THE POLAR BEARS

The King of the Polar Bears lived among the icebergs in the far north country. He was old and monstrous big; he was wise and friendly to all who knew him. His body was thickly covered with long, white hair that glistened like silver under the rays of the midnight sun. His claws were strong and sharp, that he might walk safely over the smooth ice or grasp and tear the fishes and seals upon which he fed.

The seals were afraid when he drew near, and tried to avoid him; but the gulls, both white and gray, loved him because he left the remnants of his feasts for them to devour.

Often his subjects, the polar bears, came to him for advice when ill or in trouble; but they wisely kept away from his hunting grounds, lest they might interfere with his sport and arouse his anger.

The wolves, who sometimes came as far north as

the icebergs, whispered among themselves that the King of the Polar Bears was either a magician or under the protection of a powerful fairy. For no earthly thing seemed able to harm him; he never failed to secure plenty of food, and he grew bigger and stronger day by day and year by year.

Yet the time came when this monarch of the north met man, and his wisdom failed him.

He came out of his cave among the icebergs one day and saw a boat moving through the strip of water which had been uncovered by the shifting of the summer ice. In the boat were men.

The great bear had never seen such creatures before, and therefore advanced toward the boat, sniffing the strange scent with aroused curiosity and wondering whether he might take them for friends or foes, food or carrion.

When the king came near the water's edge a man stood up in the boat and with a queer instrument made a loud "bang!" The polar bear felt a shock; his brain became numb; his thoughts deserted him; his great limbs shook and gave way beneath him and his body fell heavily upon the hard ice.

That was all he remembered for a time.

When he awoke he was smarting with pain on every inch of his huge bulk, for the men had cut away his hide with its glorious white hair and carried it with them to a distant ship.

Above him circled thousands of his friends the gulls, wondering if their benefactor were really dead and it was proper to eat him. But when they saw him raise his head and groan and tremble they knew he still lived, and one of them said to his comrades:

"The wolves were right. The king is a great magician, for even men cannot kill him. But he suffers for lack of covering. Let us repay his kindness to us by each giving him as many feathers as we can spare."

This idea pleased the gulls. One after another they plucked with their beaks the softest feathers from under their wings, and, flying down, dropped then gently upon the body of the King of the Polar Bears.

Then they called to him in a chorus:

"Courage, friend! Our feathers are as soft and beautiful as your own shaggy hair. They will guard you from the cold winds and warm you while you sleep. Have courage, then, and live!"

And the King of the Polar Bears had courage to bear his pain and lived and was strong again.

The feathers grew as they had grown upon the bodies of the birds and covered him as his own hair had done. Mostly they were pure white in color, but some from the gray gulls gave his majesty a slight mottled appearance.

The rest of that summer and all through the six months of night the king left his icy cavern only to fish or catch seals for food. He felt no shame at his feathery covering, but it was still strange to him, and he avoided meeting any of his brother bears.

During this period of retirement he thought much of the men who had harmed him, and remembered the way they had made the great "bang!" And he decided it was best to keep away from such fierce creatures. Thus he added to his store of wisdom.

When the moon fell away from the sky and the sun came to make the icebergs glitter with the gorgeous tintings of the rainbow, two of the polar bears arrived at the king's cavern to ask his advice about the hunting season. But when they saw his great body covered with feathers instead of hair they began to laugh, and one said:

"Our mighty king has become a bird! Who ever before heard of a feathered polar bear?"

Then the king gave way to wrath. He advanced upon them with deep growls and stately tread and with one blow of his monstrous paw stretched the mocker lifeless at his feet.

The other ran away to his fellows and carried the news of the king's strange appearance. The result was a meeting of all the polar bears upon a broad field of ice, where they talked gravely of the remarkable change that had come upon their monarch.

"He is, in reality, no longer a bear," said one; "nor can he justly be called a bird. But he is half bird and half bear, and so unfitted to remain our king."

"Then who shall take his place?" asked another.

"He who can fight the bird-bear and overcome him," answered an aged member of the group. "Only the strongest is fit to rule our race."

There was silence for a time, but at length a great bear moved to the front and said:

"I will fight him; I—Woof—the strongest of our race! And I will be King of the Polar Bears."

The others nodded assent, and dispatched a

messenger to the king to say he must fight the great Woof and master him or resign his sovereignty.

"For a bear with feathers," added the messenger, "is no bear at all, and the king we obey must resemble the rest of us."

"I wear feathers because it pleases me," growled the king. "Am I not a great magician? But I will fight, nevertheless, and if Woof masters me he shall be king in my stead."

Then he visited his friends, the gulls, who were even then feasting upon the dead bear, and told them of the coming battle.

"I shall conquer," he said, proudly. "Yet my people are in the right, for only a hairy one like themselves can hope to command their obedience."

The queen gull said:

"I met an eagle yesterday, which had made its escape from a big city of men. And the eagle told me he had seen a monstrous polar bear skin thrown over the back of a carriage that rolled along the street. That skin must have been yours, oh king, and if you wish I will sent an hundred of my gulls to the city to bring it back to you."

"Let them go!" said the king, gruffly. And the hundred gulls were soon flying rapidly southward.

For three days they flew straight as an arrow, until they came to scattered houses, to villages, and to cities. Then their search began.

The gulls were brave, and cunning, and wise. Upon the fourth day they reached the great metropolis, and hovered over the streets until a carriage rolled along with a great white bear robe thrown

over the back seat. Then the birds swooped down—
the whole hundred of them—and seizing the skin in
their beaks flew quickly away.

They were late. The king's great battle was upon
the seventh day, and they must fly swiftly to reach
the Polar regions by that time.

Meanwhile the bird-bear was preparing for his
fight. He sharpened his claws in the small crevasses
of the ice. He caught a seal and tested his big yellow
teeth by crunching its bones between them. And the
queen gull set her band to pluming the king bear's
feathers until they lay smoothly upon his body.

But every day they cast anxious glances into the
southern sky, watching for the hundred gulls to
bring back the king's own skin.

The seventh day came, and all the Polar bears in
that region gathered around the king's cavern.
Among them was Woof, strong and confident of his
success.

"The bird-bear's feathers will fly fast enough
when I get my claws upon him!" he boasted; and the
others laughed and encouraged him.

The king was disappointed at not having recovered his skin, but he resolved to fight bravely
without it. He advanced from the opening of his
cavern with a proud and kingly bearing, and when
he faced his enemy he gave so terrible a growl that
Woof's heart stopped beating for a moment, and he
began to realize that a fight with the wise and
mighty king of his race was no laughing matter.

After exchanging one or two heavy blows with

his foe Woof's courage returned, and he determined to dishearten his adversary by bluster.

"Come nearer, bird-bear!" he cried. "Come nearer, that I may pluck your plumage!"

The defiance filled the king with rage. He ruffled his feathers as a bird does, till he appeared to be twice his actual size, and then he strode forward and struck Woof so powerful a blow that his skull crackled like an egg-shell and he fell prone upon the ground.

While the assembled bears stood looking with fear and wonder at their fallen champion the sky became darkened.

An hundred gulls flew down from above and dripped upon the king's body a skin covered with pure white hair that glittered in the sun like silver.

And behold! the bears saw before them the well-known form of their wise and respected master, and with one accord they bowed their shaggy heads in homage to the mighty King of the Polar Bears.

THIS STORY TEACHES us that true dignity and courage depend not upon outward appearance, but come rather from within; also that brag and bluster are poor weapons to carry into battle.

CHAPTER 12

THE MANDARIN AND THE BUTTERFLY

A mandarin once lived in Kiang-ho who was so exceedingly cross and disagreeable that everyone hated him. He snarled and stormed at every person he met and was never known to laugh or be merry under any circumstances. Especially he hated boys and girls; for the boys jeered at him, which aroused his wrath, and the girls made fun of him, which hurt his pride.

When he had become so unpopular that no one would speak to him, the emperor heard about it and commanded him to emigrate to America. This suited the mandarin very well; but before he left China he stole the Great Book of Magic that belonged to the wise magician Haot-sai. Then, gathering up his little store of money, he took ship for America.

He settled in a city of the middle west and of course started a laundry, since that seems to be the natural vocation of every Chinaman, be he coolie or mandarin.

He made no acquaintances with the other Chinamen of the town, who, when they met him and saw the red button in his hat, knew him for a real mandarin and bowed low before him. He put up a red and white sign and people brought their laundry to him and got paper checks, with Chinese characters upon them, in exchange, this being the only sort of character the mandarin had left.

One day as the ugly one was ironing in his shop in the basement of 263 1/2 Main street, he looked up and saw a crowd of childish faces pressed against the window. Most Chinamen make friends with children; this one hated them and tried to drive them away. But as soon as he returned to his work they were back at the window again, mischievously smiling down upon him.

The naughty mandarin uttered horrid words in the Manchu language and made fierce gestures; but this did no good at all. The children stayed as long as they pleased, and they came again the very next day as soon as school was over, and likewise the next day, and the next. For they saw their presence at the window bothered the Chinaman and were delighted accordingly.

The following day being Sunday the children did not appear, but as the mandarin, being a heathen, worked in his little shop a big butterfly flew in at the open door and fluttered about the room.

The mandarin closed the door and chased the butterfly until he caught it, when he pinned it against the wall by sticking two pins through its beautiful wings. This did not hurt the butterfly, there being no feeling in its wings; but it made him a safe prisoner.

This butterfly was of large size and its wings were exquisitely marked by gorgeous colors laid out in regular designs like the stained glass windows of a cathedral.

The mandarin now opened his wooden chest and drew forth the Great Book of Magic he had stolen from Haot-sai. Turning the pages slowly he came to a passage describing "How to understand the language of butterflies." This he read carefully and then mixed a magic formula in a tin cup and drank it down with a wry face. Immediately thereafter he spoke to the butterfly in its own language, saying:

"Why did you enter this room?"

"I smelled bees-wax," answered the butterfly; "therefore I thought I might find honey here."

"But you are my prisoner," said the mandarin. "If I please I can kill you, or leave you on the wall to starve to death."

"I expect that," replied the butterfly, with a sigh. "But my race is shortlived, anyway; it doesn't matter whether death comes sooner or later."

"Yet you like to live, do you not?" asked the mandarin.

"Yet; life is pleasant and the world is beautiful. I do not seek death."

"Then," said the mandarin, "I will give you life —a long and pleasant life—if you will promise to obey me for a time and carry out my instructions."

"How can a butterfly serve a man?" asked the creature, in surprise.

"Usually they cannot," was the reply. "But I have a book of magic which teaches me strange things. Do you promise?"

"Oh, yes; I promise," answered the butterfly; "for even as your slave I will get some enjoyment out of life, while should you kill me—that is the end of everything!"

"Truly," said the mandarin, "butterflies have no souls, and therefore cannot live again."

"But I have enjoyed three lives already," returned the butterfly, with some pride. "I have been a caterpillar and a chrysalis before I became a butterfly. You were never anything but a Chinaman, although I admit your life is longer than mine."

"I will extend your life for many days, if you will obey me," declared the Chinaman. "I can easily do so by means of my magic."

"Of course I will obey you," said the butterfly, carelessly.

"Then, listen! You know children, do you not?— boys and girls?"

"Yes, I know them. They chase me, and try to catch me, as you have done," replied the butterfly.

"And they mock me, and jeer at me through the window," continued the mandarin, bitterly. "Therefore, they are your enemies and mine! But with your aid and the help of the magic book we shall have a fine revenge for their insults."

"I don't care much for revenge," said the butterfly. "They are but children, and 'tis natural they should wish to catch such a beautiful creature as I am."

"Nevertheless, I care! and you must obey me," retorted the mandarin, harshly. "I, at least, will have my revenge."

Then he stuck a drop of molasses upon the wall beside the butterfly's head and said:

"Eat that, while I read my book and prepare my magic formula."

So the butterfly feasted upon the molasses and the mandarin studied his book, after which he began to mix a magic compound in the tin cup.

When the mixture was ready he released the butterfly from the wall and said to it:

"I command you to dip your two front feet into this magic compound and then fly away until you meet a child. Fly close, whether it be a boy or a girl, and touch the child upon its forehead with your feet. Whosoever is thus touched, the book declares, will at once become a pig, and will remain such forever after. Then return to me and dip your legs afresh in the contents of this cup. So shall all my enemies, the children, become miserable swine, while no one will think of accusing me of the sorcery."

"Very well; since such is your command, I obey," said the butterfly. Then it dipped its front legs, which were the shortest of the six, into the contents of the tin cup, and flew out of the door and away over the houses to the edge of the town. There it alighted in a flower garden and soon forgot all about its mission to turn children into swine.

In going from flower to flower it soon brushed the magic compound from its legs, so that when the sun began to set and the butterfly finally remembered its master, the mandarin, it could not have injured a child had it tried.

But it did not intend to try.

"That horrid old Chinaman," it thought, "hates children and wishes to destroy them. But I rather like children myself and shall not harm them. Of course I must return to my master, for he is a magician, and would seek me out and kill me; but I can deceive him about this matter easily enough."

When the butterfly flew in at the door of the mandarin's laundry he asked, eagerly:

"Well, did you meet a child?"

"I did," replied the butterfly, calmly. "It was a pretty, golden-haired girl—but now 'tis a grunting pig!"

"Good! Good! Good!" cried the mandarin, dancing joyfully about the room. "You shall have molasses for your supper, and to-morrow you must change two children into pigs."

The butterfly did not reply, but ate the molasses in silence. Having no soul it had no conscience, and having no conscience it was able to lie to the mandarin with great readiness and a certain amount of enjoyment.

Next morning, by the mandarin's command, the butterfly dipped its legs in the mixture and flew away in search of children.

When it came to the edge of the town it noticed a pig in a sty, and alighting upon the rail of the sty it looked down at the creature and thought.

"If I could change a child into a pig by touching it with the magic compound, what could I change a pig into, I wonder?"

Being curious to determine this fine point in sorcery the butterfly fluttered down and touched its front feet to the pig's nose. Instantly the animal disappeared, and in its place was a shock-headed, dirty looking boy, which sprang from the sty and ran down the road uttering load whoops.

"That's funny," said the butterfly to itself. "The mandarin would be very angry with me if he knew of this, for I have liberated one more of the creatures that bother him."

It fluttered along after the boy, who had paused to throw stones at a cat. But pussy escaped by running up a tree, where thick branches protected her from the stones. Then the boy discovered a newly-planted garden, and trampled upon the beds until the seeds were scattered far and wide, and the garden was ruined. Next he caught up a switch and struck with it a young calf that stood quietly grazing in a field. The poor creature ran away with piteous bleats, and the boy laughed and followed after it, striking the frightened animal again and again.

"Really," thought the butterfly, "I do not wonder the mandarin hates children, if they are all so cruel and wicked as this one."

The calf having escaped him the boy came back to the road, where he met two little girls on their way to school. One of them had a red apple in her hand, and the boy snatched it away and began eating it. The little girl commenced to cry, but her companion, more brave and sturdy, cried out:

"You ought to be ashamed of yourself, you nasty boy!"

At this the boy reached out and slapped her pretty face, whereupon she also began to sob.

Although possessed of neither soul nor conscience, the butterfly had a very tender heart, and now decided it could endure this boy no longer.

"If I permitted him to exist," it reflected, "I should never forgive myself, for the monster would do nothing but evil from morning 'til night."

So it flew directly into his face and touched his forehead with its sticky front feet.

The next instant the boy had disappeared, but a grunting pig ran swiftly up the road in the direction of its sty.

The butterfly gave a sigh of relief.

"This time I have indeed used the mandarin's magic upon a child," it whispered, as it floated lazily upon the light breeze; "but since the child was originally a pig I do not think I have any cause to reproach myself. The little girls were sweet and gentle, and I would not injure them to save my life, but were all boys like this transformed pig, I should not hesitate to carry out the mandarin's orders."

Then it flew into a rose bush, where it remained comfortably until evening. At sundown it returned to its master.

"Have you changed two of them into pigs?" he asked, at once.

"I have," replied the butterfly. "One was a pretty, black-eyed baby, and the other a freckle-faced, red-haired, barefooted newboy."

"Good! Good! Good!" screamed the mandarin, in an ecstasy of delight. "Those are the ones who torment me the most! Change every newboy you meet into a pig!"

"Very well," answered the butterfly, quietly, and ate its supper of molasses.

Several days were passed by the butterfly in the same manner. It fluttered aimlessly about the flower gardens while the sun shone, and returned at night to the mandarin with false tales of turning children into swine. Sometimes it would be one child which was transformed, sometimes two, and occasionally three; but the mandarin always greeted the butterfly's report with intense delight and gave him molasses for supper.

One evening, however, the butterfly thought it might be well to vary the report, so that the mandarin might not grow suspicious; and when its master asked what child had been had been changed into a pig that day the lying creature answered:

"It was a Chinese boy, and when I touched him he became a black pig."

This angered the mandarin, who was in an especially cross mood. He spitefully snapped the butterfly with his finger, and nearly broke its beautiful wing; for he forgot that Chinese boys had once

134

mocked him and only remembered his hatred for American boys.

The butterfly became very indignant at this abuse from the mandarin. It refused to eat its molasses and sulked all the evening, for it had grown to hate the mandarin almost as much as the mandarin hated children.

When morning came it was still trembling with indignation; but the mandarin cried out:

"Make haste, miserable slave; for to-day you must change four children into pigs, to make up for yesterday."

The butterfly did not reply. His little black eyes were sparkling wickedly, and no sooner had he dipped his feet into the magic compound than he flew full in the mandarin's face, and touched him upon his ugly, flat forehead.

Soon after a gentleman came into the room for his laundry. The mandarin was not there, but running around the place was a repulsive, scrawny pig, which squealed most miserably.

The butterfly flew away to a brook and washed from its feet all traces of the magic compound. When night came it slept in a rose bush.

THE SEA FAIRIES

FOREWORD

THE oceans are big and broad. I believe two-thirds of the earth's surface is covered with water. What people inhabit this water has always been a subject of curiosity to the inhabitants of the land. Strange creatures come from the seas at times, and perhaps in the ocean depths are many, more strange than mortal eye has ever gazed upon.

This story is fanciful. In it the sea people talk and act much as we do, and the mermaids especially are not unlike the fairies with whom we have learned to be familiar. Yet they are real sea people, for all that, and with the exception of Zog the Magician they are all supposed to exist in the ocean's depths.

I am told that some very learned people deny that mermaids or sea-serpents have ever inhabited the oceans, but it would be very difficult for them to prove such an assertion unless they had lived under the water as Trot and Cap'n Bill did in this story.

I hope my readers who have so long followed Dorothy's adventures in the Land of Oz will be interested in Trot's equally strange experiences. The ocean has always appealed to me as a veritable wonderland, and this story has been suggested to me many times by my young correspondents in their letters. Indeed, a good many children have implored me to "write something about the mermaids," and I have willingly granted the request.

Hollywood, 1911.
L. FRANK BAUM.

CHAPTER I
TROT AND CAP'N BILL

"Nobody," said Cap'n Bill solemnly, "ever sawr a mermaid an' lived to tell the tale."

"Why not?" asked Trot, looking earnestly up into the old sailor's face.

They were seated on a bench built around a giant acacia tree that grew just at the edge of the bluff. Below them rolled the blue waves of the great Pacific. A little way behind them was the house, a neat frame cottage painted white and surrounded by huge eucalyptus and pepper trees. Still farther behind that—a quarter of a mile distant but built upon a bend of the coast—was the village, over-looking a pretty bay.

Cap'n Bill and Trot came often to this tree to sit and watch the ocean below them. The sailor man had one "meat leg" and one "hickory leg," and he often said the wooden one was the best of the two. Once Cap'n Bill had commanded and owned the

"Anemone," a trading schooner that plied along the coast; and in those days Charlie Griffiths, who was Trot's father, had been the Captain's mate. But ever since Cap'n Bill's accident, when he lost his leg, Charlie Griffiths had been the captain of the little schooner while his old master lived peacefully ashore with the Griffiths family.

This was about the time Trot was born, and the old sailor became very fond of the baby girl. Her real name was Mayre, but when she grew big enough to walk, she took so many busy little steps every day that both her mother and Cap'n Bill nicknamed her "Trot," and so she was thereafter mostly called.

It was the old sailor who taught the child to love the sea, to love it almost as much as he and her father did, and these two, who represented the "beginning and the end of life," became firm friends and constant companions.

"Why hasn't anybody seen a mermaid and lived?" asked Trot again.

"'Cause mermaids is fairies, an' ain't meant to be seen by us mortal folk," replied Cap'n Bill.

"But if anyone happens to see 'em, what then, Cap'n?"

"Then," he answered, slowly wagging his head, "the mermaids give 'em a smile an' a wink, an' they dive into the water an' gets drownded."

"S'pose they knew how to swim, Cap'n Bill?"

"That don't make any diff'rence, Trot. The mermaids live deep down, an' the poor mortals never come up again."

The little girl was thoughtful for a moment. "But

why do folks dive in the water when the mermaids smile an' wink?" she asked.

"Mermaids," he said gravely, "is the most beautiful creatures in the world—or the water, either. You know what they're like, Trot, they's got a lovely lady's form down to the waist, an' then the other half of 'em's a fish, with green an' purple an' pink scales all down it."

"Have they got arms, Cap'n Bill?"

"'Course, Trot; arms like any other lady. An' pretty faces that smile an' look mighty sweet an' fetchin'. Their hair is long an' soft an' silky, an' floats all around 'em in the water. When they comes up atop the waves, they wring the water out'n their hair and sing songs that go right to your heart. If anybody is unlucky enough to be 'round jes' then, the beauty o' them mermaids an' their sweet songs charm 'em like magic; so's they plunge into the waves to get to the mermaids. But the mermaids haven't any hearts, Trot, no more'n a fish has; so they laughs when the poor people drown an' don't care a fig. That's why I says, an' I says it true, that nobody never sawr a mermaid an' lived to tell the tale."

"Nobody?" asked Trot.

"Nobody a tall."

"Then how do you know, Cap'n Bill?" asked the little girl, looking up into his face with big, round eyes.

Cap'n Bill coughed. Then he tried to sneeze, to gain time. Then he took out his red cotton handkerchief and wiped his bald head with it, rubbing hard so as to make him think clearer. "Look, Trot; ain't that a brig out there?" he inquired, pointing to a sail far out in the sea.

"How does anybody know about mermaids if those who have seen them never lived to tell about them?" she asked again.

"Know what about 'em, Trot?"

"About their green and pink scales and pretty songs and wet hair."

"They don't know, I guess. But mermaids jes' natcherly has to be like that, or they wouldn't be mermaids."

She thought this over. "Somebody MUST have lived, Cap'n Bill," she declared positively. "Other fairies have been seen by mortals; why not mermaids?"

"P'raps they have, Trot, p'raps they have," he answered musingly. "I'm tellin' you as it was told to me, but I never stopped to inquire into the matter so close before. Seems like folks wouldn't know so much about mermaids if they hadn't seen 'em; an' yet accordin' to all accounts the victim is bound to get drownded."

"P'raps," suggested Trot softly, "someone found a fotygraph of one of 'em."

"That might o' been, Trot, that might o' been," answered Cap'n Bill.

A nice man was Cap'n Bill, and Trot knew he always liked to explain everything so she could fully understand it. The aged sailor was not a very tall man, and some people might have called him chubby, or even fat. He wore a blue sailor shirt with white anchors worked on the corners of the broad, square collar, and his blue trousers were very wide at the bottom. He always wore one trouser leg over his wooden limb and sometimes it would flutter in the wind like a flag because it was so wide and the wooden leg so slender. His rough kersey coat was a pea-jacket and came down to his waistline. In the big pockets of his jacket he kept a wonderful jack-knife, and his pipe and tobacco, and many bits of string, and matches and keys and lots of other things. Whenever Cap'n Bill thrust a chubby hand into one of his pockets, Trot watched him with breathless interest, for she never knew what he was going to pull out.

The old sailor's face was brown as a berry. He had a fringe of hair around the back of his head and a fringe of whisker around the edge of his face, running from ear to ear and underneath his chin. His eyes were light blue and kind in expression. His nose was big and broad, and his few teeth were not strong enough to crack nuts with.

Trot liked Cap'n Bill and had a great deal of confidence in his wisdom, and a great admiration for his ability to make tops and whistles and toys with that marvelous jackknife of his. In the village were many boys and girls of her own age, but she never had as much fun playing with them as she had wandering by the sea accompanied by the old sailor and listening to his fascinating stories.

She knew all about the Flying Dutchman, and Davy Jones' Locker, and Captain Kidd, and how to harpoon a whale or dodge an iceberg or lasso a seal.

Cap'n Bill had been everywhere in the world, almost, on his many voyages. He had been wrecked on desert islands like Robinson Crusoe and been attacked by cannibals, and had a host of other exciting adventures. So he was a delightful comrade for the little girl, and whatever Cap'n Bill knew Trot was sure to know in time.

"How do the mermaids live?" she asked. "Are they in caves, or just in the water like fishes, or how?"

"Can't say, Trot," he replied. "I've asked divers about that, but none of 'em ever run acrost a mermaid's nest yet, as I've heard of."

"If they're fairies," she said, "their homes must be very pretty."

"Mebbe so, Trot, but damp. They are sure to be damp, you know."

"I'd like to see a mermaid, Cap'n Bill," said the child earnestly.

"What, an' git drownded?" he exclaimed.

"No, and live to tell the tale. If they're beautiful, and laughing, and sweet, there can't be much harm in them, I'm sure."

"Mermaids is mermaids," remarked Cap'n Bill in his most solemn voice. "It wouldn't do us any good to mix up with 'em, Trot."

"May-re! May-re!" called a voice from the house.

"Yes, Mamma!"

"You an' Cap'n Bill come in to supper."

CHAPTER 2
THE MERMAIDS

The next morning, as soon as Trot had helped wipe the breakfast dishes and put them away in the cupboard, the little girl and Cap'n Bill started out toward the bluff. The air was soft and warm and the sun turned the edges of the waves into sparkling diamonds. Across the bay the last of the fisherboats was speeding away out to sea, for well the fishermen knew this was an ideal day to catch rockbass, barracuda and yellowtail.

The old man and the young girl stood on the bluff and watched all this with interest. Here was their world. "It isn't a bit rough this morning. Let's have a boat ride, Cap'n Bill," said the child.

"Suits me to a T," declared the sailor. So they found the winding path that led down the face of the cliff to the narrow beach below and cautiously began the descent. Trot never minded the steep path or the loose rocks at all, but Cap'n Bill's wooden leg was not so useful on a downgrade as on a level, and he had to be careful not to slip and take a tumble.

But by and by they reached the sands and walked to a spot just beneath the big acacia tree that grew on the bluff. Halfway to the top of the cliff hung suspended a little shed-like structure that sheltered Trot's rowboat, for it was necessary to pull the boat out of reach of the waves which beat in fury against the rocks at high tide. About as high up as Cap'n Bill could reach was an iron ring securely fastened to the cliff, and to this ring was tied a rope. The old sailor unfastened the knot and began paying out the rope, and the rowboat came out of its shed and glided slowly downward to the beach. It hung on a pair of davits and was lowered just as a boat is lowered from a ship's side. When it reached the sands, the sailor unhooked the ropes and pushed the boat to the water's edge. It was a pretty little craft, light and strong, and Cap'n Bill knew how to sail it or row it, as Trot might desire.

Today they decided to row, so the girl climbed into the bow and her companion stuck his wooden leg into the water's edge "so he wouldn't get his foot wet" and pushed off the little boat as he climbed aboard. Then he seized the oars and began gently paddling.

"Whither away, Commodore Trot?" he asked gaily.

"I don't care, Cap'n. It's just fun enough to be on the water," she answered, trailing one hand overboard. So he rowed around by the North Promontory, where the great caves were, and much as they

148

were enjoying the ride, they soon began to feel the heat of the sun.

"That's Dead Man's Cave, 'cause a skellington was found there," observed the child as they passed a dark, yawning mouth in the cliff. "And that's Bumble Cave, 'cause the bumblebees make nests in the top of it. And here's Smuggler's Cave, 'cause the smugglers used to hide things in it."

She knew all the caves well, and so did Cap'n Bill. Many of them opened just at the water's edge, and it was possible to row their boat far into their dusky depths.

"And here's Echo Cave," she continued, dreamily, as they slowly moved along the coast, "and Giant's Cave, and—oh, Cap'n Bill! Do you s'pose there were ever any giants in that cave?"

"'Pears like there must o' been, Trot, or they wouldn't o' named it that name," he replied, pausing to wipe his bald head with the red handkerchief while the oars dragged in the water.

"We've never been into that cave, Cap'n," she remarked, looking at the small hole in the cliff—an archway through which the water flowed. "Let's go in now."

"What for, Trot?"

"To see if there's a giant there."

"Hm. Aren't you 'fraid?"

"No, are you? I just don't b'lieve it's big enough for a giant to get into."

"Your father was in there once," remarked Cap'n Bill, "an' he says it's the biggest cave on the coast, but low down. It's full o' water, an' the water's deep down to the very bottom o' the ocean; but the rock roof's liable to bump your head at high tide ."

"It's low tide now," returned Trot. "And how could any giant live in there if the roof is so low down?"

"Why, he couldn't, mate. I reckon they must have called it Giant's Cave 'cause it's so big, an' not 'cause any giant man lived there."

"Let's go in," said the girl again. "I'd like to 'splore it."

"All right," replied the sailor. "It'll be cooler in there than out here in the sun. We won't go very far, for when the tide turns we mightn't get out again." He picked up the oars and rowed slowly toward the cave. The black archway that marked its entrance seemed hardly big enough to admit the boat at first, but as they drew nearer, the opening became bigger. The sea was very calm here, for the headland shielded it from the breeze.

"Look out fer your head, Trot!" cautioned Cap'n Bill as the boat glided slowly into the rocky arch. But it was the sailor who had to duck, instead of the little girl. Only for a moment, though. Just beyond the opening the cave was higher, and as the boat floated into the dim interior they found themselves on quite an extensive branch of the sea. For a time neither of them spoke and only the soft lapping of the water against the sides of the boat was heard. A beautiful sight met the eyes of the two adventurers and held them dumb with wonder and delight.

It was not dark in this vast cave, yet the light seemed to come from underneath the water, which all around them glowed with an exquisite sapphire color. Where the little waves crept up the sides of the rocks they shone like brilliant jewels, and every drop of spray seemed a gem fit to deck a queen. Trot leaned her chin on her hands and her elbows on her lap and gazed at this charming sight with real enjoyment. Cap'n Bill drew in the oars and let the boat drift where it would while he also sat silently admiring the scene.

Slowly the little craft crept farther and farther into the dim interior of the vast cavern, while its two passengers feasted their eyes on the beauties constantly revealed. Both the old seaman and the little girl loved the ocean in all its various moods. To them it was a constant companion and a genial comrade. If it stormed and raved, they laughed with glee; if it rolled great breakers against the shore, they clapped their hands joyfully; if it lay slumbering at their feet, they petted and caressed it, but always they loved it.

Here was the ocean yet. It had crept under the dome of overhanging rock to reveal itself crowned with sapphires and dressed in azure gown, revealing in this guise new and unexpected charms. "Good morning, Mayre," said a sweet voice.

Trot gave a start and looked around her in wonder. Just beside her in the water were little eddies—circles within circles—such as are caused when anything sinks below the surface. "Did—did you hear that, Cap'n Bill?" she whispered solemnly.

Cap'n Bill did not answer. He was staring with eyes that fairly bulged out at a place behind Trot's back, and he shook a little, as if trembling from cold.

Trot turned half around, and then she stared, too. Rising from the blue water was a fair face around which floated a mass of long, blonde hair. It was a sweet, girlish face with eyes of the same deep blue as the water and red lips whose dainty smile disposed two rows of pearly teeth. The cheeks were plump and rosy, the brows gracefully penciled, while the chin was rounded and had a pretty dimple in it.

"The most beauti-ful-est in all the world," murmured Cap'n Bill in a voice of horror, "an' no one has ever lived to—to tell the tale!"

There was a peal of merry laughter at this, laughter that rippled and echoed throughout the cavern. Just at Trot's side appeared a new face even fairer than the other, with a wealth of brown hair wreathing the lovely features. And the eyes smiled kindly into those of the child. "Are you a—a mermaid?" asked Trot curiously. She was not a bit afraid. They seemed both gentle and friendly.

"Yes, dear," was the soft answer.

"We are all mermaids!" chimed a laughing chorus, and here and there, all about the boat, appeared pretty faces lying just upon the surface of the water.

"Are you part fishes?" asked Trot, greatly pleased by this wonderful sight.

"No, we are all mermaid," replied the one with the brown hair. "The fishes are partly like us, because they live in the sea and must move about. And you are partly like us, Mayre dear, but have awkward stiff legs so you may walk on the land. But the mermaids lived before fishes and before mankind, so both have borrowed something from us."

"Then you must be fairies if you've lived always," remarked Trot, nodding wisely.

"We are, dear. We are the water fairies," answered the one with the blonde hair, coming nearer and rising till her slender white throat showed plainly.

"We—we're goners, Trot!" sighed Cap'n Bill with a white, woebegone face.

"I guess not, Cap'n," she answered calmly. "These pretty mermaids aren't going to hurt us, I'm sure."

"No indeed," said the first one who had spoken. "If we were wicked enough to wish to harm you, our magic could reach you as easily upon the land as in this cave. But we love little girls dearly and wish only to please them and make their lives more happy."

"I believe that!" cried Trot earnestly.

Cap'n Bill groaned.

"Guess why we have appeared to you," said another mermaid, coming to the side of the boat.

"Why?" asked the child.

"We heard you say yesterday you would like to see a mermaid, and so we decided to grant your wish."

"That was real nice of you," said Trot gratefully.

"Also, we heard all the foolish things Cap'n Bill said about us," remarked the brown-haired one smilingly, "and we wanted to prove to him that they were wrong."

"I on'y said what I've heard," protested Cap'n Bill. "Never havin' seen a mermaid afore, I couldn't be ackerate, an' I never expected to see one an' live to tell the tale."

Again the cave rang with merry laughter, and as it died away, Trot said, "May I see your scales, please? And are they green and purple and pink like Cap'n Bill said?" They seemed undecided what to say to this and swam a little way off, where the beautiful heads formed a group that was delightful to see. Perhaps they talked together, for the brown-haired mermaid soon came back to the side of the boat and asked, "Would you like to visit our kingdom and see all the wonders that exist below the sea?"

"I'd like to," replied Trot promptly, "but I couldn't. I'd get drowned."

"That you would, mate!" cried Cap'n Bill.

"Oh no," said the mermaid. "We would make you both like one of ourselves, and then you could live within the water as easily as we do."

"I don't know as I'd like that," said the child, "at least for always."

"You need not stay with us a moment longer than you please," returned the mermaid, smiling as if amused at the remark. "Whenever you are ready to return home, we promise to bring you to this place again and restore to you the same forms you are now wearing."

"Would I have a fish's tail?" asked Trot earnestly.

"You would have a mermaid's tail," was the reply.

"What color would my scales be—pink, or purple?"

"You may choose the color yourself."

"Look ahere, Trot!" said Cap'n Bill in excitement. "You ain't thinkin' o' doin' such a fool thing, are you?"

"'Course I am," declared the little girl. "We don't get such inv'tations every day, Cap'n, and if I don't go now I may never find out how the mermaids live."

"I don't care how they live, myself," said Cap'n Bill. "I jes' want 'em to let ME live."

"There's no danger," insisted Trot.

"I do' know 'bout that. That's what all the other folks said when they dove after the mermaids an' got drownded."

"Who?" asked the girl.

"I don't know who, but I've heard tell—"

"You've heard that no one ever saw a mermaid and lived," said Trot.

"To tell the tale," he added, nodding. "An' if we dives down like they says, we won't live ourselves."

All the mermaids laughed at this, and the brown-haired one said, "Well, if you are afraid, don't come. You may row your boat out of this cave and never see us again, if you like. We merely thought it would please little Mayre, and were willing to show her the sights of our beautiful home."

"I'd like to see 'em, all right," said Trot, her eyes glistening with pleasure.

"So would I," admitted Cap'n Bill, "if we would live to tell the tale."

"Don't you believe us?" asked the mermaid, fixing her lovely eyes on those of the old sailor and smiling prettily. "Are you afraid to trust us to bring you safely back?"

"N-n-no," said Cap'n Bill, "'tain't that. I've got to look after Trot."

"Then you'll have to come with me," said Trot decidedly, "for I'm going to 'cept this inv'tation. If you don't care to come, Cap'n Bill, you go home and tell mother I'm visitin' the mermaids."

"She'd scold me inter shivers!" moaned Cap'n Bill with a shudder. "I guess I'd ruther take my chance down below."

"All right, I'm ready, Miss Mermaid," said Trot. "What shall I do? Jump in, clothes and all?"

"Give me your hand, dear," answered the mermaid, lifting a lovely white arm from the water. Trot took the slender hand and found it warm and soft and not a bit "fishy."

"My name is Clia," continued the mermaid, "and I am a princess in our deep-sea kingdom."

Just then Trot gave a flop and flopped right out of the boat into the water. Cap'n Bill caught a gleam of pink scales as his little friend went overboard, and the next moment there was Trot's face in the water among those of the mermaids. She was laughing with glee as she looked up into Cap'n Bill's face and called, "Come on in, Cap'n! It didn't hurt a bit!"

CHAPTER 3
THE DEPTHS OF THE DEEP BLUE SEA

Cap'n Bill stood up in the boat as if undecided what to do. Never a sailor man was more bewildered than this old fellow by the strangeness of the adventure he had encountered. At first he could hardly believe it was all true and that he was not dreaming; but there was Trot in the water, laughing with the mermaids and floating comfortably about, and he couldn't leave his dear little companion to make the trip to the depths of the ocean alone.

"Take my hand, please, Cap'n Bill," said Princess Clia, reaching her dainty arm toward him; and suddenly the old man took courage and clasped the soft fingers in his own. He had to lean over the boat to do this, and then there came a queer lightness to his legs and he had a great longing to be in the water. So he gave a flop and flopped in beside Trot, where he found himself comfortable enough, but somewhat frightened.

"Law sakes!" he gasped. "Here's me in the water with my rheumatics! I'll be that stiff termorrer I can't wiggle."

"You're wigglin' all right now," observed Trot. "That's a fine tail you've got, Cap'n, an' its green scales is jus' beautiful."

"Are they green, eh?" he asked, twisting around to try to see them.

"Green as em'ralds, Cap'n. How do they feel?"

"Feel, Trot, feel? Why, this tail beats that ol' wooden leg all holler! I kin do stunts now that I couldn't o' done in a thousand years with ol' peg."

"And don't be afraid of the rheumatism," advised the Princess. "No mermaid ever catches cold or suffers pain in the water."

"Is Cap'n Bill a mermaid now?" asked Trot.

"Why, he's a merMAN, I suppose," laughed the pretty princess. "But when he gets home, he will be just Cap'n Bill again."

"Wooden leg an' all?" inquired the child.

"To be sure, my dear."

The sailor was now trying his newly discovered power of swimming, and became astonished at the feats he could accomplish. He could dart this way and that with wonderful speed, and turn and dive, and caper about in the water far better than he had ever been able to do on land—even before he got the wooden leg. And a curious thing about this present experience was that the water did not cling to him and wet him as it had always done before. He still wore his flannel shirt and pea jacket and his sailor cap; but although he was in the water and had been underneath the surface, the cloth still seemed dry and warm. As he dived down and came up again, the drops flashed from his head and the fringe of beard, but he never needed to wipe his face or eyes at all.

Trot, too, was having queer experiences and enjoying them. When she ducked under water, she saw plainly everything about her as easily and distinctly as she had ever seen anything above water. And by looking over her shoulder she could watch the motion of her new tail, all covered with pretty iridescent pink scales, which gleamed like jewels. She wore her dress the same as before, and the water failed to affect it in the least.

She now noticed that the mermaids were clothed, too, and their exquisite gowns were the loveliest thing the little girl had ever beheld. They seemed made of a material that was like sheeny silk, cut low in the neck and with wide, flowing sleeves that seldom covered the shapely, white arms of her new friends. The gowns had trains that floated far behind the mermaids as they swam, but were so fleecy and transparent that the sparkle of their scales might be seen reaching back of their waists, where the human form ended and the fish part began. The sea fairies wore strings of splendid pearls twined around their throats, while more pearls were sewn upon their gowns for trimmings. They did not dress their beautiful hair at all, but let it float around them in clouds.

The little girl had scarcely time to observe all

this when the princess said, "Now, my dear, if you are ready, we will begin our journey, for it is a long way to our palaces."

"All right," answered Trot, and took the hand extended to her with a trustful smile.

"Will you allow me to guide you, Cap'n Bill?" asked the blonde mermaid, extending her hand to the old sailor.

"Of course, ma'am," he said, taking her fingers rather bashfully.

"My name is Merla," she continued, "and I am cousin to Princess Clia. We must all keep together, you know, and I will hold your hand to prevent your missing the way."

While she spoke they began to descend through the water, and it grew quite dark for a time because the cave shut out the light. But presently Trot, who was eagerly looking around her, began to notice the water lighten and saw they were coming into brighter parts of the sea. "We have left the cave now," said Clia, "and may swim straight home."

"I s'pose there are no winding roads in the ocean," remarked the child, swimming swiftly beside her new friend.

"Oh yes indeed. At the bottom, the way is far from being straight or level," replied Clia. "But we are in mid-water now, where nothing will hinder our journey, unless—"

She seemed to hesitate, so Trot asked, "Unless what?"

"Unless we meet with disagreeable creatures," said the Princess. "The mid-water is not as safe as the very bottom, and that is the reason we are holding your hands."

"What good would that do?" asked Trot.

"You must remember that we are fairies," said Princess Clia. "For that reason, nothing in the ocean can injure us, but you two are mortals and therefore not entirely safe at all times unless we protect you."

Trot was thoughtful for a few moments and looked around her a little anxiously. Now and then a dark form would shoot across their pathway or pass them at some distance, but none was near enough for the girl to see plainly what it might be. Suddenly they swam right into a big school of fishes, all yellowtails and of very large size. There must have been hundreds of them lying lazily in the water, and when they saw the mermaids they merely wriggled to one side and opened a path for the sea fairies to pass through. "Will they hurt us?" asked Trot.

"No indeed," laughed the Princess. "Fishes are stupid creatures mostly, and this family is quite harmless."

"How about sharks?" asked Cap'n Bill, who was swimming gracefully beside them, his hand clutched in that of pretty Merla.

"Sharks may indeed be dangerous to you," replied Clia, "so I advise you to keep them at a safe distance. They never dare attempt to bite a mermaid, and it may be they will think you belong to our band; but it is well to avoid them if possible."

"Don't get careless, Cap'n," added Trot.

"I surely won't, mate," he replied. "You see, I didn't use to be 'fraid o' sharks 'cause if they came near I'd stick my wooden leg at 'em. But now, if they happens to fancy these green scales, it's all up with ol' Bill."

"Never fear," said Merla, "I'll take care of you on our journey, and in our palaces you will find no sharks at all."

"Can't they get in?" he asked anxiously.

"No. The palaces of the mermaids are inhabited only by themselves."

"Is there anything else to be afraid of in the sea?" asked the little girl after they had swum quite a while in silence.

"One or two things, my dear," answered Princess Clia. "Of course, we mermaids have great powers, being fairies; yet among the sea people is one nearly as powerful as we are, and that is the devilfish."

"I know," said Trot. "I've seen 'em."

"You have seen the smaller ones, I suppose, which sometimes rise to the surface or go near the shore, and are often caught by fishermen," said Clia, "but they are only second cousins of the terrible deep-sea devilfish to which I refer."

"Those ones are bad enough, though," declared Cap'n Bill. "If you know any worse ones, I don't want a interduction to 'em."

"The monster devilfish inhabit caves in the rugged, mountainous regions of the ocean," resumed the Princess, "and they are evil spirits who delight in injuring all who meet them. None lives near our palaces, so there is little danger of your meeting any while you are our guests."

"I hope we won't," said Trot.

"None for me," added Cap'n Bill. "Devils of any sort ought to be give a wide berth, an' devilfish is worser ner sea serpents."

"Oh, do you know the sea serpents?" asked Merla as if surprised.

"Not much I don't," answered the sailor, "but I've heard tell of folks as has seen 'em."

"Did they ever live to tell the tale?" asked Trot.

"Sometimes," he replied. "They're jes' ORful creatures, mate."

"How easy it is to be mistaken," said Princess Clia softly. "We know the sea serpents very well, and we like them."

"You do!" exclaimed Trot.

"Yes, dear. There are only three of them in all the world, and not only are they harmless, but quite bashful and shy. They are kind-hearted, too, and although not beautiful in appearance, they do many kind deeds and are generally beloved."

"Where do they live?" asked the child.

"The oldest one, who is king of this ocean, lives quite near us," said Clia. "His name is Anko."

"How old is he?" inquired Cap'n Bill curiously.

"No one knows. He was here before the ocean came, and he stayed here because he learned to like the water better than the land as a habitation. Perhaps King Anko is ten thousand years old, perhaps twenty thousand. We often lose track of the centuries down here in the sea."

"That's pretty old, isn't it?" said Trot. "Older than Cap'n Bill, I guess."

"Summat," chuckled the sailor man, "summat

older, mate, but not much. P'raps the sea serpent ain't got gray whiskers."

"Oh yes he has," responded Merla with a laugh. "And so have his two brothers, Unko and Inko. They each have an ocean of their own, you know; and once every hundred years they come here to visit their brother Anko. So we've seen all three many times."

"Why, how old are mermaids, then?" asked Trot, looking around at the beautiful creatures wonderingly.

"We are like all ladies of uncertain age," rejoined the Princess with a smile. "We don't care to tell."

"Older than Cap'n Bill?"

"Yes, dear," said Clia.

"But we haven't any gray whiskers," added Merla merrily, "and our hearts are ever young."

Trot was thoughtful. It made her feel solemn to be in the company of such old people. The band of mermaids seemed to all appearances young and fresh and not a bit as if they'd been soaked in water for hundreds of years. The girl began to take more notice of the sea maidens following after her. More than a dozen were in the group; all were lovely in appearance and clothed in the same gauzy robes as Merla and the Princess. These attendants did not join in the conversation but darted here and there in sportive play, and often Trot heard the tinkling chorus of their laughter. Whatever doubts might have arisen in the child's mind through the ignorant tales of her sailor friend, she now found the mermaids to be light-hearted, joyous and gay, and from the first she had not been in the least afraid of her new companions.

"How much farther do we have to go?" asked Cap'n Bill presently.

"Are you getting tired?" Merla inquired.

"No," said he, "but I'm sorter anxious to see what your palaces look like. Inside the water ain't as interestin' as the top of it. It's fine swimmin', I'll agree, an' I like it, but there ain't nuthin' special to see that I can make out."

"That is true, sir," replied the Princess. "We have purposely led you through the mid-water hoping you would see nothing to alarm you until you get more accustomed to our ocean life. Moreover, we are able to travel more swiftly here. How far do you think we have already come, Cap'n?"

"Oh, 'bout two mile," he answered.

"Well, we are now hundreds of miles from the cave where we started," she told him.

"You don't mean it!" he exclaimed in wonder.

"Then there's magic in it," announced Trot soberly.

"True, my dear. To avoid tiring you and to save time, we have used a little of our fairy power," said Clia. "The result is that we are nearing our home. Let us go downward a bit, now, for you must know that the mermaid palaces are at the very bottom of the ocean, and in its deepest part."

CHAPTER 4
THE PALACE OF QUEEN AQUAREINE

Trot was surprised to find it was not at all dark or gloomy as they descended farther into the deep sea. Things were not quite so clear to her eyes as they had been in the bright sunshine above the ocean's surface, but every object was distinct nevertheless, as if she saw through a pane of green-tainted glass. The water was very clear except for this green shading, and the little girl had never before felt so light and buoyant as she did now. It was no effort at all to dart through the water, which seemed to support her on all sides.

"I don't believe I weigh anything at all," she said to Cap'n Bill.

"No more do I, Trot," said he. "But that's nat'ral, seein' as we're under water so far. What bothers me most is how we manage to breathe, havin' no gills like fishes have."

"Are you sure we haven't any gills?" she asked, lifting her free hand to feel her throat.

"Sure. Ner the mermaids haven't any, either," declared Cap'n Bill.

"Then," said Trot, "we're breathing by magic."

The mermaids laughed at this shrewd remark, and the Princess said, "You have guessed correctly, my dear. Go a little slower, now, for the palaces are in sight."

"Where?" asked Trot eagerly.

"Just before you."

"In that grove of trees?" inquired the girl. And really, it seemed to her that they were approaching a beautiful grove. The bottom of the sea was covered with white sand, in which grew many varieties of sea shrubs with branches like those of trees. Not all of them were green, however, for the branches and leaves were of a variety of gorgeous colors. Some were purple, shading down to a light lavender; and there were reds all the way from a delicate rose-pink to vivid shades of scarlet. Orange, yellow and blue shades were there, too, mingling with the sea-greens in a most charming manner. Altogether, Trot found the brilliant coloring somewhat bewildering.

These sea shrubs, which in size were quite as big and tall as the trees on earth, were set so close together that their branches entwined; but there were several avenues leading into the groves, and at the entrance to each avenue the girl noticed several large fishes with long spikes growing upon their noses.

"Those are swordfishes," remarked the Princess as she led the band past one of these avenues.

"Are they dang'rous?" asked Trot.

"Not to us," was the reply. "The swordfishes are among our most valued and faithful servants, guarding the entrances to the gardens which surround our palaces. If any creatures try to enter uninvited, these guards fight them and drive them away. Their swords are sharp and strong, and they are fierce fighters, I assure you."

"I've known 'em to attack ships, an' stick their swords right through the wood," said Cap'n Bill.

"Those belonged to the wandering tribes of swordfishes," explained the Princess. "These, who are our servants, are too sensible and intelligent to attack ships."

The band now headed into a broad passage through the "gardens," as the mermaids called these gorgeous groves, and the great swordfishes guarding the entrance made way for them to pass, afterward resuming their posts with watchful eyes. As they slowly swam along the avenue, Trot noticed that some of the bushes seemed to have fruits growing upon them, but what these fruits might be neither she nor Cap'n Bill could guess.

The way wound here and there for some distance, till finally they came to a more open space all carpeted with sea flowers of exquisite colorings. Although Trot did not know it, these flowers resembled the rare orchids of earth in their fanciful shapes and marvelous hues. The child did not examine them very closely, for across the carpet of flowers loomed the magnificent and extensive palaces of the mermaids.

These palaces were built of coral; white, pink and yellow being used, and the colors arranged in graceful designs. The front of the main palace, which now faced them, had circular ends connecting the straight wall, not unlike the architecture we are all familiar with; yet there seemed to be no windows to the building, although a series of archways served as doors.

Arriving at one of the central archways, the band of sea maidens separated. Princess Clia and Merla leading Trot and Cap'n Bill into the palace, while the other mermaids swam swiftly away to their own quarters.

"Welcome!" said Clia in her sweet voice. "Here you are surrounded only by friends and are in perfect safety. Please accept our hospitality as freely as you desire, for we consider you honored guests. I hope you will like our home," she added a little shyly.

"We are sure to, dear Princess," Trot hastened to say.

Then Clia escorted them through the archway and into a lofty hall. It was not a mere grotto, but had smoothly built walls of pink coral inlaid with white. Trot at first thought there was no roof, for looking upward she could see the water all above them. But the princess, reading her thought, said with a smile, "Yes, there is a roof, or we would be unable to keep all the sea people out of our palace. But the roof is made of glass to admit the light."

"Glass!" cried the astonished child. "Then it must be an awful big pane of glass."

"It is," agreed Clia. "Our roofs are considered quite wonderful, and we owe them to the fairy powers of our queen. Of course, you understand there is no natural way to make glass under water."

"No indeed," said Cap'n Bill. And then he asked, "Does your queen live here?"

"Yes. She is waiting now, in her throne room, to welcome you. Shall we go in?"

"I'd just as soon," replied Trot rather timidly, but she boldly followed the princess, who glided through another arch into another small room where several mermaids were reclining upon couches of coral. They were beautifully dressed and wore many sparkling jewels.

"Her Majesty is awaiting the strangers, Princess Clia," announced one of these. "You are asked to enter at once."

"Come, then," said Clia, and once more taking Trot's hand, she led the girl through still another arch, while Merla followed just behind them, escorting Cap'n Bill. They now entered an apartment so gorgeous that the child fairly gasped with astonishment. The queen's throne room was indeed the grandest and most beautiful chamber in all the ocean palaces. Its coral walls were thickly inlaid with mother-of-pearl, exquisitely shaded and made into borders and floral decorations. In the corners were cabinets, upon the shelves of which many curious shells were arranged, all beautifully polished.

The floor glittered with gems arranged in patterns of flowers, like a brilliant carpet.

Near the center of the room was a raised platform of mother-of-pearl upon which stood a couch thickly studded with diamonds, rubies, emeralds and pearls. Here reclined Queen Aquareine, a being so lovely that Trot gazed upon her spellbound and Cap'n Bill took off his sailor cap and held it in his hands.

All about the room were grouped other mother-of-pearl couches, not raised like that of the queen, and upon each of these reclined a pretty mermaid. They could not sit down as we do, Trot readily understood, because of their tails; but they rested very gracefully upon the couches with their trailing gauzy robes arranged in fleecy folds.

When Clia and Merla escorted the strangers down the length of the great room toward the royal throne, they met with pleasant looks and smiles on every side, for the sea maidens were too polite to indulge in curious stares. They paused just before the throne, and the queen raised her head upon one elbow to observe them. "Welcome, Mayre," she said, "and welcome, Cap'n Bill. I trust you are pleased with your glimpse of the life beneath the surface of our sea."

"I am," answered Trot, looking admiringly at the beautiful face of the queen.

"It's all mighty cur'ous an' strange-like," said the sailor slowly. "I'd no idee you mermaids were like this, at all!"

"Allow me to explain that it was to correct your

wrong ideas about us that led me to invite you to visit us," replied the Queen. "We usually pay little heed to the earth people, for we are content in our own dominions; but, of course, we know all that goes on upon your earth. So when Princess Clia chanced to overhear your absurd statements concerning us, we were greatly amused and decided to let you see with your own eyes just what we are like."

"I'm glad you did," answered Cap'n Bill, dropping his eyes in some confusion as he remembered his former description of the mermaids.

"Now that you are here," continued the Queen in a cordial, friendly tone, "you may as well remain with us a few days and see the wonderful sights of our ocean."

"I'm much obliged to you, ma'am," said Trot, "and I'd like to stay ever so much, but mother worries jus' dreadfully if we don't get home in time."

"I'll arrange all that," said Aquareine with a smile.

"How?" asked the girl.

"I will make your mother forget the passage of time so she will not realize how long you are away. Then she cannot worry."

"Can you do that?" inquired Trot.

"Very easily. I will send your mother into a deep sleep that will last until you are ready to return home. Just at present she is seated in her chair by the front window, engaged in knitting." The queen paused to raise an arm and wave it slowly to and fro. Then she added, "Now your good mother is asleep, little Mayre, and instead of worries I promise her pleasant dreams."

"Won't someone rob the house while she's asleep?" asked the child anxiously.

"No, dear. My charm will protect the house from any intrusion."

"That's fine!" exclaimed Trot in delight.

"It's jes' won-erful!" said Cap'n Bill. "I wish I knew it was so. Trot's mother has a awful sharp tongue when she's worried."

"You may see for yourselves," declared the Queen, and waved her hand again. At once they saw before them the room in the cottage, with Mayre's mother asleep by the window. Her knitting was in her lap, and the cat lay curled up beside her chair. It was all so natural that Trot thought she could hear the clock over the fireplace tick. After a moment the scene faded away, when the queen asked with another smile, "Are you satisfied?"

"Oh yes!" cried Trot. "But how could you do it?"

"It is a form of mirage," was the reply. "We are able to bring any earth scene before us whenever we wish. Sometimes these scenes are reflected above the water so that mortals also observe them."

"I've seen 'em," said Cap'n Bill, nodding. "I've seen mirages, but I never knowed what caused 'em afore now."

"Whenever you see anything you do not understand and wish to ask questions, I will be very glad to answer them," said the Queen.

"One thing that bothers me," said Trot, "is why

we don't get wet, being in the ocean with water all around us."

"That is because no water really touches you," explained the Queen. "Your bodies have been made just like those of the mermaids in order that you may fully enjoy your visit to us. One of our peculiar qualities is that water is never permitted to quite touch our bodies, or our gowns. Always there remains a very small space, hardly a hair's breadth, between us and the water, which is the reason we are always warm and dry."

"I see," said Trot. "That's why you don't get soggy or withered."

"Exactly," laughed the Queen, and the other mermaids joined in her merriment.

"I s'pose that's how we can breathe without gills," remarked Cap'n Bill thoughtfully.

"Yes. The air space is constantly replenished from the water, which contains air, and this enables us to breathe as freely as you do upon the earth."

"But we have fins," said Trot, looking at the fin that stood upright on Cap'n Bill's back.

"Yes. They allow us to guide ourselves as we swim, and so are very useful," replied the Queen.

"They make us more finished," said Cap'n Bill with a chuckle. Then, suddenly becoming grave, he added, "How about my rheumatics, ma'am? Ain't I likely to get stiffened up with all this dampness?"

"No indeed," Aquareine answered. "There is no such thing as rheumatism in all our dominions. I promise no evil result shall follow this visit to us, so please be as happy and contented as possible."

CHAPTER 5
THE SEA-SERPENT

Just then Trot happened to look up at the glass roof and saw a startling sight. A big head with a face surrounded by stubby gray whiskers was poised just over them, and the head was connected with a long, curved body that looked much like a sewer pipe.

"Oh, there is King Anko," said the Queen, following the child's gaze. "Open a door and let him in, Clia, for I suppose our old friend is anxious to see the earth people."

"Won't he hurt us?" asked the little girl with a shiver of fear.

"Who, Anko? Oh no, my dear! We are very fond of the sea serpent, who is king of this ocean, although he does not rule the mermaids. Old Anko is a very agreeable fellow, as you will soon discover."

"Can he talk?" asked Trot.

"Yes indeed."

"And can we understand what he says?"

"Perfectly," replied the Queen. "I have given you power, while you remain here, to understand the language of every inhabitant of the sea."

"That's nice," said Trot gratefully.

The Princess Clia swam slowly to one of the walls of the throne room where, at a wave of her hand, a round hole appeared in the coral. The sea serpent at once observed this opening and the head left the roof of glass only to reappear presently at the round hole. Through this he slowly crawled until his head was just beneath the throne of Queen Aquareine, who said to him:

"Good morning, your Majesty. I hope you are quite well?"

"Quite well, thank your Majesty," answered Anko; and then he turned to the strangers. "I suppose these are the earth folks you were expecting?"

"Yes," returned the Queen. "The girl is named Mayre and the man Cap'n Bill."

While the sea serpent looked at the visitors, they ventured to look at him. He certainly was a queer creature, yet Trot decided he was not at all frightful. His head was round as a ball, but his ears were sharp-pointed and had tassels at the ends of them. His nose was flat, and his mouth very wide indeed, but his eyes were blue and gentle in expression. The white, stubby hairs that surrounded his face were not thick like a beard, but scattered and scraggly. From the head, the long, brown body of the sea serpent extended to the hole in the coral wall, which was just big enough to admit it; and how much more of the body remained outside the child could not tell. On the back of the body were several fins, which made the creature look more like an eel than a serpent.

"The girl is young and the man is old," said King Anko in a soft voice. "But I'm quite sure Cap'n Bill isn't as old as I am."

"How old are you?" asked the sailor.

"I can't say exactly. I can remember several thousands of years back, but beyond that my memory fails me. How's your memory, Cap'n Bill?"

"You've got me beat," was the reply. "I'll give in that you're older than I am."

This seemed to please the sea serpent. "Are you well?" he asked.

"Pretty fair," said Cap'n Bill. "How's yourself?"

"Oh, I'm very well, thank you," answered Anko. "I never remember to have had a pain but three times in my life. The last time was when Julius Sneezer was on earth."

"You mean Julius Caesar," said Trot, correcting him.

"No, I mean Julius Sneezer," insisted the Sea Serpent. "That was his real name—Sneezer. They called him Caesar sometimes just because he took everything he could lay hands on. I ought to know, because I saw him when he was alive. Did you see him when he was alive, Cap'n Bill?"

"I reckon not," admitted the sailor.

"That time I had a toothache," continued Anko, "but I got a lobster to pull the tooth with his claw, so the pain was soon over."

"Did it hurt to pull it?" asked Trot.

"Hurt!" exclaimed the Sea Serpent, groaning at the recollection. "My dear, those creatures have been called lobsters ever since! The second pain I had way back in the time of Nevercouldnever."

"Oh, I s'pose you mean Nebuchadnezzar," said Trot.

"Do you call him that now?" asked the Sea Serpent as if surprised. "He used to be called Nevercouldnever when he was alive, but this new way of spelling seems to get everything mixed up. Nebuchadnezzar doesn't mean anything at all, it seems to me."

"It means he ate grass," said the child.

"Oh no, he didn't," declared the Sea Serpent. "He was the first to discover that lettuce was good to eat, and he became very fond of it. The people may have called it grass, but they were wrong. I ought to know, because I was alive when Nevercouldnever lived. Were you alive, then?"

"No," said Trot.

"The pain I had then," remarked Anko, "was caused by a kink in my tail about three hundred feet from the end. There was an old octopus who did not like me, and so he tied a knot in my tail when I wasn't looking."

"What did you do?" asked Cap'n Bill.

"Well, first I transformed the octopus into a jellyfish, and then I waited for the tide to turn. When my tail was untied, the pain stopped."

"I—I don't understand that," said Trot, somewhat bewildered.

178

"Thank you, my dear," replied the Sea Serpent in a grateful voice. "People who are always understood are very common. You are sure to respect those you can't understand, for you feel that perhaps they know more than you do."

"About how long do you happen to be?" inquired Cap'n Bill.

"When last measured, I was seven thousand four hundred and eighty-two feet, five inches and a quarter. I'm not sure about the quarter, but the rest is probably correct. Adam measured me when Cain was a baby."

"Where's the rest of you, then?" asked Trot.

"Safe at home, I hope, and coiled up in my parlor," answered the Sea Serpent. "When I go out, I usually take along only what is needed. It saves a lot of bother and I can always find my way back in the darkest night by just coiling up the part that has been away."

"Do you like to be a sea serpent?" inquired the child.

"Yes, for I'm King of my Ocean, and there is no other sea serpent to imagine he is just as good as I am. I have two brothers who live in other oceans, but one is seven inches shorter than I am, and the other several feet shorter. It's curious to talk about feet when we haven't any feet, isn't it?"

"Seems so," acknowledged Trot.

"I feel I have much to be proud of," continued Anko in a dreamy tone. "My great age, my undisputed sway, and my exceptional length."

"I don't b'lieve I'd care to live so long," remarked Cap'n Bill thoughtfully.

"So long as seven thousand four hundred and eighty-two feet, five inches and a quarter?" asked the Sea Serpent.

"No, I mean so many years," replied the sailor.

"But what can one do if one happens to be a sea serpent?" Anko inquired. "There is nothing in the sea that can hurt me, and I cannot commit suicide because we have no carbolic acid or firearms or gas to turn on. So it isn't a matter of choice, and I'd about as soon be alive as dead. It does not seem quite so monotonous, you know. But I guess I've stayed about long enough, so I'll go home to dinner. Come and see me when you have time."

"Thank you," said Trot, and Merla added, "I'll take you over to his majesty's palace when we go out and let you see how he lives."

"Yes, do," said Anko. And then he slowly slid out of the hole, which immediately closed behind him, leaving the coral wall as solid as before.

"Oh!" exclaimed Trot. "King Anko forgot to tell us what his third pain was about."

"So he did," said Cap'n Bill. "We must ask him about that when we see him. But I guess the ol' boy's mem'ry is failin', an' he can't be depended on for pertic'lars."

CHAPTER 6
EXPLORING THE OCEAN

The queen now requested her guests to recline upon couches that they might rest themselves from their long swim and talk more at their ease. So the girl and the sailor allowed themselves to float downward until they rested their bodies on two of the couches nearest the throne, which were willingly vacated for them by the mermaids who occupied them until then.

The visitors soon found themselves answering a great many questions about their life on the earth, for although the queen had said she kept track of what was going on on the land, there were many details of human life in which all the mermaids seemed greatly interested.

During the conversation several sea-maids came swimming into the room bearing trays of sea apples and other fruit, which they first offered to the queen, and then passed the refreshments around to the company assembled. Trot and Cap'n Bill each took some, and the little girl found the fruits delicious to eat, as they had a richer flavor than any that grew upon land. Queen Aquareine was much pleased when the old sailor asked for more, but Merla warned him dinner would soon be served and he must take care not to spoil his appetite for that meal. "Our dinner is at noon, for we have to cook in the middle of the day when the sun is shining," she said.

"Cook!" cried Trot. "Why, you can't build a fire in the water, can you?"

"We have no need of fires," was the reply. "The glass roof of our kitchen is so curved that it concentrates the heat of the sun's rays, which are then hot enough to cook anything we wish."

"But how do you get along if the day is cloudy, and the sun doesn't shine?" inquired the little girl.

"Then we use the hot springs that bubble up in another part of the palace," Merla answered. "But the sun is the best to cook by." So it was no surprise to Trot when, about noon, dinner was announced and all the mermaids, headed by their queen and their guests, swam into another spacious room where a great, long table was laid. The dishes were of polished gold and dainty-cut glass, and the cloth and napkins of fine gossamer. Around the table were ranged rows of couches for the mermaids to recline upon as they ate. Only the nobility and favorites of Queen Aquareine were invited to partake of this repast, for Clia explained that tables were set for the other mermaids in different parts of the numerous palaces.

Trot wondered who would serve the meal, but her curiosity was soon satisfied when several large lobsters came sliding into the room backward, bearing in their claws trays loaded with food. Each of these lobsters had a golden band behind its neck to show it was the slave of the mermaids.

These curious waiters were fussy creatures, and Trot found much amusement in watching their odd motions. They were so spry and excitable that at times they ran against one another and upset the platters of food, after which they began to scold and argue as to whose fault it was, until one of the mermaids quietly rebuked them and asked them to be more quiet and more careful.

The queen's guests had no cause to complain of the dinner provided. First the lobsters served bowls of turtle soup, which proved hot and deliciously flavored. Then came salmon steaks fried in fish oil, with a fungus bread that tasted much like field mushrooms. Oysters, clams, soft-shell crabs and various preparations of seafoods followed. The salad was a delicate leaf from some seaweed that Trot thought was much nicer than lettuce. Several courses were served, and the lobsters changed the plates with each course, chattering and scolding as they worked, and as Trot said, "doing everything backwards" in their nervous, fussy way.

Many of the things offered them to eat were unknown to the visitors, and the child was suspicious of some of them, but Cap'n Bill asked no questions and ate everything offered him, so Trot decided to follow his example. Certain it is they found the meal very satisfying, and evidently there was no danger of their being hungry while they remained the guests of the mermaids. When the fruits came, Trot thought that must be the last course of the big dinner, but following the fruits were ice creams frozen into the shape of flowers.

"How funny," said the child, "to be eating ice cream at the bottom of the sea."

"Why does that surprise you?" inquired the Queen.

"I can't see where you get the ice to freeze it," Trot replied.

"It is brought to us from the icebergs that float in the northern parts of the ocean," explained Merla.

"O' course, Trot. You orter thought o' that. I did," said Cap'n Bill.

The little girl was glad there was no more to eat, for she was ashamed to feel she had eaten every morsel she could. Her only excuse for being so greedy was that "ev'rything tasted just splendid!" as she told the queen.

"And now," said Aquareine, "I will send you out for a swim with Merla, who will show you some of the curious sights of our sea. You need not go far this afternoon, and when you return, we will have another interesting talk together." So the blonde mermaid led Trot and Cap'n Bill outside the palace walls, where they found themselves in the pretty flower gardens.

"I'd feel all right, mate, if I could have a smoke,"

remarked the old sailor to the child, "but that's a thing as can't be did here in the water."

"Why not?" asked Merla, who overheard him.

"A pipe has to be lighted, an' a match wouldn't burn," he replied.

"Try it," suggested the mermaid. "I do not mind your smoking at all, if it will give you pleasure."

"It's a bad habit I've got, an' I'm too old to break myself of it," said Cap'n Bill. Then he felt in the big pocket of his coat and took out a pipe and a bag of tobacco. After he had carefully filled his pipe, rejoicing in the fact that the tobacco was not at all wet, he took out his matchbox and struck a light. The match burned brightly, and soon the sailor was puffing the smoke from his pipe in great contentment. The smoke ascended through the water in the shape of bubbles, and Trot wondered what anyone who happened to be floating upon the surface of the ocean would think to see smoke coming from the water.

"Well, I find I can smoke, all right," remarked Cap'n Bill, "but it bothers me to understand why."

"It is because of the air space existing between the water and everything you have about you," explained Merla. "But now, if you will come this way, I will take you to visit some of our neighbors." They passed over the carpet of sea flowers, the gorgeous blossoms swaying on their stems as the motion of the people in the water above them disturbed their repose, and presently the three entered the dense shrubbery surrounding the palace. They had not proceeded far when they came to a clearing among the bushes, and here Merla paused.

Trot and Cap'n Bill paused, too, for floating in the clear water was a group of beautiful shapes that the child thought looked like molds of wine jelly. They were round as a dinner plate, soft and transparent, but tinted in such lovely hues that no artist's brush has ever been able to imitate them. Some were deep sapphire blue; others rose pink; still others a delicate topaz color. They seemed to have neither heads, eyes nor ears, yet it was easy to see they were alive and able to float in any direction they wished to go. In shape they resembled inverted flowerpots, with the upper edges fluted, and from the centers floated what seemed to be bouquets of flowers.

"How pretty!" exclaimed Trot, enraptured by the sight.

"Yes, this is a rare variety of jellyfish," replied Merla. "The creatures are not so delicate as they appear, and live for a long time—unless they get too near the surface and the waves wash them ashore."

After watching the jellyfish a few moments, they followed Merla through the grove, and soon a low chant, like that of an Indian song, fell upon their ears. It was a chorus of many small voices and grew louder as they swam on. Presently a big rock rose suddenly before them from the bottom of the sea, rearing its steep side far up into the water overhead, and this rock was thickly covered with tiny shells that clung fast to its surface. The chorus they heard appeared to come from these shells, and Merla said to her companions, "These are the singing barnacles. They are really very amusing, and if you listen carefully, you can hear what they say."

So Trot and Cap'n Bill listened, and this is what the barnacles sang:

> *"We went to topsy-turvy land to see a*
> *man-o'-war,*
> *And we were much attached to it, be-*
> *cause we simply were;*
> *We found an anchor-ite within the mud*
> *upon the lea*
> *For the ghost of Jonah's whale he ran*
> *away and went to sea.*
> *Oh, it was awful!*
> *It was unlawful!*
> *We rallied round the flag in sev'ral*
> *millions;*
> *They couldn't shake us;*
> *They had to take us;*
> *So the halibut and cod they danced*
> *cotillions."*

"What does it all mean?" asked Trot.

"I suppose they refer to the way barnacles have of clinging to ships," replied Merla, "but usually the songs mean nothing at all. The little barnacles haven't many brains, so we usually find their songs quite stupid."

"Do they write some comic operas?" asked the child.

"I think not," answered the mermaid.

"They seem to like the songs themselves," re-marked Cap'n Bill.

"Oh yes, they sing all day long. But it never mat-ters to them whether their songs mean anything or not. Let us go in this direction and visit some other sea people."

So they swam away from the barnacle-covered rock, and Trot heard the last chorus as she slowly followed their conductor. The barnacles were singing:

> *"Oh, very well, then, I hear the curfew,*
> *Please go away and come some other*
> *day; Goliath tussels With Samson's*
> *muscles, Yet the muscles never fight*
> *in Oyster Bay."*

"It's jus' nonsense!" said Trot scornfully. "Why don't they sing 'Annie Laurie' or 'Home, Sweet Home' or else keep quiet?"

"Why, if they were quiet," replied Merla, "they wouldn't be singing barnacles."

They now came to one of the avenues which led from the sea garden out into the broad ocean, and here two swordfishes were standing guard. "Is all quiet?" Merla asked them.

"Just as usual, your Highness," replied one of the guards. "Mummercubble was sick this morning and grunted dreadfully, but he's better now and has gone to sleep. King Anko has been stirring around some, but is now taking his after-dinner nap. I think it will be perfectly safe for you to swim out for a while, if you wish."

"Who's Mummercubble?" asked Trot as they passed out into deep water.

"He's the sea pig," replied Merla. "I am glad he's asleep, for now we won't meet him."

"Don't you like him?" inquired Trot.

"Oh, he complains so bitterly of everything that he bores us," Merla answered. "Mummercubble is never contented or happy for a single minute."

"I've seen people like that," said Cap'n Bill with a nod of his head. "An' they has a way of upsettin' the happiest folks they meet."

"Look out!" suddenly cried the mermaid. "Look out for your fingers! Here are the snapping eels."

"Who? Where?" asked Trot anxiously.

And now they were in the midst of a cluster of wriggling, darting eels which sported all around them in the water with marvelous activity. "Yes, look out for your fingers and your noses!" said one of the eels, making a dash for Cap'n Bill. At first the sailor was tempted to put out a hand and push the creature away, but remembering that his fingers would thus be exposed, he remained quiet, and the eel snapped harmlessly just before his face and then darted away.

"Stop it!" said Merla. "Stop it this minute, or I'll report your impudence to Aquareine."

"Oh, who cares?" shouted the Eels. "We're not afraid of the mermaids."

"She'll stiffen you up again, as she did once before," said Merla, "if you try to hurt the earth people."

"Are these earth people?" asked one. And then they all stopped their play and regarded Trot and Cap'n Bill with their little black eyes.

"The old polliwog looks something like King Anko," said one of them.

"I'm not a polliwog!" answered Cap'n Bill angrily. "I'm a respec'ble sailor man, an' I'll have you treat me decent or I'll know why."

"Sailor!" said another. "That means to float on the water—not IN it. What are you doing down here?"

"I'm jes' a-visitin'," answered Cap'n Bill.

"He is the guest of our queen," said Merla, "and so is this little girl. If you do not behave nicely to them, you will surely be sorry."

"Oh, that's all right," replied one of the biggest eels, wriggling around in a circle and then snapping at a companion, which as quickly snapped out of his way. "We know how to be polite to company as well as the mermaids. We won't hurt them."

"Come on, fellows, let's go scare old Mummercubble," cried another; and then in a flash they all darted away and left our friends to themselves. Trot was greatly relieved.

"I don't like eels," she said.

"They are more mischievous than harmful," replied Merla, "but I do not care much for them myself."

"No," added Cap'n Bill, "they ain't respec'ful."

THE ARISTOCRATIC CODFISH

The three swam slowly along, quite enjoying the cool depths of the water. Every little while they met with some strange creature —or one that seemed strange to the earth people— for although Trot and Cap'n Bill had seen many kinds of fish, after they had been caught and pulled from the water, that was very different from meeting them in their own element, "face to face," as Trot expressed it. Now that the various fishes were swimming around free and unafraid in their deep-sea home, they were quite different from the gasping, excited creatures struggling at the end of a fishline or flopping from a net.

Before long they came upon a group of large fishes lying lazily near the bottom of the sea. They were a dark color upon their backs and silver underneath, but not especially pretty to look at. The fishes made no effort to get out of Merla's way and remained motionless except for the gentle motion of their fins and gills.

"Here," said the mermaid, pausing, "is the most aristocratic family of fish in all the sea."

"What are they?" asked the girl.

"Codfish," was the reply. "Their only fault is that they are too haughty and foolishly proud of their pedigree."

Overhearing this speech, one codfish said to another in a very dignified tone of voice, "What insolence!"

"Isn't it?" replied the other. "There ought to be a law to prevent these common mermaids from discussing their superiors."

"My sakes!" said Trot, astonished. "How stuck up they are, aren't they?"

For a moment the group of fishes stared at her solemnly. Then one of the remarked in a disdainful manner, "Come, my dear, let us leave these vulgar creatures."

"I'm not as vulgar as you are!" exclaimed Trot, much offended by this speech. "Where I come from, we only eat codfish when there's nothing else in the house to eat."

"How absurd!" observed one of the creatures arrogantly.

"Eat codfish indeed!" said another in a lofty manner.

"Yes, and you're pretty salty, too, I can tell you. At home you're nothing but a pick-up!" said Trot.

"Dear me!" exclaimed the first fish who had spoken. "Must we stand this insulting language—and from a person to whom we have never been introduced?"

"I don't need no interduction," replied the girl. "I've eaten you, and you always make me thirsty."

Merla laughed merrily at this, and the codfish said, with much dignity, "Come, fellow aristocrats, let us go."

"Never mind, we're going ourselves," announced Merla, and followed by her guests the pretty mermaid swam away.

"I've heard tell of codfish aristocracy," said Cap'n Bill, "but I never knowed 'zac'ly what it meant afore."

"They jus' made me mad with all their airs," observed Trot, "so I gave 'em a piece of my mind."

"You surely did, mate," said the sailor, "but I ain't sure they understand what they're like when they're salted an' hung up in the pantry. Folks gener'ly gets stuck-up 'cause they don't know theirselves like other folks knows 'em."

"We are near Crabville now," declared Merla. "Shall we visit the crabs and see what they are doing?"

"Yes, let's," replied Trot. "The crabs are lots of fun. I've often caught them among the rocks on the shore and laughed at the way they act. Wasn't it funny at dinnertime to see the way they slid around with the plates?"

"Those were not crabs, but lobsters and crawfish," remarked the mermaid. "They are very intelligent creatures, and by making them serve us we save ourselves much household work. Of course, they are awkward and provoke us sometimes, but no servants are perfect, it is said, so we get along with ours as well as we can."

"They're all right," protested the child, "even if they did tip things over once in a while. But it is easy to work in a sea palace, I'm sure, because there's no dusting or sweeping to be done."

"Or scrubbin'," added Cap'n Bill.

"The crabs," said Merla, "are second cousins to the lobsters, although much smaller in size. There are many families or varieties of crabs, and so many of them live in one place near here that we call it Crabville. I think you will enjoy seeing these little creatures in their native haunts."

They now approached a kelp bed, the straight, thin stems of the kelp running far upward to the surface of the water. Here and there upon the stalks were leaves, but Trot thought the growing kelp looked much like sticks of macaroni, except they were a rich red-brown color. It was beyond the kelp —which they had to push aside as they swam through, so thickly did it grow—that they came to a higher level, a sort of plateau on the ocean's bottom. It was covered with scattered rocks of all sizes, which appeared to have broken off from big shelving rocks they observed nearby. The place they entered seemed like one of the rocky canyons you often see upon the earth.

"Here live the fiddler crabs," said Merla, "but we must have taken them by surprise, it is so quiet."

Even as she spoke, there was a stirring and scrambling among the rocks, and soon scores of light-green crabs were gathered before the visitors. The crabs bore fiddles of all sorts and shapes in their claws, and one big fellow carried a leader's baton. The latter crab climbed upon a flat rock and in an excited voice called out, "Ready, now—ready, good fiddlers. We'll play Number 19, Hail to the Mermaids. Ready! Take aim! Fire away!"

At this command every crab began scraping at his fiddle as hard as he could, and the sounds were so shrill and unmusical that Trot wondered when they would begin to play a tune. But they never did; it was one regular mix-up of sounds from beginning to end. When the noise finally stopped, the leader turned to his visitors and, waving his baton toward them, asked, "Well, what did you think of that?"

"Not much," said Trot honestly. "What's it all about?"

"I composed it myself!" said the Fiddler Crab. "But it's highly classical, I admit. All really great music is an acquired taste."

"I don't like it," remarked Cap'n Bill. "It might do all right to stir up a racket New Year's Eve, but to call that screechin' music—"

Just then the crabs started fiddling again, harder than ever, and as it promised to be a long performance, they left the little creatures scraping away at their fiddles as if for dear life and swam along the rocky canyon until, on turning a corner, they came upon a new and different scene.

There were crabs here, too, many of them, and they were performing the queerest antics imaginable. Some were building themselves into a pyramid, each standing on edge, with the biggest and strongest ones at the bottom. When the crabs were five or six rows high, they would all tumble over, still clinging to one another and, having reached the ground, they would separate and commence to build the pyramid over again. Others were chasing one another around in a circle, always moving backward or sidewise, and trying to play "leapfrog" as they went. Still others were swinging on slight branches of seaweed or turning cartwheels or indulging in similar antics.

Merla and the earth people watched the busy little creatures for some time before they were themselves observed, but finally Trot gave a laugh when one crab fell on its back and began frantically waving its legs to get right-side-up again. At the sound of her laughter they all stopped their play and came toward the visitors in a flock, looking up at them with their bright eyes in a most comical way.

"Welcome home!" cried one as he turned a back somersault and knocked another crab over.

"What's the difference between a mermaid and a tadpole?" asked another in a loud voice, and without a pause continued, "Why, one drops its tail and the other holds onto it. Ha, ha! Ho, ho! Hee, hee!"

"These," said Merla, "are the clown crabs. They are very silly things, as you may already have discovered, but for a short time they are rather amusing. One tires of them very soon."

"They're funny," said Trot, laughing again. "It's almost as good as a circus. I don't think they would make me tired, but then I'm not a mermaid."

The clown crabs had now formed a row in front of them. "Mr. Johnsing," asked one, "why is a mermaid like an automobile?"

"I don't know, Tommy Blimken," answered a big crab in the middle of the row. "WHY do you think a mermaid is like an automobile?"

"Because they both get tired," said Tommy Blimken. Then all the crabs laughed, and Tommy seemed to laugh louder than the rest.

"How do the crabs in the sea know anything 'bout automobiles?" asked Trot.

"Why, Tommy Blimken and Harry Hustle were both captured once by humans and put in an aquarium," answered the mermaid. "But one day they climbed out and escaped, finally making their way back to the sea and home again. So they are quite traveled, you see, and great favorites among the crabs. While they were on land they saw a great many curious things, and so I suppose they saw automobiles."

"We did, we did!" cried Harry Hustle, an awkward crab with one big claw and one little one. "And we saw earth people with legs, awfully funny they were; and animals called horses, with legs; and other creatures with legs; and the people cover themselves with the queerest things—they even wear feathers and flowers on their heads, and—"

"Oh, we know all about that," said Trot. "We live on the earth ourselves."

"Well, you're lucky to get off from it and into the good water," said the Crab. "I nearly died on the earth; it was so stupid, dry and airy. But the circus was great. They held the performance right in front of the aquarium where we lived, and Tommy and I learned all the tricks of the tumblers. Hi! Come on, fellows, and show the earth people what you can do!"

At this the crabs began performing their antics again, but they did the same things over and over, so Cap'n Bill and Trot soon tired, as Merla said they would, and decided they had seen enough of the crab circus. So they proceeded to swim farther up the rocky canyon, and near its upper end they came to a lot of conch shells lying upon the sandy bottom. A funny-looking crab was sticking his head out from each of these shells.

"These are the hermit crabs," said one of the mermaids. "They steal these shells and live in them so no enemies can attack them."

"Don't they get lonesome?" asked Trot.

"Perhaps so, my dear. But they do not seem to mind being lonesome. They are great cowards, and think if they can but protect their lives there is nothing else to care for. Unlike the jolly crabs we have just left, the hermits are cross and unsociable."

"Oh, keep quiet and go away!" said one of the hermit crabs in a grumpy voice. "No one wants mermaids around here." Then every crab withdrew its head into its shell, and our friends saw them no more.

"They're not very polite," observed Trot, following the mermaid as Merla swam upward into the middle water.

"I know now why cross people are called 'crabbed,'" said Cap'n Bill. "They've got dispositions jes' like these 'ere hermit crabs."

Presently they came upon a small flock of mackerel, and noticed that the fishes seemed much excited. When they saw the mermaid, they cried out, "Oh, Merla! What do you think? Our Flippity has just gone to glory!"

"When?" asked the mermaid.

"Just now," one replied. "We were lying in the water, talking quietly together when a spinning, shining thing came along and our dear Flippity ate it. Then he went shooting up to the top of the water and gave a flop and—went to glory! Isn't it splendid, Merla?"

"Poor Flippity!" sighed the mermaid. "I'm sorry, for he was the prettiest and nicest mackerel in your whole flock."

"What does it mean?" asked Trot. "How did Flippity go to glory?"

"Why, he was caught by a hook and pulled out of the water into some boat," Merla explained. "But these poor stupid creatures do not understand that, and when one of them is jerked out of the water and disappears, they have the idea he has gone to glory, which means to them some unknown but beautiful sea."

"I've often wondered," said Trot, "why fishes are foolish enough to bite on hooks."

"They must know enough to know they're hooks," added Cap'n Bill musingly.

"Oh, they do," replied Merla. "I've seen fishes gather around a hook and look at it carefully for a long time. They all know it is a hook and that if they bite the bait upon it they will be pulled out of the water. But they are curious to know what will happen to them afterward, and think it means happiness instead of death. So finally one takes the hook and disappears, and the others never know what becomes of him."

"Why don't you tell 'em the truth?" asked Trot.

"Oh, we do. The mermaids have warned them many times, but it does no good at all. The fish are stupid creatures."

"But I wish I was Flippity," said one of the mackerel, staring at Trot with his big, round eyes. "He went to glory before I could eat the hook myself."

"You're lucky," answered the child. "Flippity will be fried in a pan for someone's dinner. You wouldn't like that, would you?"

"Flippity has gone to glory!" said another, and then they swam away in haste to tell the news to all they met.

"I never heard of anything so foolish," remarked Trot as she swam slowly on through the clear, blue water.

"Yes, it is very foolish and very sad," answered Merla. "But if the fish were wise, men could not catch them for food, and many poor people on your earth make their living by fishing."

"It seems wicked to catch such pretty things," said the child.

"I do not think so," Merla replied laughingly, "for they were born to become food for someone, and men are not the only ones that eat fishes. Many creatures of the sea feed upon them. They even eat one another at times. And if none was ever destroyed, they would soon become so numerous that they would clog the waters of the ocean and leave no room for the rest of us. So after all, perhaps it is just as well they are thoughtless and foolish."

Presently they came to some round balls that looked much like balloons in shape and were gaily colored. They floated quietly in the water, and Trot inquired what they were.

"Balloonfish," answered Merla. "They are helpless creatures, but have little spikes all over them so their enemies dare not bite them for fear of getting pricked."

Trot found the balloonfish quite interesting. They had little dots of eyes and dots for mouths, but she could see no noses, and their fins and tails were very small.

"They catch these fish in the South Sea Islands and make lanterns of 'em," said Cap'n Bill. "They first skin 'em and sew the skin up again to let it dry, and then they put candles inside, and the light shines through the dried skin."

Many other curious sights they saw in the ocean that afternoon, and both Cap'n Bill and Trot thoroughly enjoyed their glimpse of sea life. At last Merla said it was time to return to the palace, from which she claimed they had not at any time been very far distant. "We must prepare for dinner, as it will soon begin to grow dark in the water," continued their conductor. So they swam leisurely back to the groves that surrounded the palaces, and as they entered the gardens the sun sank, and deep shadows began to form in the ocean depths.

CHAPTER 8
A BANQUET UNDER WATER

The palaces of the mermaids were all aglow with lights as they approached them, and Trot was amazed at the sight.

"Where do the lamps come from?" she asked their guide wonderingly.

"They are not lamps, my dear," replied Merla, much amused at this suggestion. "We use electric lights in our palaces and have done so for thousands of years—long before the earth people knew of electric lights."

"But where do you get 'em?" inquired Cap'n Bill, who was as much astonished as the girl.

"From a transparent jellyfish which naturally emits a strong and beautiful electric light," was the answer. "We have many hundreds of them in our palaces, as you will presently see."

Their way was now lighted by small, phosphorescent creatures scattered about the sea gardens and which Merla informed them were hyalaea, or sea glowworms. But their light was dim when compared to that of the electric jellyfish, which they found placed in clusters upon the ceilings of all the rooms of the palaces, rendering them light as day. Trot watched these curious creatures with delight, for delicately colored lights ran around their bodies in every direction in a continuous stream, shedding splendid rays throughout the vast halls.

A group of mermaids met the visitors in the hall of the main palace and told Merla the queen had instructed them to show the guests to their rooms as soon as they arrived. So Trot followed two of them through several passages, after which they swam upward and entered a circular opening. There were no stairs here, because there was no need of them, and the little girl soon found herself in an upper room that was very beautiful indeed.

All the walls were covered with iridescent shells, polished till they resembled mother-of-pearl, and upon the glass ceiling were clusters of the brilliant electric jellyfish, rendering the room bright and cheerful with their radiance. In one corner stood a couch of white coral, with gossamer draperies hanging around it from the four high posts. Upon examining it, the child found the couch was covered with soft, amber sponges, which rendered it very comfortable to lie upon. In a wardrobe she found several beautiful gossamer gowns richly embroidered in colored seaweeds, and these Mayre was told she might wear while she remained the guest of the mermaids. She also found a toilet table with brushes, combs and other conveniences, all of which were made of polished tortoise-shell.

Really, the room was more dainty and comfortable than one might suppose possible in a palace far beneath the surface of the sea, and Trot was greatly delighted with her new quarters. The mermaid attendants assisted the child to dress herself in one of the prettiest robes, which she found to be quite dry and fitted her comfortably. Then the sea-maids brushed and dressed her hair, and tied it with ribbons of cherry-red seaweed. Finally they placed around her neck a string of pearls that would have been priceless upon the earth, and now the little girl announced she was ready for supper and had a good appetite.

Cap'n Bill had been given a similar room near Trot, but the old sailor refused to change his clothes for any others offered him, for which reason he was ready for supper long before his comrade. "What bothers me, mate," he said to the little girl as the y swam toward the great banquet hall where Queen Aquareine awaited them, "is why ain't we crushed by the pressin' of the water agin us, bein' as we're down here in the deep sea."

"How's that, Cap'n? Why should we be crushed?" she asked.

"Why, ev'r'body knows that the deeper you go in the sea, the more the water presses agin you," he explained. "Even the divers in their steel jackets can't stand it very deep down. An' here we be, miles from the top o' the water, I s'pect, an' we don't feel crowded a bit."

"I know why," answered the child wisely. "The water don't touch us, you see. If it did, it might crush us, but it don't. It's always held a little way off from our bodies by the magic of the fairy mermaids."

"True enough, Trot," declared the sailor man. "What an idjut I was not to think o' that myself!"

In the royal banquet hall were assembled many of the mermaids, headed by the lovely queen, and as soon as their earth guests arrived, Aquareine ordered the meal to be served. The lobsters again waited upon the table, wearing little white caps and aprons which made them look very funny; but Trot was so hungry after her afternoon's excursion that she did not pay as much attention to the lobsters as she did to her supper, which was very delicious and consisted of many courses. A lobster spilled some soup on Cap'n Bill's bald head and made him yell for a minute, because it was hot and he had not expected it, but the queen apologized very sweetly for the awkwardness of her servants, and the sailor soon forgot all about the incident in his enjoyment of the meal.

After the feast ended, they all went to the big reception room, where some of the mermaids played upon harps while others sang pretty songs. They danced together, too—a graceful, swimming dance, so queer to the little girl that it interested and amused her greatly. Cap'n Bill seemed a bit bashful among so many beautiful mermaids, yet he was pleased when the queen offered him a place beside her throne, where he could see and hear all the delightful entertainment provided for the royal guests.

He did not talk much, being a man of few words except when alone with Trot, but his light-blue eyes were big and round with wonder at the sights he saw.

Trot and the sailor man went to bed early and slept soundly upon their sponge-covered couches. The little girl never wakened until long after the sun was shining down through the glass roof of her room, and when she opened her eyes she was startled to find a number of big, small and middle-sized fishes staring at her through the glass. "That's one bad thing 'bout this mermaid palace," she said to herself. "It's too public. Ever'thing in the sea can look at you through the glass as much as it likes. I wouldn't mind fishes looking at me if they hadn't such big eyes, an'—goodness me! There's a monster that's all head! And there goes a fish with a sail on its back, an' here's old Mummercubble, I'm sure, for he's got a head just like a pig."

She might have watched the fishes on the roof for hours, had she not remembered it was late and breakfast must be ready. So she dressed and made her toilet, and swam down into the palace to find Cap'n Bill and the mermaids politely waiting for her to join them. The sea maidens were as fresh and lovely as ever, while each and all proved sweet tempered and merry, even at the breakfast table—and that is where people are cross, if they ever are. During the meal the queen said, "I shall take you this morning to the most interesting part of the ocean, where the largest and most remarkable sea creatures live. And we must visit King Anko, too, for the sea serpent would feel hurt and slighted if I did not bring my guests to call upon him."

"That will be nice," said Trot eagerly.

But Cap'n Bill asked, "Is there any danger, ma'am?"

"I think not," replied Queen Aquareine. "I cannot say that you will be exposed to any danger at all, so long as I'm with you. But we are going into the neighborhood of such fierce and even terrible beings which would attack you at once did they suspect you to be earth people. So in order to guard your safety, I intend to draw the Magic Circle around both of you before we start."

"What is the Magic Circle?" asked Trot.

"A fairy charm that prevents any enemy from touching you. No monster of the sea, however powerful, will be able to reach your body while you are protected by the Magic Circle," declared the Queen.

"Oh, then I'll not be a bit afraid," returned the child with perfect confidence.

"Am I to have the Magic Circle drawn around me, too?" asked Cap'n Bill.

"Of course," answered Aquareine. "You will need no other protection than that, yet both Princess Clia and I will both be with you. For today I shall leave Merla to rule our palaces in my place until we return."

No sooner was breakfast finished than Trot was anxious to start. The girl was also curious to discover what the powerful Magic Circle might prove to be, but she was a little disappointed in the ceremony. The queen merely grasped her fairy wand in her right hand and swam around the child in a circle, from left to right. Then she took her wand in her left hand and swam around Trot in another circle, from right to left. "Now, my dear," said she, "you are safe from any creature we are liable to meet."

She performed the same ceremony for Cap'n Bill, who was doubtful about the Magic Circle because he felt the same after it as he had before. But he said nothing of his unbelief, and soon they left the palace and started upon their journey.

CHAPTER 9
THE BASHFUL OCTOPUS

It was a lovely day, and the sea was like azure under the rays of the sun.

Over the flower beds and through the gardens they swam, emerging into the open sea in a direction opposite that taken by the visitors the day before. The party consisted of but four: Queen Aquareine, Princess Clia, Trot and Cap'n Bill.

"People who live upon the land know only those sea creatures which they are able to catch in nets or upon hooks or those which become disabled and are washed ashore," remarked the Queen as they swam swiftly through the clear water. "And those who sail in ships see only the creatures who chance to come to the surface. But in the deep ocean caverns are queer beings that no mortal has ever heard of or beheld, and some of these we are to visit. We shall also see some sea shrubs and flowering weeds which are sure to delight you with their beauty."

The sights really began before they had gone very far from the palace, and a school of butterfly fish, having gorgeous colors spattered over their broad wings, was first to delight the strangers. They swam just as butterflies fly, with a darting, jerky motion, and called a merry "Good morning!" to the mermaids as they passed.

"These butterfly fish are remarkably active," said the Princess, "and their quick motions protect them from their enemies. We like to meet them; they are always so gay and good-natured."

"Why, so am I!" cried a sharp voice just beside them, and they all paused to discover what creature had spoken to them.

"Take care," said Clia in a low voice. "It's an octopus."

Trot looked eagerly around. A long, brown arm stretched across their way in front and another just behind them, but that did not worry her. The octopus himself came slowly sliding up to them and proved to be well worth looking at. He wore a red coat with brass buttons, and a silk hat was tipped over one ear. His eyes were somewhat dull and watery, and he had a moustache of long, hair-like "feelers" that curled stiffly at the ends. When he tried to smile at them, he showed two rows of sharp, white teeth. In spite of his red coat and yellow-embroidered vest, his standing collar and carefully tied cravat, the legs of the octopus were bare, and Trot noticed he used some of his legs for arms, as in one of them was held a slender cane and in another a handkerchief.

"Well, well!" said the Octopus. "Are you all dumb? Or don't you know enough to be civil when you meet a neighbor?"

"We know how to be civil to our friends," replied Trot, who did not like the way he spoke.

"Well, are we not friends, then?" asked the Octopus in an airy tone of voice.

"I think not," said the little girl. "Octopuses are horrid creatures."

"OctoPI, if you please; octoPI," said the monster with a laugh.

"I don't see any pie that pleases me," replied Trot, beginning to get angry.

"OctoPUS means one of us; two or more are called octoPI," remarked the creature, as if correcting her speech.

"I suppose a lot of you would be a whole bakery!" she said scornfully.

"Our name is Latin. It was given to us by learned scientists years ago," said the Octopus.

"That's true enough," agreed Cap'n Bill. "The learned scientists named ev'ry blamed thing they come across, an' gener'ly they picked out names as nobody could understand or pernounce."

"That isn't our fault, sir," said the Octopus. "Indeed, it's pretty hard for us to go through life with such terrible names. Think of the poor little seahorse. He used to be a merry and cheerful fellow, but since they named him 'hippocampus' he hasn't smiled once."

"Let's go," said Trot. "I don't like to 'sociate with octopuses."

"OctoPI," said the creature, again correcting her.

"You're jus' as horrid whether you're puses or pies," she declared.

"Horrid!" cried the monster in a shocked tone of voice.

"Not only horrid, but horrible!" persisted the girl.

"May I ask in what way?" he inquired, and it was easy to see he was offended.

"Why, ev'rybody knows that octopuses are jus' wicked an' deceitful," she said. "Up on the earth, where I live, we call the Stannerd Oil Company an octopus, an' the Coal Trust an octopus, an'——"

"Stop, stop!" cried the monster in a pleading voice. "Do you mean to tell me that the earth people whom I have always respected compare me to the Stannerd Oil Company?"

"Yes," said Trot positively.

"Oh, what a disgrace! What a cruel, direful, dreadful disgrace!" moaned the Octopus, drooping his head in shame, and Trot could see great tears falling down his cheeks.

"This comes of having a bad name," said the Queen gently, for she was moved by the monster's grief.

"It is unjust! It is cruel and unjust!" sobbed the creature mournfully. "Just because we have several long arms and take whatever we can reach, they accuse us of being like—like—oh, I cannot say it! It is too shameful, too humiliating."

"Come, let's go," said Trot again. So they left the poor octopus weeping and wiping his watery eyes with his handkerchief and swam on their way. "I'm not a bit sorry for him," remarked the child, "for his legs remind me of serpents."

"So they do me," agreed Cap'n Bill.

"But the octopi are not very bad," said the Princess, "and we get along with them much better than we do with their cousins, the sea devils."

"Oh. Are the sea devils their cousins?" asked Trot.

"Yes, and they are the only creatures of the ocean which we greatly fear," replied Aquareine. "I hope we shall meet none today, for we are going near to the dismal caverns where they live."

"What are the sea devils like, ma'am?" inquired Cap'n Bill a little uneasily.

"Something like the octopus you just saw, only much larger and of a bright scarlet color, striped with black," answered the Queen. "They are very fierce and terrible creatures and nearly as much dreaded by the inhabitants of the ocean as is Zog, and nearly as powerful as King Anko himself."

"Zog! Who is Zog?" questioned the girl. "I haven't heard of him before now."

"We do not like to mention Zog's name," responded the Queen in a low voice. "He is the wicked genius of the sea, and a magician of great power."

"What's he like?" asked Cap'n Bill.

"He is a dreadful creature, part fish, part man, part beast and part serpent. Centuries ago they cast him off the earth into the sea, where he has caused much trouble. Once he waged a terrible war against King Anko, but the sea serpent finally conquered Zog and drove the magician into his castle, where he now stays shut up. For if ever Anko catches the monster outside of his enchanted castle, he will kill him, and Zog knows that very well."

"Seems like you have your troubles down here just as we do on top the ground," remarked Cap'n Bill.

"But I'm glad old Zog is shut up in his castle," added Trot. "Is it a sea castle like your own palace?"

"I cannot say, my dear, for the enchantment makes it invisible to all eyes but those of its inhabitants," replied Aquareine. "No one sees Zog now, and we scarcely ever hear of him, but all the sea people know he is here someplace and fear his power. Even in the old days, before Anko conquered him, Zog was the enemy of the mermaids, as he was of all the good and respectable seafolk. But do not worry about the magician, I beg of you, for he has not dared to do an evil deed in many, many years."

"Oh, I'm not afraid," asserted Trot.

"I'm glad of that," said the Queen. "Keep together, friends, and be careful not to separate, for here comes an army of sawfishes."

Even as Aquareine spoke, they saw a swirl and commotion in the water ahead of them, while a sound like a muffled roar fell upon their ears. Then swiftly there dashed upon them a group of great fishes with long saws sticking out in front of their noses, armed with sharp, hooked teeth, all set in a row. They were larger than the swordfishes and seemed more fierce and bold. But the mermaids and Trot and Cap'n Bill quietly awaited their attack, and

instead of tearing them with their saws as they expected to do, the fishes were unable to touch them
at all. They tried every possible way to get at their
proposed victims, but the Magic Circle was all powerful and turned aside the ugly saws; so our friends
were not disturbed at all. Seeing this, the sawfishes
soon abandoned the attempt and with growls and
roars of disappointment swam away and were
quickly out of sight.

Trot had been a wee bit frightened during the
attack, but now she laughed gleefully and told the
queen that it seemed very nice to be protected by
fairy powers. The water grew a darker blue as they
descended into its depths, farther and farther away
from the rays of the sun. Trot was surprised to find
she could see so plainly through the high wall of
water above her, but the sun was able to shoot its
beams straight down through the transparent sea,
and they seemed to penetrate to every nook and
crevice of the rocky bottom.

In this deeper part of the ocean some of the
fishes had a phosphorescent light of their own, and
these could be seen far ahead as if they were
lanterns. The explorers met a school of argonauts
going up to the surface for a sail, and the child
watched these strange creatures with much curiosity. The argonauts live in shells in which they are
able to hide in case of danger from prowling wolf
fishes, but otherwise they crawl out and carry their
shells like humps upon their backs. Then they
spread their skinny sails above them and sail away
under water till they come to the surface, where

they float and let the currents of air carry them along the same as the currents of water had done before. Trot thought the argonauts comical little creatures, with their big eyes and sharp noses, and to her they looked like a fleet of tiny ships.

It is said that men got their first idea of boats and of how to sail them from watching these little argonauts.

CHAPTER 10
THE UNDISCOVERED ISLAND

In following the fleet of argonauts, the four explorers had risen higher in the water and soon found they had wandered to an open space that seemed to Trot like the flat top of a high hill. The sands were covered with a growth of weeds so gorgeously colored that one who had never peered beneath the surface of the sea would scarcely believe they were not the product of a dye shop. Every known hue seemed represented in the delicate, fern-like leaves that swayed softly to and fro as the current moved them. They were not set close together, these branches of magnificent hues, but were scattered sparsely over the sandy bottom of the sea so that while from a distance they seemed thick, a nearer view found them spread out with ample spaces of sand between them.

In these sandy spaces lay the real attractiveness of the place, for here were many of those wonders of the deep that have surprised and interested people in all ages.

First were the starfishes—hundreds of them, it seemed—lying sleepily on the bottom, with their five or six points extended outward. They were of various colors, some rich and brilliant, others of dark brown hues. A few had wound their arms around the weeds or were creeping slowly from one place to another, in the latter case turning their points downward and using them as legs. But most of them were lying motionless, and as Trot looked down upon them she thought they resembled stars in the sky on a bright night, except that the blue of the heavens was here replaced by the white sand, and the twinkling diamond stars by the colored starfish.

"We are near an island," said the Queen, "and that is why so many starfishes are here, as they love to keep close to shore. Also the little seahorses love these weeds, and to me they are more interesting than the starfish."

Trot now noticed the seahorses for the first time. They were quite small—merely two or three inches high—but had funny little heads that were shaped much like the head of a horse, and bright, intelligent eyes. They had no legs, though, for their bodies ended in tails which they twined around the stems of seaweeds to support themselves and keep the currents from carrying them away.

Trot bent down close to examine one of the queer little creatures and exclaimed, "Why, the sea-horses haven't any fins or anything to swim with."

"Oh yes we have," replied the Sea Horse in a tiny but distinct voice. "These things on the side of my head are fins."

"I thought they were ears," said the girl.

"So they are. Fins and ears at the same time," answered the little sea animal. "Also, there are small fins on our backs. Of course, we can't swim as the mermaids do, or even as swiftly as fishes; but we manage to get around, thank you."

"Don't the fishes catch and eat you?" inquired Trot curiously.

"Sometimes," admitted the Sea Horse, "and there are many other living things that have a way of destroying us. But here I am, as you see, over six weeks old, and during that time I have escaped every danger. That isn't so bad, is it?"

"Phoo!" said a Starfish lying near. "I'm over three months old. You're a mere baby, Sea Horse."

"I'm not!" cried the Sea Horse excitedly. "I'm full-grown and may live to be as old as you are!"

"Not if I keep on living," said the Starfish calmly, and Trot knew he was correct in his statement.

The little girl now noticed several sea spiders creeping around and drew back because she did not think them very pretty. They were shaped not unlike the starfishes, but had slender legs and big heads with wicked-looking eyes sticking out of them.

"Oh, I don't like those things!" said Trot, coming closer to her companions.

"You don't, eh?" said a big Sea Spider in a cross voice. "Why do you come around here, then, scaring away my dinner when you're not wanted?"

"It isn't YOUR ocean," replied Trot.

"No, and it isn't yours," snapped the Spider. "But as it's big enough for us both, I'd like you to go away."

"So we will," said Aquareine gently, and at once she moved toward the surface of the water. Trot and Cap'n Bill followed, with Clia, and the child asked, "What island are we near?"

"It has no name," answered the Queen, "for it is not inhabited by man, nor has it ever yet been discovered by them. Perhaps you will be the first humans to see this island. But it is a barren, rocky place, and only fit for seals and turtles."

"Are any of them there now?" Cap'n Bill inquired.

"I think so. We will see."

Trot was astonished to find how near they were to the "top" of the ocean, for they had not ascended through the water very long when suddenly her head popped into the air, and she gave a gasp of surprise to find herself looking at the clear sky for the first time since she had started upon this adventure by rowing into Giant's Cave.

She floated comfortably in the water, with her head and face just out of it, and began to look around her. Cap'n Bill was at her side, and so were the two mermaids. The day was fair, and the surface of the sea, which stretched far away as the eye could reach, rippled under a gentle breeze. They had risen almost at the edge of a small, rocky islet, high in the middle, but gradually slanting down to the water. No trees or bushes or grass grew anywhere about; only rocks, gray and bleak, were to be seen.

Trot scarcely noticed this at first, however, for the island seemed covered with groups of forms, some still and some moving, which the old sailor promptly recognized as seals. Many were lying asleep or sunning themselves; others crept awkwardly around, using their strong fins as legs or "paddles" and caring little if they disturbed the slumbers of the others. Once in a while one of those crowded out of place would give a loud and angry bark, which awakened others and set them to barking likewise.

Baby seals were there in great numbers, and were more active and playful than their elders. It was really wonderful how they could scramble around on the land, and Trot laughed more than once at their antics.

At the edge of the water lay many huge turtles, some as big around as a wagon wheel and others much smaller in size.

"The big ones are very old," said the Queen, seeing Trot's eyes fixed on the turtles.

"How old?" asked the child.

"Hundreds of years, I think. They live to a great age, for nothing can harm them when they withdraw their legs and heads into their thick shells. We use some of the turtles for food, but prefer the younger ones. Men also fish for turtles and eat them, but of course no men ever come to this out-of-the-way place in the ocean, so the inhabitants of this little island know they are perfectly safe."

In the center of the island rose high cliffs on top of which were to be seen great flocks of seagulls, some whirling in the air, while others were perched upon the points of rock.

"What do the birds find to eat?" asked Cap'n Bill.

"They often feed upon seals which die of accident or old age, and they are expert fishermen," explained Queen Aquareine. "Curiously enough, the seals also feed upon these birds, which they are often able to catch in their strong jaws when the gulls venture too near. And then, the seals frequently rob the nests of eggs, of which they are very fond."

"I'd like a few gulls' eggs now," remarked a big seal that lay near them upon the shore. Trot had thought him sound asleep, but now he opened his eyes to blink lazily at the group in the water.

"Good morning," said the Queen. "Aren't you Chief Muffruff?"

"I am," answered the old seal. "And you are Aquareine, the mermaid queen. You see, I remember you, although you haven't been here for years. And isn't that Princess Clia? To be sure! But the other mermaids are strangers to me, especially the bald-headed one."

"I'm not a mermaid," asserted Cap'n Bill. "I'm a sailor jes' a-visitin' the mermaids."

"Our friends are earth dwellers," explained the Queen.

"That's odd," said Muffruff. "I can't remember that any earth dwellers ever came this way before. I never travel far, you see, for I'm chief of this disorderly family of seals that live on this island—on it and off it, that is."

"You're a poor chief," said a big turtle lying beside the seal. "If your people are disorderly, it is your own fault."

Muffruff gave a chuckling laugh. Then, with a movement quick as lightning, he pushed his head under the shell of the turtle and gave it a sudden jerk. The huge turtle was tossed up on edge and then turned flat upon its back, where its short legs struggled vainly to right its overturned body.

"There!" snorted the Seal contemptuously. "Perhaps you'll dare insult me again in the presence of visitors, you old mud-wallower!"

Seeing the plight of the turtle, several young seals came laughingly wabbling to the spot, and as they approached the helpless creature drew in his legs and head and closed his two shells tightly together. The seals bumped against the turtle and gave it a push that sent it sliding down the beach like a toboggan, and a minute later it splashed into the water and sank out of sight. But that was just what the creature wanted. On shore the upset turtle was quite helpless; but the mischievous seals saved him. For as soon as he touched the water, he was able to turn and right himself, which he promptly did. Then he raised his head above the water and asked:

"Is it peace or war, Muffruff?"

"Whichever you like," answered the Seal indifferently.

Perhaps the turtle was angry, for it ran on shore

with remarkable swiftness, uttering a shrill cry as it advanced. At once all the other turtles awoke to life and with upraised heads joined their comrade in the rush for the seals. Most of Chief Muffruff's band scrambled hastily down the rocks and plunged into the water of the sea without waiting for the turtles to reach them; but the chief himself was slow in escaping. It may be that he was ashamed to run while the mermaids were watching, but if this was so he made a great mistake. The turtles snapped at his fins and tail and began biting round chunks out of them so that Chief Muffruff screamed with pain and anger and floundered into the water as fast as he could go. The vengeful turtles were certainly the victors, and now held undisputed possession of the island.

Trot laughed joyously at the incident, not feeling a bit sorry for the old seal who had foolishly begun the battle. Even the gentle queen smiled as she said:

"These quarrels between the turtles and the seals are very frequent, but they are soon ended. An hour from now they will all be lying asleep together just as we found them; but we will not wait for that. Let us go."

She sank slowly beneath the water again, and the others followed after her.

CHAPTER II

CHAPTER II
ZOG THE TERRIBLE AND HIS SEA DEVILS

"The sun must be going under a cloud," said Trot, looking ahead.

They had descended far into the ocean depths again—further, the girl thought, than they had ever been before.

"No," the Queen answered after a glance ahead of them, "that is a cuttlefish, and he is dyeing the sea around him with ink so that he can hide from us. Let us turn a little to the left, for we could see nothing at all in that inky water."

Following her advice, they made a broad curve to the left, and at once the water began to darken in that direction.

"Why, there's another of 'em," said Cap'n Bill as the little party came to a sudden halt.

"So there is," returned the Queen, and Trot thought there was a little quiver of anxiety in her voice. "We must go far to the right to escape the ink."

So they again started, this time almost at a right angle to their former course, the little girl inquired:

"How can the cuttlefish color the water so very black?"

"They carry big sacks in front of them where they conceal the ink," Princess Clia answered. "Whenever they choose, the cuttlefish are able to press out this ink, and it colors the water for a great space around them."

The direction in which they were now swimming was taking them far out of their way. Aquareine did not wish to travel very far to the right, so when she thought they had gone far enough to escape the inky water, she turned to lead her party toward the left—the direction in which she DID wish to go. At once another cloud of ink stained the water and drove them to the right again.

"Is anything wrong, ma'am?" asked Cap'n Bill, seeing a frown gather upon the queen's lovely face.

"I hope not," she said. "But I must warn you that these cuttlefish are the servants of the terrible sea devils, and from the way they are acting they seem determined to drive us toward the Devil Caves, which I wished to avoid."

This admission on the part of their powerful protector, the fairy mermaid, sent a chill to the hearts of the earth people. Neither spoke for a time, but finally Cap'n Bill asked in a timid voice:

"Hadn't we better go back, ma'am?"

"Yes," decided Aquareine after a moment's

thought. "I think it will be wise to retreat. The sea devils are evidently aware of our movements and wish to annoy us. For my part, I have no fear of them, but I do not care to have you meet such creatures."

But when they turned around to abandon their journey, another inky cloud was to be seen behind them. They really had no choice but to swim in the only streak of clear water they could find, and the mermaids well knew this would lead them nearer and nearer to the caves of their enemies.

But Aquareine led the way, moving very slowly, and the others followed her. In every other direction they were hemmed in by the black waters, and they did not dare to halt, because the inky fluid crept swiftly up behind them and drove them on.

The queen and the princess had now become silent and grave. They swam on either side of their guests as if to better protect them.

"Don't look up," whispered Clia, pressing close to the little girl's side.

"Why not?" asked Trot, and then she did exactly what she had been told not to do. She lifted her head and saw stretched over them a network of scrawny, crimson arms interlaced like the branches of trees in winter when the leaves have fallen and left them bare.

Cap'n Bill gave a start and muttered "Land sakes!" for he, too, had gazed upward and seen the crimson network of limbs.

"Are these the sea devils?" asked the child, more curious than frightened.

"Yes, dear," replied the Queen. "But I advise you to pay no attention to them. Remember, they cannot touch us."

In order to avoid the threatening arms overhead, which followed them as they swam, our friends kept near to the bottom of the sea, which was here thickly covered with rough and jagged rocks. The inky water had now been left far behind, but when Trot looked over her shoulder, she shuddered to find a great crimson monster following closely after them, with a dozen long, snaky feelers stretched out as if to grab anyone that lagged behind. And there, at the side of Princess Clia, was another devil, leering silently with his cruel, bulging eyes at the pretty mermaid. Beside the queen swam still another of their enemies. Indeed, the sea devils had crept upon them and surrounded them everywhere except at the front, and Trot began to feel nervous and worried for the first time.

Cap'n Bill kept mumbling queer words under his breath, for he had a way of talking to himself when anything "upsot him," as he would quaintly remark. Trot always knew he was disturbed or in trouble when he began to "growl."

The only way now open was straight ahead. They swam slowly, yet fast enough to keep a safe distance from the dreadful creature behind them.

"I'm afraid they are driving us into a trap," whispered the Queen softly. "But whatever happens, do not lose courage, earth friends. Clia and I are here to protect you, and our fairy powers are sufficient to keep you from all harm."

"Oh, I don't mind so very much," declared Trot calmly. "It's like the fairy adventures in storybooks, and I've often thought I'd like that kind of adventures, 'cause the story always turns out the right way."

Cap'n Bill growled something just then, but the only words Trot could make out were, "never lived to tell the tale."

"Oh, pshaw, Cap'n," she said. "We may be in danger, right enough, an' to be honest, I don't like the looks of these sea devils at all. But I'm sure it's no KILLING matter, for we've got the fairy circles all around us."

"Ha ha!" laughed the monster beside her. "WE know all about the fairy circles, don't we, Migg?"

"Ho ho!" laughed the monster on the other side. "We do, Slibb, my boy, and we don't think much of fairy circles, either!"

"They have foiled our enemies many a time," declared the Princess with much dignity.

"Ha ha!" laughed one. "That's why we're here now."

"Ho ho!" laughed the other. "We've learned a trick or two, and we've got you fast this time."

Then all the sea devils—those above and the one behind, and the two on the sides—laughed all together, and their laughter was so horrible that it made even Trot shudder.

But now the queen stopped short, and the others stopped with her.

"I will go no farther," she said firmly, not caring if the monsters overheard her. "It is evident that these monsters are trying to drive us into some secret place, and it is well known that they are in league with Zog the Terrible, whom they serve because they are as wicked as he is. We must be somewhere near the hidden castle of Zog, so I prefer to stay here rather than be driven into some place far more dangerous. As for the sea devils, they are powerless to injure us in any way. Not one of those thousand arms about us can possibly touch our bodies."

The only reply to this defiant speech was another burst of horrible laughter; and now there suddenly appeared before them still another of the monsters, which thus completely hemmed them in. Then the creatures began interlacing their long arms —or "feelers"—until they formed a perfect cage around the prisoners, not an opening being left that was large enough for one of them to escape through.

The mermaids and the girl and sailor man kept huddled close together, for although they might be walled in by the sea devils, their captors could not touch them because of the protecting magic circles.

All at once Trot exclaimed, "Why, we must be moving!"

This was startling news, but by watching the flow of water past them they saw that the little girl was right. The sea devils were swimming, all together, and as the cage they were in moved forward, our friends were carried with it.

Queen Aquareine had a stern look upon her beautiful face. Cap'n Bill guessed from this look that the mermaid was angry, for it seemed much like the look Trot's mother wore when they came home late to dinner. But however angry the queen might be, she was unable to help herself or her guests just now or to escape from the guidance of the dreaded sea devils. The rest of the party had become sober and thoughtful, and in dignified silence they awaited the outcome of this strange adventure.

CHAPTER 12

THE ENCHANTED ISLAND

All at once it grew dark around them. Neither Cap'n Bill nor Trot liked this gloom, for it made them nervous not to be able to see their enemies.

"We must be near a sea cavern, if not within one," whispered Princess Clia, and even as she spoke the network of scarlet arms parted before them, leaving an avenue for them to swim out of the cage. There was brighter water ahead, too, so the queen said without hesitation:

"Come along, dear friends; but let us clasp hands and keep close together."

They obeyed her commands and swam swiftly out of their prison and into the clear water before them, glad to put a distance between themselves and the loathesome sea devils. The monsters made no attempt to follow them, but they burst into a chorus of harsh laughter which warned our friends that they had not yet accomplished their escape.

The four now found themselves in a broad, rocky passage, which was dimly lighted from some unknown source. The walls overhead, below them and at the sides all glistened as if made of silver, and in places were set small statues of birds, beasts and fishes, occupying niches in the walls and seemingly made from the same glistening material.

The queen swam more slowly now that the sea devils had been left behind, and she looked exceedingly grave and thoughtful.

"Have you ever been here before?" asked Trot.

"No, dear," said the Queen with a sigh.

"And do you know where we are?" continued the girl.

"I can guess," replied Aquareine. "There is only one place in all the sea where such a passage as that we are in could exist without my knowledge, and that is in the hidden dominions of Zog. If we are indeed in the power of that fearful magician, we must summon all our courage to resist him, or we are lost!"

"Is Zog more powerful than the mermaids?" asked Trot anxiously.

"I do not know, for we have never before met to measure our strength," answered Aquareine. "But if King Anko could defeat the magician, as he surely did, then I think I shall be able to do so."

"I wish I was sure of it," muttered Cap'n Bill.

Absolute silence reigned in the silver passage. No

fish were there; not even a sea flower grew to relieve the stern grandeur of this vast corridor. Trot began to be impressed with the fact that she was a good way from her home and mother, and she wondered if she would ever get back again to the white cottage on the cliff. Here she was, at the bottom of the great ocean, swimming through a big tunnel that had an enchanted castle at the end, and a group of horrible sea devils at the other! In spite of this thought, she was not very much afraid. Although two fairy mermaids were her companions, she relied, strange to say, more upon her tried and true friend, Cap'n Bill, than upon her newer acquaintances to see her safely out of her present trouble.

Cap'n Bill himself did not feel very confident.

"I don't care two cents what becomes o' me," he told Princess Clia in a low voice, "but I'm drea'ful worried over our Trot. She's too sweet an' young to be made an end of in this 'ere fashion."

Clia smiled at this speech. "I'm sure you will find the little girl's end a good way off," she replied. "Trust to our powerful queen, and be sure she will find some means for us all to escape uninjured."

The light grew brighter as they advanced, until finally they perceived a magnificent archway just ahead of them. Aquareine hesitated a moment whether to go on or turn back, but there was no escaping the sea devils behind them, and she decided the best way out of their difficulties was to bravely face the unknown Zog and rely upon her fairy powers to prevent his doing any mischief to herself or her friends. So she led the way, and together they approached the archway and passed through it.

They now found themselves in a vast cavern, so great in extent that the dome overhead looked like the sky when seen from earth. In the center of this immense sea cavern rose the towers of a splendid castle, all built of coral inlaid with silver and having windows of clear glass.

Surrounding the castle were beds of beautiful sea flowers, many being in full bloom, and these were laid out with great care in artistic designs. Goldfish and silverfish darted here and there among the foliage, and the whole scene was so pretty and peaceful that Trot began to doubt there was any danger lurking in such a lovely place.

As they approached to look around them, a brilliantly colored gregfish approached and gazed at them curiously with his big, saucer-like eyes. "So Zog has got you at last!" he said in a pitying tone. "How foolish you were to swim into that part of the sea where he is powerful."

"The sea devils made us," explained Clia.

"Well, I'm sorry for you, I'm sure," remarked the Greg, and with a flash of his tail, he disappeared among the sea foliage.

"Let us go to the castle," said the Queen in a determined voice. "We may as well boldly defy our fate as to wait until Zog seeks us out."

So they swam to the entrance of the castle. The doors stood wide open, and the interior seemed as well lighted as the cavern itself, although none of them could discover from whence the light came.

At each side of the entrance lay a fish such as they had never seen before. It was flat as a doormat and seemed to cling fast to the coral floor. Upon its back were quills like those of a porcupine, all pointed and sharp. From the center of the fish arose a head shaped like a round ball, with a circle of piercing, bead-like eyes set in it. These strange guardians of the entrance might be able to tell what their numerous eyes saw, yet they remained silent and watchful. Even Aquareine gazed upon them curiously, and she gave a little shudder as she did so.

Inside the entrance was a domed hall with a flight of stairs leading to an upper balcony. Around the hall were several doorways hung with curtains made of woven seaweeds. Chairs and benches stood against the wall, and these astonished the visitors because neither stairs nor chairs seemed useful in a kingdom where every living thing was supposed to swim and have a fish's tail. In Queen Aquareine's palaces benches for reclining were used, and stairs were wholly unnecessary, but in the Palace of Zog the furniture and fittings were much like those of a house upon earth, and except that every space here was filled with water instead of air, Trot and Cap'n Bill might have imagined themselves in a handsome earthly castle.

The little group paused half fearfully in the hall, yet so far there was surely nothing to be afraid of. They were wondering what to do next when the curtains of an archway were pushed aside and a boy entered. To Trot's astonishment, he had legs and walked upon them naturally and with perfect ease.

He was a delicate, frail-looking little fellow, dressed in a black velvet suit with knee breeches. The bows at his throat and knees were of colored seaweeds, woven into broad ribbons. His hair was yellow and banged across his forehead. His eyes were large and dark, with a pleasant, merry sparkle in them. Around his neck he wore a high ruff, but in spite of this Trot could see that below his plump cheeks were several scarlet-edged slits that looked like the gills of fishes, for they gently opened and closed as the boy breathed in the water by which he was surrounded. These gills did not greatly mar the lad's delicate beauty, and he spread out his arms and bowed low and gracefully in greeting.

"Hello," said Trot.

"Why, I'd like to," replied the boy with a laugh, "but being a mere slave, it isn't proper for me to hello. But it's good to see earth people again, and I'm glad you're here."

"We're not glad," observed the girl. "We're afraid."

"You'll get over that," declared the boy smilingly. "People lose a lot of time being afraid. Once I was myself afraid, but I found it was no fun, so I gave it up."

"Why were we brought here?" inquired Queen Aquareine gently.

"I can't say, madam, being a mere slave," replied the boy. "But you have reminded me of my errand. I am sent to inform you all that Zog the Forsaken, who hates all the world and is hated by all the world, commands your presence in his den."

"Do you hate Zog, too?" asked Trot.

"Oh no," answered the boy. "People lose a lot of time in hating others, and there's no fun in it at all. Zog may be hateful, but I'm not going to waste time hating him. You may do so, if you like."

"You are a queer child," remarked the Mermaid Queen, looking at him attentively. "Will you tell us who you are?"

"Once I was Prince Sacho of Sacharhineolaland, which is a sweet country, but hard to pronounce," he answered. "But in this domain I have but one title and one name, and that is 'Slave.'"

"How came you to be Zog's slave?" asked Clia.

"The funniest adventure you ever heard of," asserted the boy with eager pride. "I sailed in a ship that went to pieces in a storm. All on board were drowned but me, and I came mighty near it, to tell the truth. I went down deep, deep into the sea, and at the bottom was Zog, watching the people drown. I tumbled on his head, and he grabbed and saved me, saying I would make a useful slave. By his magic power he made me able to live under water as the fishes live, and he brought me to this castle and taught me to wait upon him as his other slaves do."

"Isn't it a dreadful, lonely life?" asked Trot.

"No indeed," said Sacho. "We haven't any time to be lonely, and the dreadful things Zog does are very exciting and amusing, I assure you. He keeps us guessing every minute, and that makes the life here interesting. Things were getting a bit slow an hour ago, but now that you are here, I'm in hopes we will all be kept busy and amused for some time."

"Are there many others in the castle besides you and Zog?" asked Aquareine.

"Dozens of us. Perhaps hundreds. I've never counted them," said the boy. "But Zog is the only master; all the rest of us are in the same class, so there is no jealousy among the slaves."

"What is Zog like?" Cap'n Bill questioned.

At this the boy laughed, and the laugh was full of mischief. "If I could tell you what Zog is like, it would take me a year," was the reply. "But I can't tell you. Every one has a different idea of what he's like, and soon you will see him yourselves."

"Are you fond of him?" asked Trot.

"If I said yes, I'd get a good whipping," declared Sacho. "I am commanded to hate Zog, and being a good servant, I try to obey. If anyone dared to like Zog, I am sure he'd be instantly fed to the turtles; so I advise you not to like him."

"Oh, we won't," promised Trot.

"But we're keeping the master waiting, and that is also a dangerous thing to do," continued the boy. "If we don't hurry up, Zog will begin to smile, and when he smiles there is trouble brewing."

The queen sighed. "Lead the way, Sacho," she said. "We will follow."

The boy bowed again, and going to an archway, held aside the curtains for them. They first swam into a small anteroom which led into a long corridor, at the end of which was another curtained arch. Through this Sacho also guided them, and now they found themselves in a cleverly constructed maze.

Every few feet were twists and turns and sharp corners, and sometimes the passage would be wide, and again so narrow that they could just squeeze through in single file. "Seems like we're gettin' further into the trap," growled Cap'n Bill. "We couldn't find our way out o' here to save our lives."

"Oh yes we could," replied Clia, who was just behind him. "Such a maze may indeed puzzle you, but the queen or I could lead you safely through it again, I assure you. Zog is not so clever as he thinks himself."

The sailor, however, found the maze very bewildering, and so did Trot. Passages ran in every direction, crossing and recrossing, and it seemed wonderful that the boy Sacho knew just which way to go. But he never hesitated an instant. Trot looked carefully to see if there were any marks to guide him, but every wall was of plain, polished marble, and every turning looked just like all the others. Suddenly Sacho stopped short. They were now in a broader passage, but as they gathered around their conductor they found further advance blocked. Solid walls faced them, and here the corridor seemed to end.

"Enter!" said a clear voice.

"But we can't!" protested Trot.

"Swim straight ahead," whispered the boy in soft tones. "There is no real barrier before you. Your eyes are merely deceived by magic."

"Ah, I understand," said Aquareine, nodding her pretty head. And then she took Mayre's hand and swam boldly forward, while Cap'n Bill followed holding the hand of Clia. And behold! the marble wall melted away before them, and they found themselves in a chamber more splendid than even the fairy mermaids had ever seen before.

CHAPTER 13

PRISONERS OF THE SEA MONSTER

The room in the enchanted castle which Zog called the "den" and in which the wicked sea monster passed most of his time was a perfectly shaped dome of solid gold. The upper part of this dome was thickly set with precious jewels—diamonds, rubies, sapphires and emeralds, which sparkled beautifully through the crystal water. The lower walls were as thickly studded with pearls, all being of perfect shape and color. Many of the pearls were larger than any which may be found upon earth, for the sea people knew where to find the very best and hide them away where men cannot discover them.

The golden floor was engraved with designs of rare beauty, depicting not only sea life, but many adventures upon land. In the room were several large, golden cabinets, the doors of which were closed and locked, and in addition to the cabinets

there were tables, chairs and sofas, the latter uphol-
stered with softest sealskins. Handsome rugs of exquisitely woven seaweeds were scattered about, the
colors of which were artistically blended together. In
one corner a fountain of air bubbled up through the
water. The entire room was lighted as brilliantly as if
exposed to the direct rays of the sun, yet where this
light came from our friends could not imagine. No
lamp or other similar device was visible anywhere.

The strangers at first scarcely glanced at all these
beautiful things, for in an easy chair sat Zog himself,
more wonderful than any other living creature, and
as they gazed upon him, their eyes seemed fasci-
nated as if held by a spell. Zog's face was the face of
a man, except that the tops of his ears were pointed
like horns and he had small horns instead of eye-
brows and a horn on the end of his chin. In spite of
these deformities, the expression of the face was not
unpleasant or repulsive. His hair was carefully
parted and brushed, and his mouth and nose were
not only perfect in shape but quite handsome.

Only the eyes betrayed Zog and made him terrible to all beholders. They seemed like coals of
glowing fire and sparkled so fiercely that no one ever
cared to meet their gaze for more than an instant.
Perhaps the monster realized this, for he usually
drooped his long lashes over his fiery eyes to shut
out their glare. Zog had two well-shaped legs which
ended in the hoofs of beasts instead of feet, and
these hoofs were shod with gold. His body was a
shapeless mass covered with richly embroidered raiment, over which a great robe of cloth of gold fell in

many folds. This robe was intended to hide the magician's body from view, but Trot noticed that the cloth moved constantly in little ripples, as if what lay underneath would not keep still.

The best features of which Zog could boast were his arms and hands, the latter being as well formed, as delicate and white as those of a well-bred woman. When he spoke, his voice sounded sweet and clear, and its tones were very gentle. He had given them a few moments to stare at him, for he was examining them in turn with considerable curiosity. "Well," said he, "do you not find me the most hateful creature you have ever beheld?"

The queen refrained from answering, but Trot said promptly, "We do. Nothing could be more horrider or more disgustin' than you are, it seems to me."

"Very good, very good indeed," declared the monster, lifting his lashes to flash his glowing eyes upon them. Then he turned toward Cap'n Bill. "Man-fish," he continued, "what do YOU think of me?"

"Mighty little," the sailor replied. "You orter be 'shamed to ask sech a question, knowin' you look worse ner the devil himself."

"Very true," answered Zog, frowning. He felt that he had received a high compliment, and the frown showed he was pleased with Cap'n Bill.

But now Queen Aquareine advanced to a position in front of their captor and said, "Tell me, Zog, why have you trapped us and brought us here?"

"To destroy you," was the quick answer, and the

magician turned for an instant to flash his eyes upon the beautiful mermaid. "For two hundred years I have been awaiting a chance to get within my power some friend of Anko the Sea Serpent—of Anko, whom I hate!" he added, smiling sweetly. "When you left your palace today, my swift spies warned me, and so I sent the sea devils to capture you. Often have they tried to do this before, but always failed. Today, acting by my command, they tricked you, and by surrounding you forced you to the entrance of my enchanted castle. The result is a fine capture of important personages. I have now in my power the queen and princess of the fairy mermaids, as well as two wandering earth people, and I assure you I shall take great pleasure in destroying you utterly."

"You are a coward," declared the Queen proudly. "You dared not meet us in the open sea."

"No, I dare not leave this castle," Zog admitted, still smiling. "But here in my own domain my power is supreme. Nothing can interfere with my vengeance."

"That remains to be seen," said Aquareine, firmly meeting the gaze of the terrible eyes.

"Of course," he answered, nodding his head with a graceful movement. "You will try to thwart me and escape. You will pit your fairy power against my powers of magic. That will give me great pleasure, for the more you struggle, the greater will be my revenge."

"But why should you seek revenge upon us?" asked Clia. "We have never harmed you."

"That is true," replied Zog. "I bear you no personal ill will. But you are friends of my great enemy, King Anko, and it will annoy him very much when he finds that you have been destroyed by me. I cannot hurt the rascally old sea serpent himself, but through you I can make him feel my vengeance."

"The mermaids have existed thousands of years," said the Queen in a tone of pride. "Do you imagine the despised and conquered Zog has power to destroy them?"

"I do not know," was the quiet answer. "It will be interesting to discover which is the more powerful."

"I challenge you to begin the test at once, vile magician!" exclaimed Aquareine.

"There is no hurry, fair Queen," answered Zog in his softest tones. "I have been so many years in accomplishing your capture that it is foolish to act hastily now. Besides, I am lonely. Here in my forced retirement I see only those uninteresting earth mortals whom I have made my slaves, for all sea dwellers are forbidden to serve me save the sea devils, and they dare not enter my castle. I have saved many mortals from drowning and brought them here to people my castle, but I do not love mortals. Two lovely mermaids are much more interesting, and before I allow you to perish, I shall have much amusement in witnessing your despair and your struggles to escape. You are now my prisoners. By slow degrees I shall wear out your fairy powers and break your hearts, as well as the hearts of these earth dwellers who have no magic powers, and I think it will be a long time before I finally permit you to die."

"That's all right," said Trot cheerfully. "The longer you take, the better I'll be satisfied."

"That's how I feel about it," added Cap'n Bill. "Don't get in a hurry to kill us Zog. It'll be such a wear an' tear on your nerves. Jes' take it easy an' let us live as long as we can."

"Don't you care to die?" asked the magician.

"It's a thing I never longed for," the sailor replied. "You see, we had no business to go on a trip with the mermaids to begin with. I've allus heard tell that mermaids is dangerous, an' no one as met 'em ever lived to tell the tale. Eh, Trot?"

"That's what you said, Cap'n Bill."

"So I guess we're done for, one way 'r 'nother, an' it don't matter much which. But Trot's a good child, an' mighty young an' tender. It don't seem like her time has come to die. I'd like to have her sent safe home to her mother. So I've got this 'ere proposition to make, Zog. If your magic could make ME die twice, or even THREE times fer good measure, why you go ahead an' do it an' I won't complain. All I ask is fer you to send this little girl safe back to dry land again."

"Don't you do it, Zog!" cried Trot indignantly, and turning to Cap'n Bill, she added, "I'm not goin' to leave you down here in all this mess, Cap'n, and don't you think it. If one of us gets out of the muddle we're in, we'll both get out, so don't you make any bargains with Zog to die twice."

Zog listened to this conversation very carefully. "The dying does not amount to much," he said. "It is the thinking about it that hurts you mortals most. I've watched many a shipwreck at sea, and the people would howl and scream for hours before the ship broke up. Their terror was very enjoyable. But when the end came, they all drowned as peacefully as if they were going to sleep, so it didn't amuse me at all."

"I'm not worrying," said Trot.

"Ner me," said Cap'n Bill. "You'll find we can take what comes jes' as easy as anybody."

"I do not expect to get much from you poor mortals," said Zog carelessly. "You are merely a side show to my circus, a sort of dessert to my feast of vengeance. When the time comes, I can find a hundred ways to kill you. My most interesting prisoners are these pretty mermaids, who claim that none of their race has ever yet died or been destroyed. The first mermaid ever created is living yet, and I am told she is none other than Queen Aquareine. So I have a pretty problem before me to invent some way to destroy the mermaids or put them out of existence. And it will require some thought."

"Also, it will require some power you do not possess," suggested the Queen.

"That may be," replied Zog softly. "But I am going to experiment, and I believe I shall be able to cause you a lot of pain and sorrow before I finally make an end of you. I have not lived twenty-seven thousand years, Aquareine, without getting a certain amount of wisdom, and I am more powerful than you suspect."

"You are a monster and a wicked magician," said the Mermaid Queen.

"I am," agreed Zog, "but I cannot help it. I was created part man, part bird, part fish, part beast and part reptile, and such a monstrosity could not be otherwise than wicked. Everybody hates me, and I hate everybody."

"Why don't you kill yourself?" asked Trot.

"I've tried that and failed," he answered. "Only one being in the world has power to destroy me, and that is King Anko, the sea serpent."

"Then you'd better let him do it," advised the little girl.

"No. Much as I long to die, I cannot allow King Anko the pleasure of killing me. He has always been my worst enemy, and it would be such a joy to him to kill me that I really cannot allow him. Indeed, I have always hoped to kill Anko. I have now been three thousand six hundred and forty-two years, eleven months and nine days figuring out a plan to destroy old Anko, and as yet I have not discovered a way."

"I'd give it up, if I were you," advised Trot. "Don't you think you could get some fun out of trying to be good?"

"No!" cried Zog, and his voice was not so soft as before. "Listen, Aquareine, you and your attendants shall be prisoners in this castle until I can manage to stop you from living. Rooms will be placed at your disposal, and I wish you to go to them at o nce, as I am tired of looking at you."

"You're no more tired than we are," remarked Trot. "It's lucky you can't see yourself, Zog."

He turned his glowing eyes full upon her. "The worst of my queer body I keep concealed," he said. "If ever you see it, you will scream with terror." He touched a bell beside him, and the girl was surprised to find how clearly its tones rang out through the water. In an instant the boy Sacho appeared and bowed low before his dreadful master. "Take the mermaids and the child to the Rose Chamber," commanded Zog, "and take the old man-fish to the Peony Room."

Sacho turned to obey. "Are the outer passages well guarded?" asked the monster.

"Yes, as you have commanded," said the boy.

"Then you may allow the prisoners to roam at will throughout the castle. Now, go!"

The prisoners followed Sacho from the room, glad to get away. The presence of this evil being had grown oppressive to them, and Zog had himself seemed ill at ease during the last few minutes. The robe so closely wound around his body moved jerkily, as if something beneath disturbed it, and at such times Zog shifted nervously in his seat.

Sacho's thin little legs trotted through the water and led the way into a different passage from the one by which they had entered. They swam slowly after him and breathed easier when they had left the golden domed chamber where their wicked enemy sat enthroned. "Well, how do you like him?" asked Sacho with a laugh.

"We hate him!" declared Trot emphatically.

"Of course you do," replied Sacho. "But you're wasting time hating anything. It doesn't do you any good, or him any harm. Can you sing?"

"A little," said Trot, "but I don't feel like singing now."

"You're wrong about that," the boy asserted. "Anything that keeps you from singing is foolishness, unless it's laughter. Laughter, joy and song are the only good things in the world."

Trot did not answer this queer speech, for just then they came to a flight of stairs, and Sacho climbed up them while the others swam. And now they were in a lofty, broad corridor having many doors hung with seaweed draperies. At one of these doorways Sacho stopped and said, "Here is the Rose Chamber where the master commands you to live until you die. You may wander anywhere in the castle as you please; to leave it is impossible. Whenever you return to the Rose Chamber, you will know it by this design of roses sewn in pearls upon the hangings. The Peony Room where the man-fish is to live is the next one farther on."

"Thank you," replied Queen Aquareine. "Are we to be fed?"

"Meals will be served in your rooms. If you desire anything, ring the bell and some of the slaves will be sure to answer it. I am mostly in attendance upon my master, but whenever I am at liberty I will look after your comfort myself."

Again they thanked the strange boy, and he turned and left them. They could hear him whistle and sing as he returned along the passage. Then Princess Clia parted the curtains that her queen and companions might enter the Rose Chamber.

Again Clia thanked the strange boy, and he
turned and left them. They could hear him whistle
and sing as he returned along the passage. Then
Princess Clia opened the curtains that her queen and
companions might enter the Rose Chamber.

CHAPTER 14
CAP'N JOE AND CAP'N BILL

The rooms Zog had given his prisoners were
as handsome as all other parts of this
strange enchanted castle. Gold was used
plentifully in the decorations, and in the Rose
Chamber occupied by the mermaids and Trot
golden roses formed a border around the entire
room. The sea maidens had evidently been expected,
for the magician had provided couches for them to
recline upon similar to the ones used in the mermaid
palaces. The frames were of mother of pearl and the
cushions of soft, white sponges. In the room were
toilet tables, mirrors, ornaments and many articles
used by earth people, which they afterward learned
had been plundered by Zog from sunken ships and
brought to his castle by his allies, the sea devils.

While the mermaids were examining and admiring their room, Cap'n Bill went to the Peony
Room to see what it was like and found his quarters

were very cozy and interesting. There were pictures on the wall, portraits of grave-looking porpoises, bashful seals, and smug and smiling walruses. Some of the wall panels were formed of mirrors and re-flected clearly the interior of the room. Around the ceiling was a frieze of imitation peonies in silver, and the furniture was peony-shaped, the broad leaves being bent to form seats and couches. Beside a pretty dressing table hung a bell cord with a tassel at the end. Cap'n Bill did not know it was a bell cord, so he pulled it to see what would happen and was puzzled to find that nothing seemed to happen at all, the bell being too far away for him to hear it. Then he began looking at the treasures contained in this royal apartment, and was much pleased with a golden statue of a mermaid that resembled Princess Clia in feature. A silver flower vase upon a stand contained a bouquet of gorgeous peonies, "as nat'ral as life," said Cap'n Bill, although he saw plainly that they must be made of metal.

Trot came in just then to see how her dear friend was located. She entered from the doorway that connected the two rooms and said, "Isn't it pretty, Cap'n? And who'd ever think that awful creature Zog owned such a splendid castle and kept his pris-oners in such lovely rooms?"

"I once heard tell," said the sailor, "of a foreign people that sacrificed humans to please their pagan gods, an' before they killed 'em outright they stuffed the victims full of good things to eat an' dressed 'em in pretty clothes an' treated 'em like princes. That's why I don't take much comfort in our fine surroundin's, Trot. This Zog is a pagan, if ever there was one, an' he don't mean us any good, you may depend on 't."

"No," replied Trot soberly, "I'm sure he does not expect us to be happy here. But I'm going to fool him and have just as good a time as I can." As she spoke they both turned around—an easy thing to do with a single flop of their flexible tails—and Cap'n Bill uttered a cry of surprise. Just across the room stood a perfect duplicate of himself. The round head, with its bald top and scraggly whiskers, the sailor cap and shirt, the wide pantaloons, even the wooden leg, each and every one were exact copies of those owned by Cap'n Bill. Even the expression in the light-blue eyes was the same, and it is no wonder the old sailor stared at his "double" in amazement. But the next minute he laughed and said, "Why, Trot, it's ME reflected in a mirror. But at first I thought it was someone else."

Trot was staring, too. "Look, Cap'n!" she whispered. "Look at the wooden leg."

"Well, it's MY wooden leg, ain't it?" he inquired.

"If it is, it can't be a reflection in a mirror," she argued, "for YOU haven't got a wooden leg. You've got a fish's tail."

The old sailor was so startled by this truth that he gave a great flop with his tail that upset his balance and made him keel a somersault in the water before he got right side up again. Then he found the other sailor man laughing at him and was horrified to find the "reflection" advancing toward them by stumping along on its wooden leg. "Keep away! Get out, there!" yelled Cap'n Bill. "You're a ghost, the ghost o' me that once was, an' I can't bear the sight o' you. Git out!"

"Did you ring jes' to tell me to git out?" asked the other in a mild voice.

"I—I didn't ring," declared Cap'n Bill.

"You did. You pulled that bell cord," said the one-legged (one or more lines missing here in this edition)

"Oh, did pullin' that thing ring a bell?" inquired the Cap'n, a little ashamed of his ignorance and re-assured by hearing the "ghost" talk.

"It surely did," was the reply, "and Sacho told me to answer your bell and look after you. So I'm a-lookin' after you."

"I wish you wouldn't," protested Cap'n Bill. "I've no use fer—fer ghostses, anyhow."

The strange sailor began to chuckle at hearing this, and his chuckle was just like Cap'n Bill's chuckle, so full of merry humor that it usually made everyone laugh with him.

"Who are you?" asked Trot, who was very curious and much surprised.

"I'm Cap'n Joe," was the reply. "Cap'n Joe Wee-dles, formerly o' the brig 'Gladsome' an' now a slave o' Zog at the bottom o' the sea."

"J—J—Joe Wee-Weedles!" gasped Cap'n Bill, amazed. "Joe Weedles o' the 'Gladsome'! Why, dash my eyes, mate, you must be my brother!"

"Are YOU Bill Weedles?" asked the other. And then he added, "But no, you can't be. Bill wasn't no mermaid. He were a human critter like myself."

"That's what I am," said Cap'n Bill hastily. "I'm a human critter, too. I've jes' borrered this fish tail to swim with while I'm visitin' the mermaids."

"Well, well," said Cap'n Joe in astonishment. "Who'd o' thought it! An' who'd ever o' thought as I'd find my long-lost brother in Zog's enchanted castle full fifty fathoms deep down in the wet, wet water!"

"Why, as fer that," replied Cap'n Bill, "it's YOU as is the long-lost brother, not me. You an' your ship disappeared many a year ago, an' ain't never been heard of since, while, as you see, I'm livin' on earth yet."

"You don't look it to all appearances," remarked Cap'n Joe in a reflective tone of voice. "But I'll agree it's many a year since I saw the top o' the water, an' I'm not expectin' to ever tramp on dry land again."

"Are you dead, or drownded, or what?" asked Cap'n Bill.

"Neither one nor t'other," was the answer. "But Zog gave me gills so's I could live in the water like fishes do, an' if I got on land I couldn't breathe air any more'n a fish out o' water can. So I guess as long as I live, I'll hev to stay down here."

"Do you like it?" asked Trot.

"Oh, I don't objec' much," said Cap'n Joe. "There ain't much excitement here, fer we don't catch a flock o' mermaids ev'ry day, but the work is easy an' the rations fair. I might o' been worse off, you know, for when my brig was wrecked, I'd 'a' gone to Davy Jones's Locker if Zog hadn't happened to find me an' made me a fish."

"You don't look as much like a fish as Cap'n Bill does," observed Trot.

"P'raps not," said Cap'n Joe, "but I notice Bill ain't got any gills an' breathes like you an' the mermaids does. When he gets back to land, he'll have his two legs again an' live in comfort breathin' air."

"I won't have two legs," asserted Cap'n Bill, "for when I'm on earth I'm fitted with one wooden leg, jes' the same as you are, Joe."

"Oh, I hadn't heard o' that, Bill, but I'm not surprised," replied Brother Joe. "Many a sailor gets to wear a wooden leg in time. Mine's hick'ry."

"So's mine," said Cap'n Bill with a air of pride. "I'm glad I've run across you, Joe, for I often wondered what had become of you. Seems too bad, though, to have to spend all your life under water."

"What's the odds?" asked Cap'n Joe. "I never could keep away from the water since I was a boy, an' there's more dangers to be met floatin' on it than there is soakin' in it. An' one other thing pleases me when I think on it: I'm parted from my wife, a mighty good woman with a tongue like a two-edge sword, an' my pore widder'll get the insurance money an' live happy. As fer me, Bill, I'm a good deal happier than I was when she kep' scoldin' me from mornin' to night every minute I was home."

"Is Zog a kind master?" asked Trot.

"I can't say he's kind," replied Cap'n Joe, "for he's as near a devil as any livin' critter CAN be. He grumbles an' growls in his soft voice all day, an' hates himself an' everybody else. But I don't see much of him. There's so many of us slaves here that

Zog don't pay much attention to us, an' we have a pretty good time when the ol' magician is shut up in his den, as he mostly is."

"Could you help us to escape?" asked the child.

"Why, I don't know how," admitted Cap'n Joe. "There's magic all around us, and we slaves are never allowed to leave this great cave. I'll do what I can, o' course, but Sacho is the boy to help you if anyone can. That little chap knows a heap, I can tell you. So now, if nothin' more's wanted, I must get back to work."

"What work do you do?" Cap'n Bill asked.

"I sew buttons on Zog's clothes. Every time he gets mad, he busts his buttons off, an' I have to sew 'em on again. As he's mad most o' the time, it keeps me busy."

"I'll see you again, won't I, Joe?" said Cap'n Bill.

"No reason why you shouldn't, if you manage to keep alive," said Cap'n Joe. "But you mustn't forget, Bill, this Zog has his grip on you, an' I've never known anything to escape him yet."

Saying this, the old sailor began to stump toward the door, but tripped his foot against his wooden leg and gave a swift dive forward. He would have fallen flat had he not grabbed the drapery at the doorway and saved himself by holding fast to it with both hands. Even then he rolled and twisted so awkwardly before he could get upon his legs that Trot had to laugh outright at his antics. "This hick'ry leg," said Cap'n Joe, "is so blamed light that it always wants to float. Agga-Groo, the goldworker, has promised me a gold leg that will stay down, but he never has time to make it. You're mighty lucky, Bill, to have a merman's tail instead o' legs."

"I guess I am, Joe," replied Cap'n Bill, "for in such a wet country the fishes have the best of it. But I ain't sure I'd like this sort o' thing always."

"Think o' the money you'd make in a side show," said Cap'n Joe with his funny chuckling laugh. Then he pounded his wooden leg against the hard floor and managed to hobble from the room without more accidents.

When he had gone, Trot said, "Aren't you glad to find your brother again, Cap'n Bill?"

"Why, so-so," replied the sailor. "I don't know much about Joe, seein' as we haven't met before for many a long year, an' all I remember about our boyhood days is that we fit an' pulled hair most o' the time. But what worries me most is Joe's lookin' so much like me myself, wooden leg an' all. Don't you think it's rather cheeky an' unbrotherly, Trot?"

"Perhaps he can't help it," suggested the child. "And anyhow, he'll never be able to live on land again."

"No," said Cap'n Bill with a sigh. "Joe's a fish, now, an' so he ain't likely to be took for me by one of our friends on the earth."

CHAPTER 15

THE MAGIC OF THE MERMAIDS

When Trot and Cap'n Bill entered the Rose Chamber they found the two mermaids reclining before an air fountain that was sending thousands of tiny bubbles up through the water.

"These fountains of air are excellent things," remarked Queen Aquareine, "for they keep the water fresh and sweet, and that is the more necessary when it is confined by walls, as it is in this castle. But now, let us counsel together and decide what to do in the emergency that confronts us."

"How can we tell what to do without knowing what's going to happen?" asked Trot.

"Somethin's sure to happen," said Cap'n Bill.

As if to prove his words, a gong suddenly sounded at their door and in walked a fat little man clothed all in white, including a white apron and white cap. His face was round and jolly, and he had a big mustache that curled up at the ends.

"Well, well!" said the little man, spreading out his legs and putting his hands on his hips as he stood looking at them. "Of all the queer things in the sea, you're the queerest! Mermaids, eh?"

"Don't bunch us that way!" protested Cap'n Bill.

"You are quite wrong," said Trot. "I'm a—a girl."

"With a fish's tail?" he asked, laughing at her.

"That's only just for a while," she said, "while I'm in the water, you know. When I'm at home on the land I walk just as you do, an' so does Cap'n Bill."

"But we haven't any gills," remarked the Cap'n, looking closely at the little man's throat, "so I take it we're not as fishy as some others."

"If you mean me, I must admit you are right," said the little man, twisting his mustache. "I'm as near a fish as a man can be. But you see, Cap'n, without the gills that make me a fish, I could not live under water."

"When it comes to that, you've no business to live under water," asserted the sailor. "But I s'pose you're a slave and can't help it."

"I'm chief cook for that old horror Zog. And that reminds me, good mermaids, or good people, or good girls and sailors, or whatever you are, that I'm sent here to ask what you'd like to eat."

"Good to see you, sir," said Cap'n Bill. "I'm nearly starved, myself."

"I had it in mind," said the little man, "to prepare a regular mermaid dinner, but since you're not mermaids—"

"Oh, two of us are," said the Queen, smiling. "I, my good cook, am Aquareine, the ruler of the mermaids, and this is the Princess Clia."

"I've often heard of you, your Majesty," returned the chief cook, bowing respectfully, "and I must say I've heard only good of you. Now that you have unfortunately become my master's prisoners, it will give me pleasure to serve you as well as I am able."

"We thank you, good sir," said Aquareine.

"What have you got to eat?" inquired Trot. "Seems to me I'm hollow way down to my toes—my tail, I mean—and it'll take a lot to fill me up. We haven't eaten a morsel since breakfast, you know."

"I think I shall be able to give you almost anything you would like," said the cook. "Zog is a wonderful magician and can procure anything that exists with no more effort than a wiggle of his thumb. But some eatables, you know, are hard to serve under water, because they get so damp that they are soon ruined."

"Ah, it is different with the mermaids," said Princess Clia.

"Yes, all your things are kept dry because they are surrounded by air. I've heard how the mermaids live. But here it is different."

"Take this ring," said the Queen, handing the chief cook a circlet which she drew from her finger. "While it is in your possession, the food you prepare will not get wet, or even moist."

"I thank your Majesty," returned the cook, taking

the ring. "My name is Tom Atto, and I'll do my best to please you. How would you like for luncheon some oysters on the half-shell, clam broth, shrimp salad, broiled turtle steak and watermelon?"

"That will do very nicely," answered the Queen.

"Do watermelons grow in the sea?" asked Trot.

"Of course, that is why they are called watermelons," replied Tom Atto. "I think I shall serve you a water ice, in addition to the rest. Water ice is an appropriate sea food."

"Have some watercress with the salad," said Cap'n Bill.

"I'd thought of that," declared the cook. "Doesn't my bill of fare make your mouths water?"

"Hurry up and get it ready," suggested Trot.

Tom Atto at once bowed and retired, and when they were done, Cap'n Bill said to the queen, "Do you think, ma'am, we can manage to escape from Zog and his castle?"

"I hope we shall find a way," replied Aquareine. "The evil powers of magic which Zog controls may not prove to be as strong as the fairy powers I possess, but of course I cannot be positive until I discover what this wicked magician is able to do."

Princess Clia was looking out of one of the windows. "I think I can see an opening far up in the top of the dome," she said. They all hastened to the windows to look, and although Trot and Cap'n Bill could see nothing but a solid dome above the castle —perhaps because it was so far away from them— the sharp eyes of Aquareine were not to be deceived.

"Yes," she announced, "there is surely an

opening in the center of the great dome. A little thought must convince us that such an opening is bound to exist, for otherwise the water confined within the dome would not be fresh or clear."

"Then if we could escape from this castle, we could swim up to the hole in the dome and get free!" exclaimed Trot.

"Why, Zog has probably ordered the opening well guarded, as he has all the other outlets," responded the Queen. "Yet it may be worth while for us to make the attempt to get back into the broad ocean this way. The night would be the best time, when all are asleep, and surely it will be quicker to reach the ocean through this hole in the roof than by means of the long, winding passages by which we entered."

"But we will have to break out of the castle in some way," observed Cap'n Bill.

"That will not be difficult," answered Aquareine. "It will be no trouble for me to shatter one of these panes of glass, allowing us to pass out and swim straight up to the top of the dome."

"Let's do it now!" said Trot eagerly.

"No, my dear, we must wait for a good opportunity when we are not watched closely. We do not wish the terrible Zog to thwart our plan," answered the Queen gently.

Presently two sailor boys entered bearing trays of food, which they placed upon a large table. They were cheery-faced young fellows with gills at their throats, but had laughing eyes, and Trot was astonished not to find any of the slaves of Zog weeping or miserable. Instead, they were as jolly and good-natured as could be and seemed to like their life under the water. Cap'n Bill asked one of the boys how many slaves were in the castle, and the youth replied that he would try to count them and let him know.

Tom Atto had, they found, prepared for them an excellent meal, and they ate heartily because they were really hungry. After luncheon Cap'n Bill smoked his pipe contentedly, and they renewed their conversation, planning various ways to outwit Zog and make their escape. While thus engaged, the gong at the door sounded and Sacho entered.

"My diabolical master commands you to attend him," said the boy.

"When?" asked Aquareine.

"At once, your Majesty."

"Very well, we will follow you," she said. So they swam down the corridors following Sacho until they again reached the golden-domed room they had formerly visited. Here sat Zog just as they had left him, seemingly, but when his prisoners entered, the magician arose and stood upon his cloven feet and then silently walked to a curtained archway.

Sacho commanded the prisoners to follow, and beyond the archway they found a vast chamber that occupied the center of the castle and was as big as a ballroom. Zog, who seemed to walk with much difficulty because his ungainly body swayed back and forth, did not go far beyond the arched entrance. A golden throne was set nearby, and in this the monster seated himself. At one side of the throne stood a group of slaves. They were men, women and children. All had broad gold bands clasped around their ankles as a badge of servitude, and at each throat were the fish's gills that enabled them to breathe and live under water. Yet every face was smiling and serene, even in the presence of their dread master. In parts of the big hall were groups of other slaves.

Sacho ranged the prisoners in a circle before Zog's throne, and slowly the magician turned his eyes, glowing like live coals, upon the four. "Captives," said he, speaking in his clear, sweet voice, "in our first interview you defied me, and both the mermaid queen and the princess declared they could not die. But if that is a true statement, as I have yet to discover, there are various ways to make you miserable and unhappy, and this I propose to do in order to amuse myself at your expense. You have been brought here to undergo the first trial of strength between us." None of the prisoners replied to this speech, so Zog turned to one of his slaves and said, "Rivivi, bring in the Yell-Maker."

Rivivi was a big fellow, brown of skin and with flashing, black eyes. He bowed to his master and left the room by an archway covered with heavy draperies. The next moment these curtains were violently pushed aside, and a dreadful sea creature swam into the hall. It had a body much like that of a crab, only more round and of a jet-black color. Its eyes were bright yellow balls set on the ends of two horns that stuck out of its head. They were cruel-looking eyes, too, and seemed able to see every person in the room at the same time. The legs of the Yell-Maker, however, were the most curious part of the creature. There were six of them, slender and black as coal, and each extended twelve to fifteen feet from its body when stretched out in a straight line. They were hinged in several places so they could be folded up or extended at will. At the ends of these thin legs were immense claws shaped like those of a lobster, and they were real "nippers" of a most dangerous sort.

The prisoners knew, as soon as they saw the awful claws, why the thing was called the "Yell-Maker," and Trot gave a little shiver and crept closer to Cap'n Bill. Zog looked with approval upon the creature he had summoned and said to it, "I give you four victims, the four people with fish's tails. Let me hear how loud they can yell."

The Yell-Maker uttered a grunt of pleasure and in a flash stretched out one of its long legs toward the queen's nose, where its powerful claws came together with a loud noise. Aquareine did not stir; she only smiled. Both Zog and the creature that had attacked her seemed much surprised to find she was unhurt. "Again!" cried Zog, and again the Yell-Maker's claw shot out and tried to pinch the queen's pretty ear. But the magic of the fairy mermaid was proof against this sea-rascal's strength and swiftness, nor could he touch any part of Aquareine, although he tried again and again, roaring with anger like a mad bull.

Trot began to enjoy this performance, and as her merry, childish laughter rang out, the Yell-Maker turned furiously upon the little girl, two of the dreadful claws trying to nip her at the same time.

She had no chance to cry out or jump backward, yet she remained unharmed. For the Fairy Circle of Queen Aquareine kept her safe. Now Cap'n Bill was attacked, and Princess Clia as well. The half-dozen slender legs darted in every direction like sword thrusts to reach their victims, and the cruel claws snapped so rapidly that the sound was like the rattling of castanets. But the four prisoners regarded their enemy with smiling composure, and no yell greeted the Yell-Maker's efforts.

"Enough!" said Zog, softly and sweetly. "You may retire, my poor Yell-Maker, for with these people you are powerless."

The creature paused and rolled its yellow eyes. "May I nip just one of the slaves, oh Zog?" it asked pleadingly. "I hate to leave without pleasing your ears with a single yell."

"Let my slaves alone," was Zog's answer. "They are here to serve me and must not be injured. Go, feeble one."

"Not so!" cried the Queen. "It is a shame, Zog, that such an evil thing should exist in our fair sea." With this, she drew her fairy wand from a fold of her gown and waved it toward the creature. At once the Yell-Maker sank down unconscious upon the floor; its legs fell apart in many pieces, the claws tumbling in a heap beside the body. Then all grew withered and lost shape, becoming a pulpy mass, like gelatin. A few moments later the creature had melted away to nothing at all, forever disappearing from the ocean where it had caused so much horror and pain.

Zog watched this destruction with surprising

patience. When it was all over, he nodded his head and smiled, and Trot noticed that whenever Zog smiled, his slaves lost their jolly looks and began to tremble. "That is very pretty magic, Aquareine," said the monster. "I myself learned the trick several thousand years ago, so it does not astonish me. Have you fairies nothing that is new to show me?"

"We desire only to protect ourselves," replied the Queen with dignity.

"Then I will give you a chance to do so," said Zog. As he spoke, the great marble blocks in the ceiling of the room directly over the heads of the captives gave way and came crashing down upon them. Many tons of weight were in these marble blocks, and the magician had planned to crush his victims where they stood. But the four were still unharmed. The marble, being unable to touch them, was diverted from its course, and when the roar of the great crash had died away, Zog saw his intended victims standing quietly in their places and smiling scornfully at his weak attempts to destroy them.

CHAPTER 16
THE TOP OF THE GREAT DOME

Cap'n Bill's heart was beating pretty vast, but he did not let Zog know that. Trot was so sure of the protection of the fairy mermaids that she would not allow herself to become frightened. Aquareine and Clia were as calm as if nothing had happened.

"Please excuse this little interruption," said Zog. "I knew very well the marble blocks would not hurt you. But the play is over for a time. You may now retire to your rooms, and when I again invite you to my presence, I shall have found some better ways to entertain you."

Without reply to this threat, they turned and followed Sacho from the hall, and the boy led them straight back to their own rooms.

"Zog is making a great mistake," said Sacho with a laugh. "He has no time for vengeance, but the great magician does not know that."

"What is he trying to do, anyway?" asked Trot.

"He does not tell me all his secrets, but I've an idea he wants to kill you," replied Sacho. "How absurd it is to be plotting such a thing when he might spend his time in laughing and being jolly! Isn't it, now?"

"Zog is a wicked, wicked creature!" exclaimed Trot.

"But he had his good points," replied Sacho cheerfully. "There is no one about in the world so bad that there is nothing good about him."

"I'm not so sure of that," said Cap'n Bill. "What are Zog's good points?"

"All his slaves were saved from drowning, and he is kind to them," said Sacho.

"That is merely the kindness of selfishness," said Aquareine. "Tell me, my lad, is the opening in the great dome outside guarded?"

"Yes indeed," was the reply. "You cannot hope to escape in that way, for the prince of the sea devils, who is the largest and fiercest of his race, lies crouched over the opening night and day, and none can pass his network of curling legs."

"Is there no avenue that is not guarded?" continued Aquareine.

"None at all, your Majesty. Zog is always careful to be well guarded, for he fears the approach of an enemy. What this enemy can be to terrify the great magician I do not know, but Zog is always afraid and never leaves an entrance unguarded. Besides, it is an enchanted castle, you know, and none in the ocean can see it unless Zog

273

wishes him to. So it will be very hard for his enemy
to find him."

"We wish to escape," said Clia. "Will you help us,
Sacho?"

"In any way I can," replied the boy.

"If we succeed, we will take you with us," continued the Princess.

But Sacho shook his head and laughed. "I would
indeed like to see you escape Zog's vengeance," said
he, "for vengeance is wrong, and you are too pretty
and too good to be destroyed. But I am happy here
and have no wish to go away, having no other home
or friends other than my fellow slaves."

Then he left them, and when they were again
alone, Aquareine said, "We were able to escape Zog's
attacks today, but I am quite sure he will plan more
powerful ways to destroy us. He has shown that he
knows some clever magic, and perhaps I shall not be
able to foil it. So it will be well for us to escape
tonight if possible."

"Can you fight and conquer the big sea devil up
in the dome?" asked Trot.

The queen was thoughtful, and did not reply to
this question at once. But Cap'n Bill said uneasily, "I
can't abide them devil critters, an' I hopes, for my
part, we won't be called on to tackle 'em. You see,
Trot, we're in consider'ble of a bad mess, an' if we
ever live to tell the tale—"

"Why not, Cap'n?" asked the child. "We're safe
enough so far. Can't you trust our good friend, the
queen?"

"She don't seem plumb sure o' things herself,"

remarked the sailor. "The mermaids is all right an' friendly, mate, but this 'ere magic maker, ol' Zog, is a bad one, out 'n' out, an' means to kill us if he can."

"But he can't!" cried Trot bravely.

"I hope you're right, dear. I wouldn't want to bet on Zog's chances jes' yet, an' at the same time it would be riskin' money to bet on our chances. Seems to me it's a case of luck which wins."

"Don't worry, friend," said the Queen. "I have a plan to save us. Let us wait patiently until nightfall." They waited in the Rose Chamber a long time, talking earnestly together, but the brilliant light that flooded both the room and the great dome outside did not fade in the least. After several hours had passed away, the gong sounded and Tom Atto again appeared, followed by four slaves bearing many golden dishes upon silver trays. The friendly cook had prepared a fine dinner, and they were all glad to find that, whatever Zog intended to do to them, he had no intention of starving them. Perhaps the magician realized that Aquareine's fairy powers, if put to the test, would be able to provide food for her companions, but whatever his object may have been, their enemy had given them splendid rooms and plenty to eat.

"Isn't it nearly nighttime?" asked the Queen as Tom Atto spread the table with a cloth of woven seaweed and directed his men to place the dishes upon it.

"Night!" he exclaimed as if surprised. "There is no night here."

"Doesn't it ever get dark?" inquired Trot.

"Never. We know nothing of the passage of time or of day or night. The light always shines just as you see it now, and we sleep whenever we are tired and rise again as soon as we are rested."

"What causes the light?" Princess Clia asked.

"It's magic, your Highness," said the cook solemnly. "It's one of the curious things Zog is able to do. But you must remember all this place is a big cave in which the castle stands, so the light is never seen by anyone except those who live here."

"But why does Zog keep his light going all the time?" asked the Queen.

"I suppose it is because he himself never sleeps," replied Tom Atto. "They say the master hasn't slept for hundreds of years, not since Anko, the sea serpent, defeated him and drove him into this place."

They asked no more questions and began to eat their dinner in silence. Before long, Cap'n Joe came in to visit his brother and took a seat at the table with the prisoners. He proved a jolly fellow, and when he and Cap'n Bill talked about their boyhood days, the stories were so funny that everybody laughed and for a time forgot their worries.

When dinner was over, however, and Cap'n Joe had gone back to his work of sewing on buttons and the servants had carried away the dishes, the prisoners remembered their troubles and the fate that awaited them. "I am much disappointed," said the Queen, "to find there is no night here and that Zog never sleeps. It will make our escape more difficult. Yet we must make the attempt, and as we are tired and a great struggle is before us, it will be best for us to sleep and refresh ourselves."

They agreed to this, for the day had been long and adventurous, so Cap'n Bill kissed Trot and went in to the Peony Room, where he lay down upon his spongy couch and fell fast asleep. The mermaids and Trot followed this example, and I think none of them was much worried, after all, because they quickly sank into peaceful slumber and forgot all the dangers that threatened them.

CHAPTER 17

THE QUEEN'S GOLDEN SWORD

"Goodness me!" exclaimed Trot, raising herself by a flirt of her pink-scaled tail and a wave of her fins, "isn't it dreadful hot here?"

The mermaids had risen at the same time, and Cap'n Bill came swimming in from the Peony Room in time to hear the little girl's speech.

"Hot!" echoed the sailor. "Why, I feel like the inside of a steam engine!"

The perspiration was rolling down his round, red face, and he took out his handkerchief and carefully wiped it away, waving his fish tail gently at the same time.

"What we need most in this room," said he, "is a fan."

"What's the trouble, do you s'pose?" inquired Trot.

"It is another trick of the monster Zog," answered the Queen calmly. "He has made the water in our rooms boiling hot, and if it could touch us, we would be well cooked by this time. Even as it is, we are all made uncomfortable by breathing the heated air."

"What shall we do, ma'am?" the sailor man asked with a groan. "I expected to get into hot water afore we've done with this foolishness, but I don't like the feel o' bein' parboiled, jes' the same."

The queen was waving her fairy wand and paid no attention to Cap'n Bill's moans. Already the water felt cooler, and they began to breathe more easily. In a few moments more, the heat had passed from the surrounding water altogether, and all danger from this source was over.

"This is better," said Trot gratefully.

"Do you care to sleep again?" asked the Queen.

"No, I'm wide awake now," answered the child.

"I'm afraid if I goes to sleep ag'in, I'll wake up a pot roast," said Cap'n Bill.

"Let us consider ways to escape," suggested Clia. "It seems useless for us to remain here quietly until Zog discovers a way to destroy us."

"But we must not blunder," added Aquareine cautiously. "To fail in our attempt would be to acknowledge Zog's superior power, so we must think well upon our plan before we begin to carry it out. What do you advise, sir?" she asked, turning to Cap'n Bill.

"My opinion, ma'am, is that the only way for us to escape is to get out o' here," was the sailor's vague answer. "How to do it is your business, seein' as I ain't no fairy myself," either in looks or in eddication."

The queen smiled and said to Trot, "What is your opinion, my dear?"

"I think we might swim out the same way we came in," answered the child. "If we could get Sacho to lead us back through the maze, we would follow that long tunnel to the open ocean, and—"

"And there would be the sea devils waitin' for us," added Cap'n Bill with a shake of his bald head. "They'd drive us back inter the tunnel like they did the first time, Trot. It won't do, mate, it won't do."

"Have you a suggestion, Clia?" inquired the Queen.

"I have thought of an undertaking," replied the pretty princess, "but it is a bold plan, your Majesty, and you may not care to risk it."

"Let us hear it, anyway," said Aquareine encouragingly.

"It is to destroy Zog himself and put him out of the world forever. Then we would be free to go home whenever we pleased."

"Can you suggest a way to destroy Zog?" asked Aquareine.

"No, your Majesty," Clia answered. "I must leave the way for you to determine."

"In the old days," said the Queen thoughtfully, "the mighty King Anko could not destroy this monster. He succeeded in defeating Zog and drove him into this great cavern, but even Anko could not destroy him."

"I have heard the sea serpent explain that it was

because he could not reach the magician," returned Clia. "If King Anko could have seized Zog in his coils, he would have made an end of the wicked monster quickly. Zog knows this, and that is why he does not venture forth from his retreat. Anko is the enemy he constantly dreads. But with you, my queen, the case is different. You may easily reach Zog, and the only question is whether your power is sufficient to destroy him."

For a while Aquareine remained silent. "I am not sure of my power over him," she said at last, "and for that reason I hesitate to attack him personally. His slaves and his allies, the sea devils, I can easily conquer, so I prefer to find a way to overcome the guards at the entrances rather than to encounter their terrible master. But even the guards have been given strength and power by the magician, as we have already discovered, so I must procure a weapon with which to fight them."

"A weapon, ma'am?" said Cap'n Bill, and then he took a jackknife from his coat pocket and opened the big blade, afterward handing it to the queen. "That ain't a bad weapon," he announced.

"But it is useless in this case," she replied, smiling at the old sailor's earnestness. "For my purpose I must have a golden sword."

"Well, there's plenty of gold around this castle," said Trot, looking around her. "Even in this room there's enough to make a hundred golden swords."

"But we can't melt or forge gold under water, mate," the Cap'n said.

"Why not? Don't you s'pose all these gold roses

and things were made under water?" asked the little girl.

"Like enough," remarked the sailor, "but I don't see how."

Just then the gong at the door sounded, and the boy Sacho came in smiling and cheerful as ever. He said Zog had sent him to inquire after their health and happiness. "You may tell him that his water became a trifle too warm, so we cooled it," replied the Queen. Then they told Sacho how the boiling water had made them uncomfortable while they slept.

Sacho whistled a little tune and seemed thoughtful. "Zog is foolish," said he. "How often have I told him that vengeance is a waste of time. He is worried to know how to destroy you, and that is wasting more time. You are worried for fear he will injure you, and so you also are wasting time. My, my! What a waste of time is going on in this castle!"

"Seems to me that we have so much time it doesn't matter," said Trot. "What's time for, anyhow?"

"Time is given us to be happy, and for no other reason," replied the boy soberly. "When we waste time, we waste happiness. But there is no time for preaching, so I'll go."

"Please wait a moment, Sacho," said the Queen.

"Can I do anything to make you happy?" he asked, smiling again.

"Yes," answered Aquareine. "We are curious to know who does all this beautiful gold work and ornamentation."

"Some of the slaves here are goldsmiths, having

been taught by Zog to forge and work metal under water," explained Sacho. "In parts of the ocean lie many rocks filled with veins of pure gold and golden nuggets, and we get large supplies from sunken ships as well. There is no lack of gold here, but it is not as precious as it is upon the earth because here we have no need of money."

"We would like to see the goldsmiths at work," announced the Queen.

The boy hesitated a moment. Then he said, "I will take you to their room, where you may watch them for a time. I will not ask Zog's permission to do this, for he might refuse. But my orders were to allow you the liberty of the castle, and so I will let you see the goldsmiths' shop."

"Thank you," replied Aquareine quietly, and then the four followed Sacho along various corridors until they came to a large room where a dozen men were busily at work. Lying here and there were heaps of virgin gold, some in its natural state and some already fashioned into ornaments and furniture of various sorts. Each man worked at a bench where there was a curious iron furnace in which glowed a vivid, white light. Although this workshop was all under water and the workmen were all obliged to breathe as fishes do, the furnaces glowed so hot that the water touching them was turned into steam. Gold or other metal held over a furnace quickly softened or melted, when it could be forged or molded into any shape desired.

"The furnaces are electric," explained Sacho, "and heat as well under water as they would in the open air. Let me introduce you to the foreman, who will tell you of his work better than I can."

The foreman was a slave named Agga-Groo, who was lean and lank and had an expression more surly and unhappy than any slave they had yet seen. Yet he seemed willing to leave his work and explain to the visitors how he made so many beautiful things out of gold, for he took much pride in this labor and knew its artistic worth. Moreover, since he had been in Zog's castle these were the first strangers to enter his workshop, so he welcomed them in his own gruff way.

The queen asked him if he was happy, and he shook his head and replied, "It isn't like Calcutta, where I used to work in gold before I was wrecked at sea and nearly drowned. Zog rescued me and brought me here a slave. It is a stupid life we lead, doing the same things over and over every day, but perhaps it is better than being dead. I'm not sure. The only pleasure I get in life is in creating pretty things out of gold."

"Could you forge me a golden sword?" asked the Queen, smiling sweetly upon the goldsmith.

"I could, madam, but I won't unless Zog orders me to do it."

"Do you like Zog better than you do me?" inquired Aquareine.

"No," was the answer. "I hate Zog."

"Then won't you make the sword to please me and to show your skill?" pleaded the pretty mermaid.

"I'm afraid of my master. He might not like it," the man replied.

"But he will never know," said Princess Clia.

"You cannot say what Zog knows or what he doesn't know," growled the man. "I can't take chances of offending Zog, for I must live with him always as a slave." With this he turned away and resumed his work, hammering the leaf of a golden ship.

Cap'n Bill had listened carefully to this conversation, and being a wise old sailor in his way, he thought he understood the nature of old Agga-Groo better than the mermaids did. So he went close to the goldsmith, and feeling in the pockets of his coat drew out a silver compass shaped like a watch. "I'll give you this if you'll make the queen the golden sword," he said.

Agga-Groo looked at the compass with interest and tested its power of pointing north. Then he shook his head and handed it back to Cap'n Bill. The sailor dived into his pocket again and pulled out a pair of scissors, which he placed beside the compass on the palm of his big hand. "You may have them both," he said.

Agga-Groo hesitated, for he wanted the scissors badly, but finally he shook his head again. Cap'n Bill added a piece of cord, an iron thimble, some fish-hooks, four buttons and a safety pin, but still the goldsmith would not be tempted. So with a sigh the sailor brought out his fine, big jackknife, and at sight of this Agga-Groo's eyes began to sparkle. Steel was not to be had at the bottom of the sea, although gold was so plentiful. "All right, friend," he said. "Give me that lot of trinkets and I'll make you a pretty gold sword. But it won't be any good except to look at, for our gold is so pure that it is very soft."

"Never mind that," replied Cap'n Bill. "All we want is the sword."

The goldsmith set to work at once, and so skillful was he that in a few minutes he had forged a fine sword of yellow gold with an ornamental handle. The shape was graceful and the blade keen and slender. It was evident to them all that the golden sword would not stand hard use, for the edge of the blade would nick and curl like lead, but the queen was delighted with the prize and took it eagerly in her hand.

Just then Sacho returned to say that they must go back to their rooms, and after thanking the goldsmith, who was so busy examining his newly acquired treasure that he made no response, they joyfully followed the boy back to the Rose Chamber. Sacho told them that he had just come from Zog, who was still wasting time in plotting vengeance. "You must be careful," he advised them, "for my cruel master intends to stop you from living, and he may succeed. Don't be unhappy, but be careful. Zog is angry because you escaped his Yell-Maker and the falling stones and the hot water. While he is angry he is wasting time, but that will not help you. Take care not to waste any time yourselves."

"Do you know what Zog intends to do to us next?" asked Princess Clia.

"No," said Sacho, "but it is reasonable to guess

that, being evil, he intends evil. He never intends to do good, I assure you." Then the boy went away.

"I am no longer afraid," declared the Mermaid Queen when they were alone. "When I have bestowed certain fairy powers upon this golden sword, it will fight its way against any who dare oppose us, and even Zog himself will not care to face so powerful a weapon. I am now able to promise you that we shall make our escape."

"Good!" cried Trot joyfully. "Shall we start now?"

"Not yet, my dear. It will take me a little while to charm this golden blade so that it will obey my commands and do my work. There is no need of undue haste, so I propose we all sleep for a time and obtain what rest we can. We must be fresh and ready for our great adventure."

As their former nap had been interrupted, they readily agreed to Aquareine's proposal and at once went to their couches and composed themselves to slumber. When they were asleep, the fairy mermaid charmed her golden sword and then she also lay down to rest herself.

CHAPTER 18
A DASH FOR LIBERTY

Trot dreamed that she was at home in her own bed, but the night seemed chilly and she wanted to draw the coverlet up to her chin. She was not wide awake, but realized that she was cold and unable to move her arms to cover herself up. She tried, but could not stir. Then she roused herself a little more and tried again. Yes, it was cold, very cold! Really, she MUST do something to get warm, she thought. She opened her eyes and stared at a great wall of ice in front of her.

She was awake now, and frightened, too. But she could not move because the ice was all around her. She was frozen inside of it, and the air space around her was not big enough to allow her to turn over.

At once the little girl realized what had happened. Their wicked enemy Zog had by his magic art frozen all the water in their room while they slept, and now they were all imprisoned and helpless. Trot and Cap'n Bill were sure to freeze to death in a short time, for only a tiny air space remained between their bodies and the ice, and this air was like that of a winter day when the thermometer is below zero.

Across the room Trot could see the mermaid queen lying on her couch, for the solid ice was clear as crystal. Aquareine was imprisoned just as Trot was, and although she held her fairy wand in one hand and the golden sword in the other, she seemed unable to move either of them, and the girl remembered that the queen always waved her magic wand to accomplish anything. Princess Clia's couch was behind that of Trot, so the child could not see her, and Cap'n Bill was in his own room, probably frozen fast in the ice as the others were.

The terrible Zog has surely been very clever in this last attempt to destroy them. Trot thought it all over, and she decided that inasmuch as the queen was unable to wave her fairy wand, she could do nothing to release herself or her friends.

But in this the girl was mistaken. The fairy mermaid was even now at work trying to save them, and in a few minutes Trot was astonished and delighted to see the queen rise from her couch. She could not go far from it at first, but the ice was melting rapidly all around her so that gradually Aquareine approached the place where the child lay. Trot could hear the mermaid's voice sounding through the ice as if from afar off, but it grew more distinct until she could make out that the queen was saying, "Courage, friends! Do not despair, for soon you will be free."

Before very long the ice between Trot and the queen had melted away entirely, and with a cry of joy the little girl flopped her pink tail and swam to the side of her deliverer.

"Are you very cold?" asked Aquareine.

"N-not v-v-very!" replied Trot, but her teeth chattered and she was still shivering.

"The water will be warm in a few minutes," said the Queen. "But now I must melt the rest of the ice and liberate Clia."

This she did in an astonishingly brief time, and the pretty princess, being herself a fairy, had not been at all affected by the cold surrounding her.

They now swam to the door of Cap'n Bill's room and found the Peony Chamber a solid block of ice. The queen worked her magic power as hard as she could, and the ice flowed and melted quickly before her fairy wand. Yet when they reached the old sailor, he was almost frozen stiff, and Trot and Clia had to rub his hands and nose and ears very briskly to warm him up and bring him back to life.

Cap'n Bill was pretty tough, and he came around, in time, and opened his eyes and sneezed and asked if the blizzard was over. So the queen waved her wand over his head a few times to restore him to his natural condition of warmth, and soon the old sailor became quite comfortable and was able to understand all about the strange adventure from which he had so marvelously escaped.

"I've made up my mind to one thing, Trot," he said confidentially. "If ever I get out o' this mess I'm in, I won't be an Arctic explorer, whatever else happens. Shivers an' shakes ain't to my likin', an' this ice business ain't what it's sometimes cracked up to be. To be friz once is enough fer anybody, an' if I was a gal like you, I wouldn't even wear frizzes on my hair."

"You haven't any hair, Cap'n Bill," answered Trot, "so you needn't worry."

The queen and Clia had been talking together very earnestly. They now approached their earth friends, and Aquareine said:

"We have decided not to remain in this castle any longer. Zog's cruel designs upon our lives and happiness are becoming too dangerous for us to endure. The golden sword now bears a fairy charm, and by its aid I will cut a way through our enemies. Are you ready and willing to follow me?"

"Of course we are!" cried Trot.

"It don't seem 'zactly right to ask a lady to do the fightin'," remarked Cap'n Bill, "but magic ain't my strong p'int, and it seems to be yours, ma'am. So swim ahead, and we'll wiggle the same way you do, an' try to wiggle out of our troubles."

"If I chance to fail," said the Queen, "try not to blame me. I will do all in my power to provide for our escape, and I am willing to risk everything, because I well know that to remain here will mean to perish in the end."

"That's all right," said Trot with fine courage. "Let's have it over with."

"Then we will leave here at once," said Aquareine.

She approached the window of the room and

with one blow of her golden sword shattered the thick pane of glass. The opening thus made was large enough for them to swim through if they were careful not to scrape against the broken points of glass. The queen went first, followed by Trot and Cap'n Bill, with Clia last of all.

And now they were in the vast dome in which the castle and gardens of Zog had been built. Around them was a clear stretch of water, and far above— full half a mile distant—was the opening in the roof guarded by the prince of the sea devils. The mermaid queen had determined to attack this monster. If she succeeded in destroying it with her golden sword, the little band of fugitives might then swim through the opening into the clear waters of the ocean. Although this prince of the sea devils was said to be big and wise and mighty, there was but one of him to fight; whereas, if they attempted to escape through any of the passages, they must encounter scores of such enemies.

"Swim straight for the opening in the dome!" cried Aquareine, and in answer to the command, the four whisked their glittering tails, waved their fins, and shot away through the water at full speed, their course slanting upward toward the top of the dome.

CHAPTER 19

KING ANKO TO THE RESCUE

The great magician Zog never slept. He was always watchful and alert. Some strange power warned him that his prisoners were about to escape.

Scarcely had the four left the castle by the broken window when the monster stepped from a doorway below and saw them. Instantly he blew upon a golden whistle, and at the summons a band of wolf-fish appeared and dashed after the prisoners. These creatures swam so swiftly that soon they were between the fugitives and the dome, and then they turned and with wicked eyes and sharp fangs began a fierce attack upon the mermaids and the earth dwellers.

Trot was a little frightened at the evil looks of the sea wolves, whose heads were enormous, and whose jaws contained rows of curved and pointed teeth. But Aquareine advanced upon them with her golden sword, and every touch of the charmed weapon instantly killed an enemy, so that one by one the wolf-fish rolled over upon their backs and sank helplessly downward through the water, leaving the prisoners free to continue their way toward the opening in the dome.

Zog witnessed the destruction of his wolves and uttered a loud laugh that was terrible to hear. Then the dread monster determined to arrest the fugitives himself, and in order to do this he was forced to discover himself in all the horror of his awful form, a form he was so ashamed of and loathed so greatly that he always strove to keep it concealed, even from his own view. But it was important that his prisoners should not escape. Hastily casting off the folds of the robe that enveloped him, Zog allowed his body to uncoil and shoot upward through the water in swift pursuit of his victims. His cloven hoofs, upon which he usually walked, being now useless, were drawn up under him, while coil after coil of his eel-like body wriggled away like a serpent. At his shoulders two broad, feathery wings expanded, and these enabled the monster to cleave his way through the water with terrific force.

Zog was part man, part beast, part fish, part fowl, and part reptile. His undulating body was broad and thin and like the body of an eel. It was as repulsive as one could well imagine, and no wonder Zog hated it and kept it covered with his robe. Now, with his horned head and its glowing eyes thrust forward, wings flapping from his shoulders and his eely body—ending in a fish's tail—wriggling far behind him, this strange and evil creature was a thing of terror even to the sea dwellers, who were accustomed to remarkable sights.

The mermaids, the sailor and the child, one after another looking back as they swam toward liberty and safety, saw the monster coming and shuddered with uncontrollable fear. They were drawing nearer to the dome by this time, yet it was still some distance away. The four redoubled their speed, darting through the water with the swiftness of skyrockets. But fast as they swam, Zog swam faster, and the good queen's heart began to throb as she realized she would be forced to fight her loathesome foe.

Presently Zog's long body was circling around them like a whirlwind, lashing the water into foam and gradually drawing nearer and nearer to his victims. His eyes were no longer glowing coals, they were balls of flame, and as he circled around them, he laughed aloud that horrible laugh which was far more terrifying than any cry of rage could be. The queen struck out with her golden sword, but Zog wrapped a coil of his thin body around it and, wrestling it from her hand, crushed the weapon into a shapeless mass. Then Aquareine waved her fairy wand, but in a flash the monster sent it flying away through the water.

Cap'n Bill now decided that they were lost. He drew Trot closer to his side and placed one arm around her. "I can't save you, dear little mate," he said sadly, "but we've lived a long time together, an' now we'll die together. I knew, Trot, when first we sawr them mermaids, as we'd—we'd—"

"Never live to tell the tale," said the child. "But never mind, Cap'n Bill, we've done the best we could, and we've had a fine time."

"Forgive me! Oh, forgive me!" cried Aquareine despairingly. "I tried to save you, my poor friends, but—"

"What's that?" exclaimed the Princess, pointing upward. They all looked past Zog's whirling body, which was slowly enveloping them in its folds, toward the round opening in the dome. A dark object had appeared there, sliding downward like a huge rope and descending toward them with lightning rapidly. They gave a great gasp as they recognized the countenance of King Anko, the sea serpent, its gray hair and whiskers bristling like those of an angry cat, and the usually mild blue eyes glowing with a ferocity even more terrifying than the orbs of Zog.

The magician gave a shrill scream at sight of his dreaded enemy, and abandoning his intended victims, Zog made a quick dash to escape. But nothing in the sea could equal the strength and quickness of King Anko when he was roused. In a flash the sea serpent had caught Zog fast in his coils, and his mighty body swept round the monster and imprisoned him tightly. The four, so suddenly rescued, swam away to a safer distance from the struggle, and then they turned to watch the encounter between the two great opposing powers of the ocean's depths. Yet there was no desperate fight to observe, for the combatants were unequal. The end came before they were aware of it. Zog had been taken by surprise, and his great fear of Anko destroyed all of his magic power. When the sea serpent slowly released those awful coils, a mass of jelly-like pulp floated downward through the water with no remnant of life remaining in it, no form to show it had once been Zog, the Magician.

Then Anko shook his body that the water might cleanse it, and advanced his head toward the group of four whom he had so opportunely rescued. "It is all over, friends," said he in his gentle tones, while a mild expression once more reigned on his comical features. "You may go home at any time you please, for the way through the dome will be open as soon as I get my own body through it."

Indeed, so amazing was the length of the great sea serpent that only a part of him had descended through the hole into the dome. Without waiting for the thanks of those he had rescued, he swiftly retreated to the ocean above, and with grateful hearts they followed him, glad to leave the cavern where they had endured so much anxiety and danger.

CHAPTER 20

THE HOME OF THE OCEAN MONARCH

Trot sobbed quietly with her head on Cap'n Bill's shoulder. She had been a brave little girl during the trying times they had experienced and never once had she given way to tears, however desperate their fate had seemed to be. But now that the one enemy in all the sea to be dreaded was utterly destroyed and all dangers were past, the reaction was so great that she could not help having "just one good cry," as she naively expressed it.

Cap'n Bill was a big sailor man hardened by age and many adventures, but even he felt a "Lump in his throat" that he could not swallow, try as hard as he might. Cap'n Bill was glad. He was mostly glad on Trot's account, for he loved his sweet, childish companion very dearly, and did not want any harm to befall her.

They were now in the wide, open sea, with liberty to go wherever they wished, and if Cap'n Bill could have "had his way," he would have gone straight home and carried Trot to her mother. But the mermaids must be considered. Aquareine and Clia had been true and faithful friends to their earth guests while dangers were threatening, and it would not be very gracious to leave them at once. More-over, King Anko was now with them, his big head keeping pace with the mermaids as they swam, and this mighty preserver had a distinct claim upon Trot and Cap'n Bill. The sailor felt that it would not be polite to ask to go home so soon.

"If you people had come to visit me as I invited you to do," said the Sea Serpent, "all this bother and trouble would have been saved. I had my palace put in order to receive the earth dwellers and sat in my den waiting patiently to receive you. Yet you never came at all."

"That reminds me," said Trot, drying her eyes, "you never told us about that third pain you once had."

"Finally," continued Anko, "I sent to inquire as to what had become of you, and Merla said you had been gone from the palace a long time and she was getting anxious about you. Then I made inquiries. Everyone in the sea loves to serve me—except those sea devils and their cousins, the octopi—and it wasn't long before I heard you had been captured by Zog."

"Was the third pain as bad as the other two?" asked Trot.

"Naturally this news disturbed me and made me unhappy," said Anko, "for I well knew, my

Aquareine, that the magician's evil powers were greater than your own fairy accomplishments. But I had never been able to find Zog's enchanted castle, and so I was at a loss to know how to save you from your dreadful fate. After I had wasted a good deal of time thinking it over, I decided that if the sea devils were slaves of Zog, the prince of the sea devils must know where the enchanted castle was located.

"I knew this prince and where to find him, for he always lay on a hollow rock on the bottom of the sea and never moved from that position. His people brought food to him and took his commands. So I had no trouble in finding this evil prince, and I went to him and asked the way to Zog's castle. Of course, he would not tell me. He was even cross and disrespectful, just as I had expected him to be, so I allowed myself to become angry and killed him, thinking he was much better dead than alive. But after the sea devil was destroyed, what was my surprise to find that all these years he had been lying over a round hole in the rock and covering it with his scarlet body!

"A light shone through this hole, so I thrust my head in and found a great domed cave underneath with a splendid silver castle built at the bottom. You, my friends, were at that moment swimming toward me as fast as you could come, and the monster Zog, my enemy for centuries past, was close behind you. Well, the rest of the story you know. I would be angry with all of you for so carelessly getting captured, had the incident not led to the destruction of the one evil genius in all my ocean. I shall rest easier and be much happier now that Zog is dead. He has defied me for hundreds of years."

"But about that third pain," said Trot. "If you don't tell us now, I'm afraid that I'll forget to ask you."

"If you should happen to forget, just remind me of it," said Anko, "and I'll be sure to tell you."

While Trot was thinking this over, the swimmers drew near to a great, circular palace made all of solid alabaster polished as smooth as ivory. Its roof was a vast dome, for domes seemed to be fashionable in the ocean houses. There were no doors or windows, but instead of these, several round holes appeared in different parts of the dome, some being high up and some low down and some in between. Out of one of these holes, which it just fitted, stretched the long, brown body of the sea serpent. Trot, being astonished at this sight, asked, "Didn't you take all of you when you went to the cavern, Anko?"

"Nearly all, my dear," was the reply, accompanied by a cheerful smile, for Anko was proud of his great length. "But not quite all. Some of me remained, as usual, to keep house while my head was away. But I've been coiling up ever since we started back, and you will soon be able to see every inch of me all together."

Even as he spoke, his head slid into the round hole, and at a signal from Aquareine they all paused outside and waited. Presently there came to them four beautiful winged fishes with faces like doll babies. Their long hair and eyelashes were of a purple color, and their cheeks had rosy spots that looked as if they had been painted upon them. "His Majesty bids you welcome," said one of the doll fishes in a sweet voice. "Be kind enough to enter the royal palace, and our ocean monarch will graciously receive you."

"Seems to me," said Trot to the queen, "these things are putting on airs. Perhaps they don't know we're friends of Anko."

"The king insists on certain formalities when anyone visits him," was Aquareine's reply. "It is right that his dignity should be maintained."

They followed their winged conductors to one of the upper openings, and as they entered it Aquareine said in a clear voice, "May the glory and power of the ocean king continue forever!" Then she touched the palm of her hand to her forehead in token of allegiance, and Clia did the same, so Cap'n Bill and Trot followed suit. The brief ceremony being ended, the child looked curiously around to see what the palace of the mighty Anko was like.

An extensive hall lined with alabaster was before them. In the floor were five of the round holes. Upon the walls were engraved many interesting scenes of ocean life, all chiseled very artistically by the tusks of walruses who, Trot was afterward informed, are greatly skilled in such work. A few handsome rugs of woven sea grasses were spread upon the floor, but otherwise the vast hall was bare of furniture. The doll-faced fishes escorted them to an upper room where a table was set, and here the revelers were invited to refresh themselves. As all four were exceedingly hungry, they welcomed the repast, which was served by an army of lobsters in royal purple aprons and caps.

The meal being finished, they again descended to the hall, which seemed to occupy all the middle of the building. And now their conductors said, "His Majesty is ready to receive you in his den."

They swam downward through one of the round holes in the floor and found themselves in a brilliantly lighted chamber which appeared bigger than all the rest of the palace put together. In the center was the quaint head of King Anko, and around it was spread a great coverlet of purple and gold woven together. This concealed all of his body and stretched from wall to wall of the circular room. "Welcome, friends!" said Anko pleasantly. "How do you like my home?"

"It's very grand," replied Trot.

"Just the place for a sea serpent, seems to me," said Cap'n Bill.

"I'm glad you admire it," said the King. "Perhaps I ought to tell you that from this day you four belong to me."

"How's that?" asked the girl, surprised.

"It is a law of the ocean," declared Anko, "that whoever saves any living creature from violent death owns that creature forever afterward, while life lasts. You will realize how just this law is when you remember that had I not saved you from Zog, you would now be dead. The law was suggested by Captain Kid Glove, when he once visited me."

"Do you mean Captain Kidd?" asked Trot. "Because if you do—"

"Give him his full name," said Anko. "Captain Kid Glove was—"

"There's no glove to it," protested Trot. "I ought to know, 'cause I've read about him."

"Didn't it say anything about a glove?" asked Anko.

"Nothing at all. It jus' called him Cap'n Kidd," replied Trot.

"She's right, ol' man," added Cap'n Bill.

"Books," said the Sea Serpent, "are good enough as far as they go, but it seems to me your earth books don't go far enough. Captain Kid Glove was a gentleman pirate, a kid-glove pirate. To leave off the glove and call him just Kidd is very disrespectful."

"Oh! You told me to remind you of that third pain," said the little girl.

"Which proves my friendship for you," returned the Sea Serpent, blinking his blue eyes thoughtfully. "No one likes to be reminded of a pain, and that third pain was—was—"

"What was it?" asked Trot.

"It was a stomach ache," replied the King with a sigh.

"What made it?" she inquired.

"Just my carelessness," said Anko. "I'd been away to foreign parts, seeing how the earth people were getting along. I found the Germans dancing the german and the Dutch making dutch cheese and the Belgians combing their belgian hares and the Turks eating turkey and the Sardinians sardonically pickling sardines. Then I called on the Prince of Whales, and—"

"You mean the Prince of Wales," corrected Trot.

"I mean what I say, my dear. I saw the battlefield where the Bull Run but the Americans didn't, and when I got to France I paid a napoleon to see Napoleon with his boney apart. He was—"

"Of course you mean—" Trot was beginning, but the king would not give her a chance to correct him this time.

"He was very hungry for Hungary," he continued, "and was Russian so fast toward the Poles that I thought he'd discover them. So as I was not accorded a royal welcome, I took French leave and came home again."

"But the pain—"

"On the way home," continued Anko calmly, "I was a little absent-minded and ate an anchor. There was a long chain attached to it, and as I continued to swallow the anchor I continued to eat the chain. I never realized what I had done until I found a ship on the other end of the chain. Then I bit it off."

"The ship?" asked Trot.

"No, the chain. I didn't care for the ship, as I saw it contained some skippers. On the way home the chain and anchor began to lie heavily on my stomach. I didn't seem to digest them properly, and by the time I got to my palace, where you will notice there is no throne, I was thrown into throes of severe pain. So I at once sent for Dr. Shark—"

"Are all your doctors sharks?" asked the child.

"Yes, aren't your doctors sharks?" he replied.

"Not all of them," said Trot.

"That is true," remarked Cap'n Bill. "But when you talk of lawyers—"

"I'm not talking of lawyers," said Anko reprovingly. "I'm talking about my pain. I don't imagine anyone could suffer more than I did with that stomach ache."

"Did you suffer long?" inquired Trot.

"Why, about seven thousand four hundred and eighty-two feet and—"

"I mean a long time."

"It seemed like a long time," answered the King. "Dr. Shark said I ought to put a mustard poultice on my stomach, so I uncoiled myself and summoned my servants, and they began putting on the mustard plaster. It had to be bound all around me so it wouldn't slip off, and I began to look like an express package. In about four weeks fully one-half of the pain had been covered by the mustard poultice, which got so hot that it hurt me worse than the stomach ache did."

"I know," said Trot. "I had one, once."

"One what?" asked Anko.

"A mustard plaster. They smart pretty bad, but I guess they're a good thing."

"I got myself unwrapped as soon as I could," continued the King, "and then I hunted for the doctor, who hid himself until my anger had subsided. He has never sent in a bill, so I think he must be terribly ashamed of himself."

"You're lucky, sir, to have escaped so easy," said Cap'n Bill. "But you seem pretty well now."

"Yes, I'm more careful of what I eat," replied the Sea Serpent. "But I was saying when Trot interrupted me, that you all belong to me, because I have saved your lives. By the law of the ocean, you must obey me in everything."

The sailor scowled a little at hearing this, but Trot laughed and said, "The law of the ocean isn't OUR law, 'cause we live on land."

"Just now you are living in the ocean," declared Anko, "and as long as you live here, you must obey my commands."

"What are your commands?" inquired the child.

"Ah, that's the point I was coming to," returned the King with his comical smile. "The ocean is a beautiful place, and we who belong here love it dearly. In many ways it's a nicer place for a home than the earth, for we have no sunstroke, mosquitoes, earthquakes or candy ships to bother us. But I am convinced that the ocean is no proper dwelling place for earth people, and I believe the mermaids did an unwise thing when they invited you to visit them."

"I don't," protested the girl. "We've had a fine time, haven't we, Cap'n Bill?"

"Well, it's been diff'rent from what I expected," admitted the sailor.

"Our only thought was to give the earth people pleasure, your Majesty," pleaded Aquareine.

"I know, I know, my dear Queen, and it was very good of you," replied Anko. "But still it was an unwise act, for earth people are as constantly in danger under water as we would be upon the land. So having won the right to command you all, I order you to take little Mayre and Cap'n Bill straight home, and there restore them to their natural forms. It's a dreadful condition, I know, and they must each have two stumbling legs instead of a strong, beautiful fish tail, but it is the fate of earth dwellers, and they cannot escape it."

"In my case, your Majesty, make it ONE leg," suggested Cap'n Bill.

"Ah yes, I remember. One leg and a wooden stick to keep it company. I issue this order, dear friends, not because I am not fond of your society, but to keep you from getting into more trouble in a country where all is strange and unnatural to you. Am I right, or do you think I am wrong?"

"You're quite correct, sir," said Cap'n Bill, nodding his head in approval.

"Well, I'm ready to go home," said Trot. "But in spite of Zog, I've enjoyed my visit, and I shall always love the mermaids for being so good to me." That speech pleased Aquareine and Clia, who smiled upon the child and kissed her affectionately.

"We shall escort you home at once," announced the Queen.

"But before you go," said King Anko, "I will give you a rare treat. It is one you will remember as long as you live. You shall see every inch of the mightiest sea serpent in the world, all at one time!"

As he spoke, the purple and gold cloth was lifted by unseen hands and disappeared from view. And now Cap'n Bill and Trot looked down upon thousands and thousands of coils of the sea serpent's body, which filled all of the space at the bottom of the immense circular room. It reminded them of a great coil of garden hose, only it was so much bigger around and very much longer.

Except for the astonishing size of the Ocean King, the sight was not an especially interesting one, but they told old Anko that they were pleased to see him, because it was evident he was very fond of his figure. Then the cloth descended again and covered all but the head, after which they bade the king goodbye and thanked him for all his kindness to them.

"I used to think sea serpents were horrid creatures," said Trot, "but now I know they are good and —and—and—"

"And big," added Cap'n Bill, realizing his little friend could not find another word that was complimentary.

CHAPTER 21
KING JOE

As they swam out of Anko's palace and the doll-faced fishes left them, Aquareine asked:

"Would you rather go back to our mermaid home for a time and rest yourselves or would you prefer to start for Giant's Cave at once?"

"I guess we'd better go back home," decided Trot. "To our own home, I mean. We've been away quite a while, and King Anko seemed to think it was best."

"Very well," replied the Queen. "Let us turn in this direction, then."

"You can say goodbye to Merla for us," continued Trot. "She was very nice to us, an' 'specially to Cap'n Bill."

"So she was, mate," agreed the sailor, "an' a prettier lady I never knew, even if she is a mermaid, beggin' your pardon, ma'am."

"Are we going anywhere near Zog's castle?" asked the girl.

"Our way leads directly past the opening in the dome," said Aquareine.

"Then let's stop and see what Sacho and the others are doing," suggested Trot. "They can't be slaves any longer, you know, 'cause they haven't any master. I wonder if they're any happier than they were before?"

"They seemed to be pretty happy as it was," remarked Cap'n Bill.

"It will do no harm to pay them a brief visit," said Princess Clia. "All danger disappeared from the cavern with the destruction of Zog."

"I really ought to say goodbye to Brother Joe," observed the sailor man. "I won't see him again, you know, and I don't want to seem unbrotherly."

"Very well," said the Queen, "we will reenter the cavern, for I, too, am anxious to know what will be the fate of the poor slaves of the magician."

When they came to the hole in the top of the dome, they dropped through it and swam leisurely down toward the castle. The water was clear and undisturbed and the silver castle looked very quiet and peaceful under the radiant light that still filled the cavern. They met no one at all, and passing around to the front of the building, they reached the broad entrance and passed into the golden hall.

Here a strange scene met their eyes. All the slaves of Zog, hundreds in number, were assembled in the room, while standing before the throne formerly occupied by the wicked magician was the boy

Sacho, who was just beginning to make a speech to his fellow slaves. "At one time or another," he said, "all of us were born upon the earth and lived in the thin air, but now we are all living as the fishes live, and our home is in the water of the ocean. One by one we have come to this place, having been saved from drowning by Zog, the Magician, and by him given power to exist in comfort under water. The powerful master who made us his slaves has now passed away forever, but we continue to live, and are unable to return to our native land, where we would quickly perish. There is no one but us to inherit Zog's possessions, and so it will be best for us to remain in this fine castle and occupy ourselves as we have done before, in providing for the comforts of the community. Only in labor is happiness to be found, and we may as well labor for ourselves as for others.

"But we must have a king. Not an evil, cruel master like Zog, but one who will maintain order and issue laws for the benefit of all. We will govern ourselves most happily by having a ruler, or head, selected from among ourselves by popular vote. Therefore I ask you to decide who shall be our king, for only one who is accepted by all can sit in Zog's throne."

The slaves applauded this speech, but they seemed puzzled to make the choice of a ruler. Finally the chief cook came forward and said, "We all have our duties to perform and so cannot spend the time to be king. But you, Sacho, who were Zog's own attendant, have now no duties at all. So it will be best for you to rule us. What say you, comrades? Shall we make Sacho king?"

"Yes, yes!" they all cried.

"But I do not wish to be king," replied Sacho. "A king is a useless sort of person who merely issues orders for others to carry out. I want to be busy and useful. Whoever is king will need a good attendant as well as an officer who will see that his commands are obeyed. I am used to such duties, having served Zog in this same way."

"Who, then, has the time to rule over us?" asked Agga-Groo, the goldsmith.

"It seems to me that Cap'n Joe is the proper person for king," replied Sacho. "His former duty was to sew buttons on Zog's garments, so now he is out of a job and has plenty of time to be king, for he can sew on his own buttons. What do you say, Cap'n Joe?"

"Oh, I don't mind," agreed Cap'n Joe. "That is, if you all want me to rule you."

"We do!" shouted the slaves, glad to find someone willing to take the job.

"But I'll want a few pointers," continued Cap'n Bill's brother. "I ain't used to this sort o' work, you know, an' if I ain't properly posted I'm liable to make mistakes."

"Sacho will tell you," said Tom Atto encouragingly. "And now I must go back to the kitchen and look after my dumplings, or you people won't have any dinner today."

"Very well," announced Sacho. "I hereby proclaim Cap'n Joe elected King of the Castle, which is the Enchanted Castle no longer. You may all return to your work."

The slaves went away well contented, and the boy and Cap'n Joe now came forward to greet their visitors. "We're on our way home," explained Cap'n Bill, "an' we don't expec' to travel this way again. But it pleases me to know, Joe, that you're the king o' such a fine castle, an' I'll rest easier now that you're well pervided for."

"Oh, I'm all right, Bill," returned Cap'n Joe. "It's an easy life here, an' a peaceful one. I wish you were as well fixed."

"If ever you need friends, Sacho, or any assistance or counsel, come to me," said the Mermaid Queen to the boy.

"Thank you, madam," he replied. "Now that Zog has gone, I am sure we shall be very safe and contented. But I shall not forget to come to you if we need you. We are not going to waste any time in anger or revenge or evil deeds, so I believe we shall prosper from now on."

"I'm sure you will," declared Trot.

They now decided that they must continue their journey, and as neither Sacho nor King Joe could ascend to the top of the dome without swimming in the human way, which was slow and tedious work for them, the goodbyes were said at the castle entrance, and the four visitors started on their return. Trot took one last view of the beautiful silver castle from the hole high up in the dome, which was now open and unguarded, and the next moment she was in the broad ocean again, swimming toward home beside her mermaid friends.

CHAPTER 22
TROT LIVES TO TELL THE TALE

Aquareine was thoughtful for a time. Then she drew from her finger a ring, a plain gold band set with a pearl of great value, and gave it to the little girl.

"If at any period of your life the mermaids can be of service to you, my dear," she said, "you have but to come to the edge of the ocean and call 'Aquareine.' If you are wearing the ring at the time, I shall instantly hear you and come to your assistance."

"Thank you!" cried the child, slipping the ring over her own chubby finger, which it fitted perfectly. "I shall never forget that I have good and loyal friends in the ocean, you may be sure."

Away and away they swam, swiftly and in a straight line, keeping in the middle water where they were not liable to meet many sea people. They passed a few schools of fishes, where the teachers were explaining to the young ones how to swim properly, and to conduct themselves in a dignified manner, but Trot did not care to stop and watch the exercises.

Although the queen had lost her fairy wand in Zog's domed chamber, she had still enough magic power to carry them all across the ocean in wonderfully quick time, and before Trot and Cap'n Bill were aware of the distance they had come, the mermaids paused while Princess Clia said:

"Now we must go a little deeper, for here is the Giant's Cave and the entrance to it is near the bottom of the sea."

"What, already?" cried the girl joyfully, and then through the dark water they swam, passing through the rocky entrance, and began to ascend slowly into the azure-blue water of the cave.

"You've been awfully good to us, and I don't know jus' how to thank you," said Trot earnestly.

"We have enjoyed your visit to us," said beautiful Queen Aquareine, smiling upon her little friend, "and you may easily repay any pleasure we have given you by speaking well of the mermaids when you hear ignorant earth people condemning us."

"I'll do that, of course," exclaimed the child.

"How about changin' us back to our reg'lar shapes?" inquired Cap'n Bill anxiously.

"That will be very easy," replied Princess Clia with her merry laugh. "See! Here we are at the surface of the water."

They pushed their heads above the blue water and looked around the cave. It was silent and deserted. Floating gently near the spot where they had left it was their own little boat. Cap'n Bill swam to it, took hold of the side, and then turned an inquiring face toward the mermaids. "Climb in," said the Queen. So he pulled himself up and awkwardly tumbled forward into the boat. As he did so, he heard his wooden leg clatter against the seat, and turned around to look at it wonderingly.

"It's me, all right!" he muttered. "One meat one, an' one hick'ry one. That's the same as belongs to me!"

"Will you lift Mayre aboard?" asked Princess Clia.

The old sailor aroused himself, and as Trot lifted up her arms, he seized them and drew her safely into the boat. She was dressed just as usual, and her chubby legs wore shoes and stockings. Strangely enough, neither of them were at all wet or even damp in any part of their clothing.

"I wonder where our legs have been while we've been gone?" mused Cap'n Bill, gazing at his little friend in great delight.

"And I wonder what's become of our pretty pink and green scaled tails!" returned the girl, laughing with glee, for it seemed good to be herself again.

Queen Aquareine and Princess Clia were a little way off, lying with their pretty faces just out of the water while their hair floated in soft clouds around them.

"Goodbye, friends!" they called.

"Goodbye!" shouted both Trot and Cap'n Bill,

and the little girl blew two kisses from her fingers toward the mermaids.

Then the faces disappeared, leaving little ripples on the surface of the water.

Cap'n Bill picked up the oars and slowly headed the boat toward the mouth of the cave.

"I wonder, Trot, if your ma has missed us," he remarked uneasily.

"Of course not," replied the girl. "She's been sound asleep, you know."

As the boat crept out into the bright sunlight, they were both silent, but each sighed with pleasure at beholding their own everyday world again.

Finally Trot said softly, "The land's the best, Cap'n."

"It is, mate, for livin' on," he answered.

"But I'm glad to have seen the mermaids," she added..

"Well, so'm I, Trot," he agreed. "But I wouldn't 'a' believed any mortal could ever 'a' seen 'em an'—an'—"

Trot laughed merrily.

"An' lived to tell the tale!" she cried, her eyes dancing with mischief. "Oh, Cap'n Bill, how little we mortals know!"

"True enough, mate," he replied, "but we're a-learnin' something ev'ry day."

THE END

www.ingramcontent.com/pod-product-compliance
Lightning Source LLC
Chambersburg PA
CBHW010423120726
47992CB00008B/3300